LISA CUTTS

Lost Lives

SIMON &
SCHUSTER

London · New York · Sydney · Toronto · New Delhi

A CBS COMPANY

First published in Great Britain by Simon & Schuster UK Ltd, 2018
A CBS COMPANY

3 5 7 9 10 8 6 4 2

Simon & Schuster UK Ltd
1st Floor
222 Gray's Inn Road
London WC1X 8HB

Simon & Schuster Australia, Sydney
Simon & Schuster India, New Delhi

www.simonandschuster.co.uk
www.simonandschuster.com.au
www.simonandschuster.co.in

A CIP catalogue record for this book
is available from the British Library

Paperback ISBN: 978-1-4711-6829-1
eBook ISBN: 978-1-4711-6830-7

Typeset in the UK by M Rules
Printed and bound by CPI Group (UK) Ltd, Croydon, CR0 4YY

For Rachel Harris.
For twenty-two years of friendship,
wine and putting the world to rights

Prologue

Hungary
Five weeks earlier

The tatty white minibus lurched from side to side. Some of the roads taken by the ugly pock-marked driver were unmade and unlit. Still, Anna was warmer than she had been in days. Her family home wasn't much to talk about and it certainly let in the draughts, even in the mildest weather.

Life in the United Kingdom couldn't be any worse than the hardship she'd already endured at home, with little chance of prospects or income. Things were surely on the up for her and her tiny family.

She squeezed a tear from the corner of her eye as she tried to forget where she was going and remember her reasons for leaving them behind.

It still didn't make it any easier for her.

Once she reached England, she would start earning a living and would pay back the money her family had promised for her safe passage and new job.

1

Wrapping her arms around herself, Anna tried to take her mind off the jolting minibus and the queasy feeling she was fighting, and instead imagine the hotel she would be working in.

The windows began to steam up, just as Budapest was coming into sight. She wrapped her hand in the sleeve of her denim jacket and wiped it across the glass.

Anna was sitting two rows behind the driver and was shaken from her reverie as she caught snatches of the muttered conversation between him and his right-hand man.

The man driving them to their – as yet unknown – destination made the hairs on the back of her neck stand up.

There was something about his expression.

Yet everything was going so well. The conversation between her great-uncle and the woman who had arranged her passage to the UK was still fresh in her mind.

This was a new opportunity. A new beginning.

A part of her, though, was still questioning her decision to leave Hungary; a feeling deep in the pit of her stomach urging her to stay. But Anna wanted more from life; she wanted to make a success of herself, make her family proud. Make up for what she had done.

The thought of what she had put everyone through sent a shiver down her spine, causing her teeth to chatter. She realized the temperature had dropped, the only source of warmth in the van now apparently turned off.

She glanced towards the driver to ask why it had all of a sudden got so cold.

His ugly pock-marked face looked up. Their eyes met in the rear-view mirror and a whole new chill raced through her body.

She read lust in his look: a sleazy, threatening expression that froze her soul.

Whatever lay ahead, she instinctively knew that she would have to keep her distance from this man. He spelled trouble.

Anna concentrated on why she was taking this journey – not to mention the *risk* – and thought of all that she was putting on hold. Her stomach lurched – her almost empty stomach. Yet she loved the idea of starting a new life and the excitement almost overwhelmed her.

That was until she caught the driver's eye once more. His look told her things wouldn't be as easy as she had hoped. She looked away, the knot in her stomach tightening.

Once she got to England, she would be safe. The arrangements were in place for her to share a house with other women her age. She would have her own room, away from predatory men. With that thought in mind to comfort her, she sat back and followed the road signs to the railway station where they were to pick up a couple more passengers.

There was little point in denying it: the driver seemed to have taken a liking to her, something that made her want to squeeze herself into the tightest ball she could manage. She tried to slow her galloping heartbeat, make herself as invisible as she could. This wasn't the time or the place for unwanted attention. She couldn't afford to get this wrong. Returning home ashamed and in debt wasn't worth thinking about.

The lingering, suggestive look he gave her once he had pulled the minibus over at the railway station left no room for uncertainty: this man wasn't going to take no for an answer.

Anna looked around, thought about clambering out of the minibus and running home. Her parents would be furious about the several hundred euros they now owed, all because of her. And with no way to pay it back.

For the first time it dawned on her: she was trapped.

Chapter 1

East Rise
Early hours of Monday 12 February

Three o'clock in the morning was the best time.

There was less chance of being discovered.

Not that any of that would matter, because as soon as it was over they would disappear.

Just like last time.

The car drove along Kitchener Street at a steady speed, both of its occupants checking whether the lights were on in the target premises, as promised.

Their briefing was simple: send a message, loud and clear. But they wouldn't hesitate to murder the problem if it came down to it.

The driver pulled the car over, giving the passenger barely enough time to jump out and slam the door before he drove off again, on his way to their meeting point.

The passenger reached the front of the large Georgian house, sliced into six flats many decades ago.

He glanced up and down the road before unzipping his jacket – doing little to keep out the biting wind – and taking out a gun. Three shots would be plenty.

Holding the gun steady, he took aim at the window, pointed and fired. Despite being confident that he would get away if anyone were foolish enough to tackle him – he was, after all, *armed* – as soon as the third bullet left the barrel he ran across the road to the nearby alley and raced in the direction of the rendez-vous point.

He was chosen for his ability to take off from the scene at speed. The coldness of the night combined with his agility meant he hadn't even broken into a sweat and was breathing only slightly harder than usual. He stopped at the boot of his accomplice's car, heard a soft click as the catch was released from inside and hid the gun underneath the carpet, all in a few seconds. He then peeled off his latex gloves and shoved them in his pocket before shutting the boot and climbing back inside the Nissan Qashqai.

Detective Inspector Harry Powell's mobile phone rang next to him on the bedside cabinet. In those first few waking moments, especially when rudely jolted from his slumber, he forgot that his ex-wife was no longer lying beside him, but was miles away in Dorset with their children and most of his furniture.

He let out a slow breath and allowed his eyes to adjust to the darkness, the room illuminated only by the faint glow of the digital alarm clock and his phone's dimmed screen settings. His ex-wife had always complained when his phone had 'lit up the room like Blackpool Illuminations'.

Harry threw off the covers, sat up and answered, his voice belying the tiredness he felt. It was the third time he'd been called out in as many days of being the on-call senior investigating officer.

Sitting on the edge of his bed, clad in tartan pyjamas, Harry listened as he was given the address of his latest enquiry – an apparent drive-by shooting at a very interesting location. At the end of the call, for just one minute, he remained where he was as he gathered his thoughts and summoned up enough mental energy to tackle what lay ahead of him and his team.

Harry knew the address was a Georgian house converted into six flats, and he also knew two of the occupants: one a convicted sex offender and the other a police officer from his own incident room.

The list of likely suspects would be endless, and would push his already overstretched team to their limits.

Chapter 2

Anna knew that it was 4 a.m. and she should be out of bed before the Controller stormed into the room and kicked her in the ribs. The bruises from last week still remained, now faded to a dirty yellow on her pale, skinny body. She was unbelievably tired, not to mention hungry.

At least her filthy mattress was away from the window. It had rained a few nights ago and the water had seeped through the ill-fitting window and dripped onto the floor. Lili, one of the newest arrivals, had inched her mattress away from the damp, rousing complaints from the other five women in the room. They had grumbled and muttered rather than shouted at her – the last time one of them raised their voice, the entire household was fined for causing upset. It was bad enough not getting paid, but no money meant no food. And it didn't make them very popular with the eight men who lived in the rest of the house.

Anna got to her feet, feeling much older than her twenty-four years, and shuffled towards the bathroom.

A splash of cold water on her face was about as much as her morning ablutions allowed. The toilet had never worked in the five weeks she had been living there and a shower was out of the question.

Surprised to find the bathroom empty, Anna went inside, but before she could close the door behind her, her gag reflex told her something was wrong, far before her brain did.

This was bad, very bad.

There was a strict rota for emptying the bucket in the corner. Failure to take care of it resulted in problems for them all, so they didn't dare not to. Only as her eyes found themselves reluctantly seeking the far side of the room did she spy the almost empty metal bucket. She was wrong: the stench was coming from the toilet.

Anna felt the panic rising along with the bile. If someone had used the broken toilet in the middle of the night, they were all in for another fine, not to mention what would happen to the culprit.

They couldn't find her in here. They would blame her. She couldn't take another beating, not so soon after the last one. Holding her breath and walking on tiptoe, she crept back to the bedroom.

Lili opened the door as Anna covered the short distance across the wooden boards, avoiding the planks she knew made the most noise.

Anna gestured for the younger woman to go back inside. She could have let her take the blame, and in those few seconds she considered it. They weren't friends, just two lost souls from poor Hungarian families who found themselves in the United Kingdom. Exactly where, neither of them knew.

Part of the reason Anna didn't want Lili to take the blame was because she wanted to do the decent thing, and besides, she knew the young girl wasn't responsible for the contents of the broken toilet bowl. She was pretty sure it was the middle-aged man called Dominik something-or-other who had got on at Budapest and travelled with her on the two-day minibus journey. He always seemed to have something wrong with him.

But the overwhelming reason Anna didn't want the blame to land on Lili was because she had a very good idea of the way things were heading. She had a vested interest in Lili's well-being.

Despite the conditions they lived in – poor sanitation and wearing the same clothes for weeks on end – Lili stood out from the rest of them.

Under the circumstances they now found themselves in, being beautiful would almost certainly seal Lili's fate. And Anna would do everything she could to use the young woman's beauty for her own gains.

Chapter 3

By 4 a.m., DI Harry Powell had showered, downed a cup of tea, scoffed a slice of toast, dressed and driven to the crime scene. He glanced at his reflection in the car mirror, shrugged at the stubble on his face that he hadn't bothered to shave and made his way towards the police cordon at the front of the building.

'Morning, Harry,' said Josh Walker, Harry's uniformed counterpart. 'I know it's early, but you might have taken five minutes to shave.'

'Don't start. I only had time for one cup of tea this morning. It was either burnt toast or shave. My stomach won.'

'The speed your facial hair grows, it'll be back by sunrise anyway,' said Josh. 'Sign in and I'll show you what we've got so far.'

Harry greeted the PC on the cordon, signed the scene log and followed Josh inside the building.

'You know who lives here?' said Josh, glancing in the direction of the next floor up to where one of Harry's officers, Detective Constable Gabrielle Royston, resided.

'Yeah,' said Harry as he scratched at his chin. 'I'll go up and see her myself in a minute. And I take it that you know who else lives here?' He tilted his head to the left, indicating the ground-floor flat the other side of the wall. It was one of only two with its own front door opening onto Kitchener Street.

'Only too well,' said Josh. 'One of my officers was with her – Martha Lipton – a few minutes ago. She's pretty shaken up by all accounts. She asked for you.'

'My day just keeps getting better and better,' replied Harry as he paused on the stairs. 'I take it there's no more information than what you already told me on the phone?'

'You know what I know. Someone fired off shots at the building, seemed to be aiming for the first floor, and then they made off. No one heard or saw a car, though the assumption is that nobody would be blasé enough to do it on foot, so we're checking the cameras and ANPR for any movement or registration numbers around 3 a.m.'

Harry steadied himself against the banister, looked once more up the staircase before changing his mind and heading back down. 'It's going to be a very long day.'

'How's my favourite sex offender?' said Harry to Martha Lipton.

'Are you going to come inside?' she replied, head

resting against the door jamb, one long leg in front of the other, hand on hip.

Harry noted the smile on her lips, fought down the bile in his throat and looked away.

'What you doing, Harry,' she asked, 'lowering yourself to come and see the likes of me?'

He slowly turned his head in her direction.

'As detestable as you are,' he said, 'someone's taken shots at your building. And as much as it sticks in my throat, as a police officer I'm here to protect and serve the public. You're the public.'

'Don't make me laugh. Last time we spoke, you threatened to throw me off a cliff. Now you've got my back?'

'How about we don't do this again?' he said, battling down a sigh. 'It's the early hours of the morning. Shall we just get on with it?'

His words were met with a stare equally as harsh. Then her beautiful face broke into a smile. 'Come on in.' As she turned and stepped inside she called over her shoulder, 'Tea or coffee?'

He let out a slow, silent breath and followed her, closing the door of the ground-floor flat.

'It goes against the grain to break bread with you, but for the sake of crime detection, I'll make an exception.'

'It's not bread,' she called from the other side of the kitchen door, barely a stone's throw from the front door, 'it's PG Tips or Nescafé. Take your pick.'

He walked towards the kitchen, taking in the tidy

home, smart fitted worktops, and the courtyard garden faintly illuminated through the window.

'Tea, then,' he said.

Harry couldn't help but watch her as she moved around the room, gliding from the tap to the kettle and reaching up for the box of tea before stretching over to the fridge for the milk.

Everything about her made him angry.

Sexually abusing her own daughter was bad enough, made worse by the fact that she could still be called attractive, even if only physically. Not something Harry would ever admit to out loud.

'So, what do you want to know?' she said over the noise of the kettle.

'You wanted to see me,' he stated, failing to keep the annoyance out of his voice.

She turned in his direction and leaned back against the sink, the harsh glare of the ceiling spotlights on her flawless face.

'There's a chance I can help,' she said.

'Go on.'

He paused, watched her closely. Her features didn't alter, but then they rarely did. He'd watched her police interviews from before she was convicted of her unspeakable crimes, and she'd barely raised an eyebrow even then.

The silence was all the more noticeable now that the kettle had finished boiling.

'Despite all the things I am, all the things I've done, I would never lie to you,' she said before turning her back on him once more to finish making the drinks.

'So what exactly do you know?' he asked. Harry hated himself for needing something from her, having to keep her onside, but he knew he had to. She could have information that could help. He'd make sure that his suit went to the cleaner's and he had a hot shower as soon as this hideous tour of duty was finished.

A pout, one hand up to ruffle through her hair, before she said, 'I keep my ear to the ground around here. I know people. Perhaps I can find out who's behind this. I've helped you before, I can do it again.' She looked at Harry, chin jutting towards him, eyes narrowed. 'But you couldn't live with yourself, even if I were of actual use to you.'

She handed him his drink. He took a tentative sip and pulled an expression of mild surprise at its pleasant taste before answering her. 'Unless you've actually got something I can go and investigate, set my team on, this conversation is at an end. If you're scared, I understand that: we can find you somewhere else to stay. But if this is just a game you're playing, I'll get another officer to take your statement and we'll leave it there.'

He stared at her, unwilling to walk away if she actually did have something of use for him, yet praying for any source that wasn't her.

She gave him a stare full of malice.

'I thought as much. Thanks for the tea. I'll see myself out.'

Chapter 4

Harry made his way through the main entrance to the flats, past the uniformed officer on the cordon and upstairs to flat number four, not entirely sure what he was going to say to the strange young woman who lived there.

DC Gabrielle Royston had been on his team for over a year, yet he still hadn't worked her out. He had been very surprised to find out where she lived and had thought long and hard about telling her that one of her neighbours had been to prison for sexually abusing her own daughter. In the end, it had turned out Gabrielle already knew.

As he lifted his hand to knock, he shook his head as he recalled how indifferent to it Gabrielle had seemed.

Without warning, the door opened. Gabrielle stood in her hallway wearing tartan pyjamas, very similar to the ones he'd been wearing not much more than an hour ago.

'Gabs,' he said. 'How're you doing, girl?'

'They didn't shoot my windows,' she nodded, loose hair falling over her shoulders, 'so I'm okay, I suppose.'

'Well, that's terrific. Is it all right if I come in?'

Without answering, she stood back against the wall leaving him just enough room to get by her.

He deliberately turned his back to avoid brushing past her face to face. As he did so, a black-and-white photograph on the wall caught his eye.

'Is this the harbour?' he asked her.

'Yeah,' she replied. 'I got up at four one morning to go down there and take it. I love photography. It's what I spend most of my spare time doing.'

'It's very good. You've obviously got a good eye for lining up a shot. I didn't know you were into this.'

'I've sold a few too.'

Even though he was trying to keep a safe distance from the young woman in her nightwear, he turned in the confines of the hallway to stare down at her, their height differences all the more obvious, what with her bare feet.

'Don't look so worried, sir,' she said. 'I've got secondary employment clearance.'

Harry couldn't help but give a little chuckle. 'I wasn't worried about you making a few undeclared bob on the side, I'm in awe. Got any others I can see?'

'In the living room.' She gestured towards the door, a soft light showing through the gap.

The room was much larger than Harry had expected from the narrow hallway. It must have been almost ten metres long, almost the same across, with a very high ceiling, something he hadn't appreciated in the communal area. The room didn't contain much in the way of furniture: a three-seater sofa, large television on the wall and a bookcase with half a dozen paperbacks and a handful of knick-knacks. A coffee table in the centre of the room with seemingly little practical use as it was so far from the sofa was the only other item. But what really caught Harry's attention were the photographs on two of the walls, one a riot of colour, the other black and white.

'Did you take all of these?' he asked, standing in front of the colour photos.

'Yes,' she replied, beside him, gazing at her own work.

'These are incredible. Where was this one taken?'

She stepped forward and brushed the edge of the silver frame with her fingertips. 'I went to Rwanda to see the gorillas.'

'And this?' he said, pointing to another photograph.

'Yep, that one was in Botswana. The elephants were so close I could have reached out and touched them, though they probably would have ripped my arm off, so I stayed in my seat in the boat.'

'Fucking hell, Gabs.' Harry turned a slow 360 degrees, taking in the twenty or so wildlife photographs and a similar number of natural wonders adorning the adjoining wall. 'That's got to be the Northern Lights. It's incredible.'

As blown away as he was by the hidden talents of one of his team, he wondered where she got the money to go away so much, and how she managed to keep so quiet about it.

'My uncle got me interested in photography. He's

given me a lot of the equipment and has taken me on a couple of trips with him.'

'Not David Bailey, is it?'

She gave him a half-smile, then said, 'I love nature and I love animals. People I can do without. Would you like tea?'

Her question jolted him, reminding him why he was standing in one of his DCs' living rooms so early in the morning.

'You wouldn't have a coffee, would you? I think I'll need the extra caffeine for the day ahead.'

'Regular, cappuccino or latte?'

'Blimey, wasn't expecting that. Just a regular one, please.'

He spent the next couple of minutes as he waited for his coffee wandering from photograph to photograph, shaking his head every now and again. The jaws of a lion as it roared caught his eye, the picture showing every tiny detail, including insects flying around the huge mane. He heard Gabrielle come back into the room behind him.

'You weren't tempted to photoshop the flies out of this one?' he asked her, eyes still on the photograph.

'Life's not perfect, and besides, the flies are still better than some people.'

He turned to look at her and saw that she'd changed into black trousers and a sweatshirt. Somehow, it made her look younger than she'd appeared in her pyjamas.

Gabrielle handed him his coffee and sat at one end of the sofa. With nowhere else to sit, he sat on the other end, notebook balanced on one knee.

'Do you need a table to lean on, sir?'

He glanced over at the low coffee table. 'That's probably not going to work.'

'No,' she smiled, her face lighting up for one brief and rare moment. 'I've got one in the bedroom.' Her smile was replaced by the briefest drop of her jaw and a flash of red across her cheeks. 'No, no, I didn't mean that we should go in there. What I meant was, I've got a portable table.'

Harry was all too aware that Gabrielle had had a crush on him when she'd first started at East Rise incident room. It had been very subtle and he had never encouraged it further, but still, he didn't want to cause her any embarrassment or give any indication that a spark, no matter how small, was about to ignite.

'I'm only grateful you weren't about to suggest I sit on the floor,' he said. 'At my age, getting up's a bit of a struggle.'

'I have some terrible neighbours. I'd move, but apart from not being able to afford anything else nearly so large and central, I love the flat ... Are you able to tell me why someone shot at the front of the building?'

'No,' he said pausing while he took a sip of his coffee. 'And not because you're a witness, but simply because we don't know yet. It does seem that the shots were fired at your neighbour and not you. The window was broken and he's suffered from a few cuts, nothing life-threatening. The question is why?'

'His name's John Kersley,' said Gabrielle. 'You'll know that already, but what you probably won't know is that he's had people staying with him from time to time.'

'People?'

'Men. There were two last week and one the week before. I keep myself to myself, as you'd probably expect, although, last Thursday, I had some bags of shopping and I couldn't find my door key, so I was standing on the landing for about a minute or so as I went through my handbag.'

She paused and fidgeted in her seat, hands tightened around the coffee cup.

'I suppose I wasn't making much noise, just scrabbling around in the bottom of my bag, so they didn't even notice I was there. Someone opened John's front door and I looked over and saw two men. They were white, but didn't look English, and quite frankly they seemed really shocked to see anyone. I couldn't say what language they were speaking, possibly Polish, Romanian, I'm not sure. Then I heard another male voice – probably John – say, "Get back inside." Perhaps something to do with them?'

She gave a little shrug, then added, 'Certainly isn't something I've really thought about since – until now, that is.'

Harry listened to everything she said with a growing sense of dread. Going by the recent intelligence meetings he had attended regarding the state of the town's new visitors, plus the urgent training afternoons he had been on, it was likely one of his detective constables was living next door to a people trafficker.

Chapter 5

No one wanted to look the Controller in the eye.

All fourteen of them were lined up, heads bowed, silent.

Fourteen adults, not one of them prepared to stand up to the three men and one woman who stood before them.

Anna hated the Controller. Well, they all hated her, but Anna in particular. She tried to concentrate on the angry words spitting from the Controller's mouth: *She wasn't there to tend to their every need; did they have any idea how difficult it was for her to get them work, how hard it was for her to look after them all, and what did she have to show for it?*

'And you.' She stopped in front of Anna, jabbed a forefinger under her chin and forced the slave's eyes up to meet hers. 'You were the last one seen coming out of the bathroom. Did you leave that disgusting mess in there?'

'No, no, I promise, it wasn't me.' Anna closed her eyes in anticipation of a punch that didn't come, not at that moment anyway.

'I've been good to you,' said the Controller, face

centimetres from Anna's. The gentle waft of perfume from her tormentor was almost too much to bear. Anna hadn't washed properly in weeks; she was covered in sores and had only two sets of clothes. Most of her others were filthy from the time she had gone through the bins at the back of a supermarket trying to find food. Surely things would get better when she was free of this.

She tried to stare back, yet simply couldn't do it. Defiance was as much of a luxury as a decent meal.

'Your family owe me a lot of money for bringing you here.' The Controller dug her manicured fingernail into Anna's chin. 'I've even managed to get you a job packing vegetables. You want to work with the chicken catchers?'

'No, I like my job packing vegetables. It's good work. I'm grateful, very grateful.'

Anna closed her eyes and swallowed. She couldn't risk not getting paid again. Her family had taken on so much debt to get her out of Hungary and into the UK. She knew it was going to take time to pay it off, especially as she was only earning 250 euros a week. At least, that was what she'd been promised, even though she had yet to see any of it herself. She couldn't lose another week's wages.

She opened her eyes, the Controller still centimetres from her face, her henchmen staring at her.

Anna couldn't help it. She was tired, hungry, broken. Her eyes flitted to the man next to her: Dominik.

He was the one they had stopped to pick up at Budapest train station. The driver told them they would only stop twice before they reached the ferry in France, but Dominik was having issues with something he'd eaten, causing them to stop a third time. That increased the price of a seat in the minibus from 110 euros to 150 euros. His digestion problems and the stench on the bus had cost all twelve of them crammed in an extra 40 euros each.

Well, it definitely wasn't her who caused the problems on either occasion, so why should she be made to suffer?

At least, that was what she comforted herself with as one of the Controller's bodyguards stepped forward and aimed a punch at Dominik. It connected with his nose, which exploded with a sickening crunch. He hadn't even had time to hold up his bleeding, raked, ruined hands to shield himself. Then he was on the floor, two of them kicking him while the third looked on with their boss.

Anna shuddered as their heavy boots went in time and time again, kick after kick, until the Controller held her hand up.

'Don't kill him,' she said. 'The last time that happened, we had to beat up a lot of family members before I got the 23,000 euros I was owed for bringing the useless bastard here. This one's passed out now. Leave him there and he can make up his lost wages when he can walk again.'

She looked up and down the line. 'Now you can all fuck off out to work. The nightshift will be here any minute and will want your mattresses.'

Anna watched the Controller as she stepped over Dominik and made towards the bolted front door.

Chapter 6

Harry Powell stayed at Gabrielle's flat for another half-hour or so, unable to persuade her to leave for a relative's house or a police-funded hotel room, and then made his way to East Rise incident room.

When he arrived at 5.30, even the cleaners hadn't yet appeared. He started to work out what he was going to say at the 'morning prayers': a time for various departments and senior officers from East Rise to row over who would be involved in an investigation. Any kind of firearms incident always attracted a lot of attention, and rightly so. This one, however, hadn't resulted in a murder, not even a serious injury. That always made the detectives lose a bit of interest, especially when the victim was being particularly unhelpful.

The division night-duty DC had done her best with John Kersley, despite his insistence that there wasn't a soul on the planet who would wish him any harm. At that time, however, no one had spoken to Gabrielle or the rest of Kersley's neighbours.

Harry would feel satisfied once his own team had

spoken to the victim, the other residents, and particularly Martha Lipton, once more. He had a good team and trusted them to do everything they could to get to the bottom of the investigation. That wasn't to say they were better at their jobs than others at the police station, but they had the time to do things properly, as opposed to having a caseload of forty burglaries, assaults and frauds to deal with.

He had once been at a meeting where the head of the Sexual Offences Investigations Team announced that his staff had over two hundred rapes to investigate, and the team consisted of three full-time DCs, one of whom was pregnant and about to start thirteen months' maternity leave, and a part-time civilian. No one had argued when Harry had said, 'Well, that's a fucking fiasco.'

As he got to his office, just along the corridor from the main incident room where his team sat and worked, he stopped and looked round at the empty banks of desks, blank computer screens and the whiteboard adorned with photos of various office Christmas parties and drunken nights out. A snapshot of two of his DCs – Pierre Rainer and Hazel Hamilton – caught his eye. He stopped and smiled at it. He had been on that particular night out, had taken the photo himself. Pierre had his arm draped around Hazel's shoulder. It was shortly after she had finished a very lengthy trial at the Crown Court and Harry felt that he had, at long last, got his girlfriend back. Things were certainly going well in Harry's life.

He took his phone out of his pocket to text her, then hesitated. It was so early in the morning, yet he knew she'd be up and out of bed. Not only did Hazel find lying in difficult, she'd taken a day off work to look after someone's dog, and it turned out to be very needy as well as an early riser.

Unsure whether he should call her or not, he erred on the side of caution and returned the phone to his jacket pocket.

Harry looked back at the photograph and made up his mind that Pierre was going to be the one to deal with John Kersley. If anyone could get him talking, it was Pierre. He was probably the best detective constable the department had. He was also one of the most flexible in terms of his working arrangements, something Harry knew he took advantage of.

Ensconced in his office, Harry began working out the priorities of the investigation and the initial response so far. He'd ask for as many staff as he could get away with and give the budget as much of a beating as he was allowed.

One matter that was pressing on his mind was what Gabrielle had said about John Kersley's visitors. He was really no expert on modern-day slavery – it didn't tend to feature very much in his incident room – but he was aware it was a lucrative business, more so than drugs or weapons.

And the one thing the planet had a lot of was people. An easily exploited commodity.

Chapter 7

Still unable to forgive herself for what she had done to Dominik, Anna made her way out of the house through the back garden, opened the unlocked gate and walked to her pick-up point.

The house they were kept in was unremarkable. Weeks ago, Anna had stopped thinking of the ideal England she used to see in her head. The house was terraced and on a run-down street, in a run-down neighbourhood somewhere in the south-east of this godless country. No one in the nearby houses looked at them, talked to them or even seemed to notice them. Even if they had, Anna knew the script as well as the others. They were tested on it often enough.

She went as fast as she could manage, all too aware that Lili was behind her, flanked by two of the men from the house.

Lili caught up with Anna as she approached the first corner. She placed a hand on the older woman's arm and muttered, 'It wasn't your fault, Anna.'

'Please,' she replied, 'I need to concentrate on this

route. They've changed it once already this week. It's left and then second right, isn't it?'

She heard a sigh and then Lili said, 'There is a way out of this, you know.'

It was Anna's turn to let out an audible breath. She looked at the hand still on her arm, patted the not yet worn and broken skin and said, 'If you're contemplating what I think you are, you know it won't end there.'

'But she told me it would pay my debt off.'

'Don't you think we've been deceived enough as it is?' said Anna with a shake of her head. 'I know you're younger than me and you've only been here two weeks, but believe me when I say it won't help you. No one can help you. You have to accept that this is how things are now and hope you don't fall sick.'

'What happens if I'm ill?' Lili asked, at last letting go of Anna's arm.

'Look, this is our turning,' she said. 'The minibus will be here soon. Don't talk about it in the bus and definitely not in front of those two.' She indicated the two men behind them, angry looks and whispered conversation aimed in her direction, no doubt down to her betrayal of Dominik.

'But it'll only be one night,' insisted Lili. 'How bad could it possibly be?'

'Come on. If we miss the minibus, not only will we still have to pay the 7 euros for the lift, but they'll dock our wages too. Then you'll never pay your debt off, no matter what you decide.'

The sound of their transport turning into the top of

29

the road was enough to make both women run, followed closely by the men. Anna started to lag behind, despite the short distance to the bus.

The pain shot across her ribs as soon as she began to move faster than a steady walk. Even so, she knew she couldn't afford to miss the only way she had of getting to work. She had never thought the most pressing thing on her mind would be running for a bus that cost such a huge amount of money to take her to a ten-hour shift of packing vegetables. Still, it was better than being a chicken catcher.

The pain now searing, she continued to run, beads of sweat across her forehead. The two men reached the bus. She saw them glance back at her, jump in and then hold their hands out to haul Lili inside.

Then she saw the door begin to close, yet still she pounded along the pavement as fast as she could, unable to accept defeat.

At first, Anna couldn't hear the raised voices above the pounding in her own ears, then she heard Lili's voice loud and clear, 'You have to wait for her, you have to.'

Relief surged through Anna as she saw the white minibus door slide open and Lili lean towards her, the driver refusing to stop completely as she was pulled inside, broken ribs and all.

Chapter 8

Detective Constable Pierre Rainer parked the unmarked police car in one of the designated bays outside the entrance to Queen Elizabeth the Queen Mother Hospital. It was one of the few left in the county that had free police parking: the taxpayer still footed the bill, only this way he avoided handfuls of loose change, a detective's expenses form and a trip to three different people to get the money back.

Grateful that one of the bays was free, Pierre put his *On official police business* card complete with his mobile number on the dashboard, locked the car and made his way to the check-in desk with his investigator's notebook under his arm.

He had listened patiently to DI Harry Powell at six o'clock that morning when he'd called Pierre to request he urgently visit their newest victim. Never one to avoid an early start, Pierre was already showered and eating breakfast when the call came, so he simply got dressed and went to work.

All the information he'd been given about John

Kersley, victim of a shooting in Kitchener Street, had come to him third-hand. He tried to clear his mind of everything he'd been told so far and reserve any judgement. That John was a bit jumpy and evasive was to be expected – after all, he had been shot at – but his lack of co-operation was proving tricky.

Pierre was directed to a small room in the far corner of A & E. The area was already buzzing with medical staff, paramedics and members of the public. Even though it didn't take much detective work to establish which room John Kersley was in, largely due to the armed police officer outside his door, Pierre introduced himself to the staff, both out of politeness and to see if they had any important information. It was always useful to know if the patient was completely off their face from morphine or about to die, for example.

There was no such concern about John Kersley, at least when it came to his injuries.

Pierre exchanged pleasantries with the armed officer, someone he knew from his uniform days, and then went inside the room to introduce himself to the victim.

His initial impression of the man – pale white skin, short brown hair, stubbled chin, eyes closed – was that he was soundly sleeping. But the noise of Pierre's shoes on the hard, pale blue surface as he made his way to the bedside caused John's eyelids to snap open.

Any impression of tranquillity vanished.

John's bloodshot eyes darted beyond Pierre towards his armed protector. At the same time his hands, which had been at his sides, came up to clutch at the thin cotton sheet halfway up his chest.

'It's okay, John,' said Pierre, holding out his warrant card for inspection. 'I'm a police officer, a detective constable.'

'All right, John?' said the armed officer at the door. 'I said that one of the suits would be along soon to speak to you. You're in very good hands with Pierre. I'll be out here for another few hours.'

This seemed to calm the jumpy young man in the bed, who nodded and waved one of his hands in reply, before throwing his head back against the propped-up pillow.

'I didn't mean to startle you,' explained Pierre, moving the wipe-down armchair from its position against the wall so he was side-on to John. 'I'll sit here, unless it's painful for you to turn this way towards me.'

"S'okay,' he muttered, making a play of taking hold of the bed's remote to elevate himself. 'Just didn't know who you were, suddenly appearing like that. I expected a detective inspector.'

'What I'm here for,' continued Pierre, 'is to find out from you exactly what happened and get to the bottom of who shot at your window.'

'At me, you mean.' John's words were accompanied by a frown, swiftly followed by a pursing of the lips.

'At you?'

'Well, I . . . I don't know that, do I? Obviously, I said me, because, well it's my flat, but it could have been a case of mistaken identity, someone messing around.

Anything. You're the police, so you tell me. That's your job to work out, not mine.'

'And rest assured, John, we will work it out.'

Pierre hadn't thought it possible for the patient in the bed to become any paler, but at these words he went whiter than the sheet he was once again clutching to his trembling body.

Chapter 9

The journey to the farm took an hour and a half in the minibus. The pain in Anna's ribs felt as though someone was sticking red-hot rods into her side. There was little point in complaining: as she'd said to Lili, getting sick would only mean no wages. There was absolutely no chance of a doctor attending to them, and a hospital was out of the question. She couldn't speak any English and had no identification. The last time she'd seen her passport was when it was taken from her as they drove away from the immigration officers at Dover.

To take her mind off the pain and to distract herself from the whispered conversation between her two disgruntled housemates, Anna looked out of the grimy window at the street signs in a language she had never been given the chance to learn. The letters meant nothing to her, so working out where she was was near impossible. Not that it would do her much good if she knew.

Her ears pricked up as Tamas, one of the men sitting

behind her, said, 'Dominik's hands were infected, too, from the chicken scratches. He had some terrible marks on them. Really nasty and deep, some of them.'

'I know,' came the reply, 'and we'll have to work even harder today as we're one down.'

A not completely unexpected jab to Anna's shoulder made her move forward on her seat out of their reach.

'Hope you can live with yourself,' said a voice in her ear. 'Stupid bitch. You don't remember Adam Varga, do you?'

She squeezed her eyes shut in anticipation of what was coming.

'No, you probably don't,' Tamas continued, well aware that everyone crowded into the minibus was listening to him, not just the intended recipient of his tale. 'He got sick, made too many mistakes and was seen speaking to one of the bosses at the factory where he worked. Never seen again, but he's still at the factory. Well, most of him is, anyway.'

A rare flash of anger made Anna turn in her seat, a movement that caused her to wince with pain. She was about to tell him to shut up when Lili leaned across, the three of them heads bent together, faces centimetres apart in the confines of the bus.

'You've no idea if that's true,' said Lili to Tamas. 'It's to scare us. We've no idea whether this Adam person even existed, let alone went missing.'

'He existed, trust me, he existed,' said Tamas.

He glanced up to see the driver staring at him in the rear-view mirror. The driver said something to the man beside him who turned in his seat and shouted, 'Be quiet. Save your energy for work, unless you don't want to get paid this week. We're already running late so you can expect to make up the time.'

'It'll be fine,' said Lili as she rested her hand on top of Anna's. 'We'll look out for one another. It'll make things much easier if we do.'

Her words were met with a slow shake of Anna's head and a barely audible sigh. 'You still don't get it, do you?' she whispered. 'We get moved after a few weeks. The only one who arrived with me was Dominik. Everyone else was dropped off at different places, and two to three weeks is usually the longest anyone stays in one house. I don't know why I've been left for so long, but I reckon I'll be moved any day now. You too, probably.'

'Can't we ask to stay together?'

Anna would have laughed if she hadn't felt so wretched. 'We could. We could also ask for food, not to be threatened and ask what happened to the 250 euros a week we were told to expect. Last week I got 30 euros for five days' work. What about you?'

For a few seconds Lili was silent.

'We could run,' she said. 'They'd never find us.'

To hide what she was really thinking, Anna concentrated on the back of the seat in front of her and then said, 'I have a family. They'll find them, hurt them. I can't take the chance, at least not yet.'

'Well,' muttered Lili as she squeezed Anna's hand, 'there's another way.'

'I'm begging you not to. I've seen what happens. Please promise me you won't.'

Lili moved her hand, linked her fingers and failed to answer her companion.

Germany
Five weeks earlier

At the rate they were going, Anna didn't think they would ever reach England. Since picking up a man called Dominik at the train station in Budapest, they'd already had to make an unscheduled stop for him. He had spent most of the journey clutching his stomach and groaning.

It was only when the driver shouted, 'If you don't shut up, I'm going to pull over and throw you out,' that he stopped.

His ceasing to groan didn't put paid to the smell. Several of them moved away from him, including Anna, who preferred to lean against the cold metal of the minibus's side than breathe in the foul stench emanating from Dominik.

It was dark outside, the motorway lights and headlights from other vehicles on the road the only illumination. She passed the time trying to read the road signs, although most of them didn't mean anything to her.

Anna knew they were in Germany, and had possibly seen signs for Switzerland and France. She would have asked which way they were heading, but other than not wanting to engage in any sort of exchange with the men in charge, she felt the route they took was of little importance.

There wasn't much conversation in the minibus, most keeping to themselves, all except Dominik, who asked several times if they were due to stop again soon.

'Are you going to be a nuisance the entire time?' said the driver with a shake of his head.

'Sorry, I don't usually have this problem,' said Dominik. 'I guess it's nerves and excitement. If we can stop once more, I'm sure I'll be okay then.'

'If it stops this smell,' called out a young man from the back of the bus, 'then I'm all for it.'

A few others murmured their agreement; even Anna nodded her head, the smell being particularly bad now.

With a sigh, the driver indicated at some services up ahead and pulled off the autobahn.

Anna peered out of the window and saw a long line of parked cars and vans along the road leading to the services. Whether the driver was being particularly malicious or simply didn't want to chance there being no spaces up ahead, he drew to a stop about three hundred metres or so from the services.

'Last chance to get out before the ferry tomorrow,' shouted the driver as he turned off the ignition, put the keys in his pocket and jumped out.

Fearing that if she didn't take the opportunity to use the toilet herself she would be the next one asking to stop, Anna hurried after the others. And it might actually be warm inside.

Teeth chattering, she raced to keep up. She didn't want to chance their leaving without her.

Anna managed to get in and out of the toilets in record time, and hearing two of the men laughing that Dominik was still in a cubicle making noises like they'd never heard before, she risked stopping to buy something to eat.

The prices were astounding. She could feel her empty belly churning at the idea of food, but she wasn't sure she should spend almost 5 euros on a sandwich. The couple of snacks she had brought with her were long gone and she didn't expect the food on the ferry to be any cheaper. Besides, that wasn't until tomorrow.

Her hand hovered over the sandwiches. She looked up to see the pock-marked face of the driver.

'You buying that?' he said.

'No, it's too expensive.'

'Here,' he said, stepping forward. 'Let me get it for you.'

He picked up a cheese sandwich and said, 'Was it this one?'

'No, no really,' she insisted. 'I'm ... I'm not that hungry. I've already eaten.'

'Come on,' he said, 'you're paying, what, 110 euros for the trip? The least I can do is buy you a sandwich.'

He smiled at her, his cruel face refusing to soften even while he was trying to be nice. Or pretending to be.

Anna might have come from a poor family in a remote part of the Hungarian countryside, but she was far from stupid. Something about this wasn't right, yet she couldn't seem to do anything to get out of the situation.

She gave a miserable smile in return as he turned and walked towards the cashier, clutching her meagre meal.

There was only one more day to go.

In the meantime, Anna would have to keep her wits about her until she got to her job in the hotel. At least then she wouldn't have to see this driver ever again.

The last thing she wanted was to be around someone she was indebted to. She was supposed to be leaving all her previous troubles behind, not surrounding herself with new ones.

Once she got to England, she'd be able to count down the days until her little girl could join her. It would be a new life for them both.

That thought was the only thing keeping her going.

Chapter 10

The incident room was at last starting to come alive. Both police and civilian staff were taking their seats, the words 'A job's broken' uttered up and down the lines of desks as news got out about the overnight shooting. A few looked stressed at the thought of more work adding to their growing list of tasks to complete, a few looked intrigued at the prospect of something new, and some spoke of their surprise at a firearms incident in their seaside town.

Thankfully, shootings were still unusual, but often involved drugs and, almost without fail, some kind of organized criminal gang, whatever their particular illegal enterprise.

Detective Sergeant Sandra Beckinsale strode into the room, a pile of investigator's notebooks in her hands, and approached several members of the team, telling them that there was a briefing in fifteen minutes. No one she approached complained – not to her face, anyway.

'She's still full of cheer this morning, then,' said Tom

Delayhoyde to another of the incident room's detective constables, Sophia Ireland.

'I'm not in too good a mood myself,' she replied. 'I've been told to go to the briefing for the shooting even though I've got a six-page defence statement for my series of rapes to take care of. They've requested so much material despite the fact the idiot defence twats have already had most of it. They really are a bunch of shit-for-brains. Still, it could be worse, they could be defending someone who actually was innocent and making a complete pig's ear of it.'

'Oooh, someone's tired.'

'And I need you like a hole in the head,' said Sophia as she threw a pen at him.

'I'm not sure you should be throwing police-issued equipment about like that either,' said Tom. 'People get sacked for less these days.'

She flopped down in the chair and massaged her temples. 'Sorry, mate. I've got enough to do without a new job that'll take my time up for a week or so. I've had sleepless nights thinking about this rapist bastard. If I don't get this right, how many more women is he going to date-rape? He'd drugged six before anyone came forward.'

'Never your fault, Soph.'

'Feels like it.'

'Hey,' said Tom, leaning towards her, head low to the desk's surface, 'I know what'll cheer you up.'

'Go on,' she said, grin creeping across her face.

'Rumour has it, there's at least one detective sergeant

across the whole of Major Crime who knows how to put a case file together.'

'Now that's fucking funny,' she replied. 'I heard one of them left the building last week too, and not just to get lunch.'

To the sound of titters from those around them, Harry Powell walked into the incident room. No one noticed him until he bellowed, 'Good morning, top tecs,' at them. If he had heard the conversation, he'd chosen to ignore it. 'Briefing in fifteen minutes. Anyone seen Pierre? He was going to try to get back here.'

'He's texted me,' called Sandra from the DS's office. 'He won't be back in time. The victim's not being very forthcoming.'

'Oh good,' said Sophia, 'while nine rape victims are relying on me, I've got to drop everything for some daft twat who's been shot at but won't tell us what happened. This isn't going to be a waste of my time at all.'

'I know, Soph, I know,' said Harry. 'I've tried ringing the other two MIR DCIs and they're all copping a deaf 'un. Once Barbara gets in, it'll be a case of "My DCI can shout louder than yours". We'll get some more staff and you can get back to what you're supposed to be doing. I know your trial isn't far away. Best I can do. Sorry.'

The DC tucked her wavy brown hair behind her ears, sought out her temples with her fingertips and said, 'It's so frustrating that we never have time to get things done properly any more. We're going to start losing jobs at court. That would never have happened a few years ago.'

Something that resembled annoyance flashed across Harry's face. The red from his hair appeared to leak down onto his cheeks, the parts that were visible, anyway, through his stubble.

'Sorry, sir,' she said. 'I didn't sleep very well. I woke up at three this morning worrying about this case file.'

'Just before I was called out to the shooting,' he said, face returning to its normal colour. 'We can be grumpy bastards together for the rest of the day, then.'

The DI turned and walked off in the direction of the kitchen.

As soon as Harry was out of earshot, Tom raised his eyebrows at his colleague. 'Nice one,' he said, 'you've only been on duty ten minutes and you've managed to really cheese the DI off.'

Sophia felt her face redden at Tom's comment. 'I'd rather annoy Harry than let down nine victims of rape and have the offender walk free because I've not completed the bloody paperwork. You know what'll happen if I mess up – it'll all be my fault, but if I get a conviction, it'll be a different story. Everyone comes crawling out of the woodwork for their fake certificate of commendation.'

'Tell you one thing,' said Tom. 'I really hope you don't work with me today. You're in a bloody awful mood. Let's at least go to the briefing and find out why the victim is so reluctant to tell us what happened.'

Sophia let out a slow breath.

'Come on, misery,' he said. 'I'll even make you tea.' She resigned herself to leaving behind the case file that had kept her awake for weeks, stopped her eating, increased her drinking and, unsurprisingly, made her ulcer come back with a vengeance.

DI Harry Powell returned to his office with a cup of strong tea, shut the door and wondered how he was going to get through another day. He didn't want to let on to his team that there was a chance they weren't going to get to the bottom of the Kitchener Street shooting. If he came across as despondent so early in the day, the rest of them were bound to follow suit. The trouble was, he knew that Sophia had an ever-burdening workload, they all did. But what could he do about it? Tell the chief constable they were closed until further notice? That would go down well.

An email flashed up on Harry's computer, causing him to pause mid-sip. He clicked on the attachment and began to read. As he did so, his landline started to ring. Without taking his eyes off the words in front of him, he picked up the phone and said, 'Morning. Harry Powell.'

He listened to the voice on the other end, eyes widening as the chief inspector of operations told him about the latest raids to take place up and down the county, complete with a summary of the ten-page attachment he had barely had a chance to read the first paragraph of.

When at last the newest tale of horrors was finished, Harry said the first thing he could think of: 'I'm going to need more staff. This is only going to get worse.'

Chapter 11

After the briefing, which lived up to its name as shock-ingly little was known about the incident, Harry drove out of East Rise, past fields and orchards, towards a farm on the outskirts of Riverstone, the county town. There were farms like this all over the south-east of the country, only here there were over a dozen marked police vehicles, as well as a number of ambulances, a van dispensing hot drinks to the crowds and a scatter-ing of people wearing identification lanyards around their necks.

These people were clearly on official business, yet most definitely were not police officers: Harry didn't recognize a single person in plain clothes as he drove across the rutted track leading to the melee. Though he hadn't expected to, after being told by Chief Inspector Ops over the phone that the police officers raiding the farm would be accompanied by staff from the Gangmasters and Labour Abuse Authority, the National Crime Agency and the Salvation Army.

Harry cast an eye over the scene before him and

guessed that the Salvation Army would be the ones handing out the beverages. They certainly looked the most cheerful and contented. It was either their unshakeable faith in God, or the fact that they wouldn't have as much paperwork as everybody else when all of this was done.

He pulled up beside a marked police van, the car behind him containing Sophia Ireland and Tom Delayhoyde stopping next to him.

Harry glanced over and saw the scowl on Sophia's face. He liked her, she was a good worker and usually very upbeat, but the cutbacks and ever-increasing workload were getting to them all.

There was a time when hardly anyone left the police with more than fifteen years' service unless it was time to retire, or they had been fired. He had an uneasy feeling that Sophia, with her sixteen years of shifts, murders and rapes, would probably find another job soon. And she wouldn't be the last to opt out of a failing organization for a better standard of living.

Doing as all good management did when faced with a problem they could do little about, Harry ignored it. He got out of the car and walked towards the only two detectives he could spare to bring along.

'This will probably take a few hours, Soph,' he said to the frowning woman as she got out of the driver's seat. 'I'll get you back to your case file as soon as I can. I appreciate your help today, but I'm totally stuck.'

'It's all right, sir,' she acquiesced. 'I like the smell of a farm in the morning.'

'What is that stench?' said Tom as he walked round to join them.

'I think it's chicken shit,' said the DI as all three looked in the direction of one of the large buildings' corrugated sides and the faint squawk of something that might have been poultry-like reached their ears.

'Living the dream,' muttered Sophia.

'Right,' said Harry, 'I'm off to find someone in charge. Follow me and we'll find out exactly what this has to do with our shooting at Kitchener Street.'

He turned his back on the other two and didn't doubt for one second that there was some eyebrow-raising being exchanged between them.

The three of them couldn't help but wonder at what was going on around them. Men and women were being led from one part of the farm to another, some on the arms of police officers and paramedics, some with anger etched on their faces at being escorted so unceremoniously away from whatever they had been doing.

As they got closer to the chicken shed, the stench increased.

'Think I'll give KFC a miss for a while,' said Sophia as they made their way towards a mobile incident room, which was, for all intents and purposes, a very large van.

'What do you think's going to happen to all of these people?' said Tom as he walked beside her, pushing his foppish, boy-band hair out of his face in the same breeze that was carrying the smell straight to their nostrils.

'Perhaps some of them work here legally,' said Sophia

as she searched the faces of those streaming by her for any readable signs. 'They all look so wretched.'

'Wouldn't you be?' said Tom. 'The smell's bad enough from here. I can't imagine what it's like inside.'

'Think of the chickens,' she said. 'Have they got the same magnified sense of smell as dogs?'

'What the fuck are you on about? How the hell should I know?'

Their exchange halted as Harry stopped to speak to a uniformed officer with the insignia of a chief inspector.

'How's it going?' he asked as he shook the hand of the woman outranking him.

'It's the chaos you see,' she replied, casting her eye over the stream of people moving between the farm buildings and disused shipping containers dotted across the land. 'Farmer's swearing he didn't have any idea that the three metal shipping units you can see over there were used to house twenty migrant workers each. We had to cut the chains off when we got here. The sun's up, so they looked like moles coming up out of the earth's core. I'm Jean Patterson, by the way.'

'Harry Powell. Where are they from?' he asked as he put a hand up to shield his eyes from the mid-morning sun and follow the CI's gaze across the patch of England's green and pleasant land.

'This lot here are from Hungary, though today is the tip of the iceberg. These days, the majority of new ones come from Romania and Hungary, whereas it used to be Poland and Lithuania. Anywhere exploitable. Poor bastards.'

'They all work here on this farm?' said Harry, incredulous that he had, on numerous occasions, driven along the very road that took him past this way. It had always looked like an idyllic piece of the countryside: comforting, homely, reassuring.

'Not all of them,' she said, giving him a tight smile from under the shadow of her flat cap. 'Some are loaded into a minibus and taken to other places, while others come and go on a daily basis. I want to show you something.'

The two officers turned to walk in the direction of the temporary shelter set up for processing the workers. It was little more than a large tent, and the queue was growing.

Harry's attention was caught by a battered old white minibus in the distance as it chugged along the country road running alongside the farmland. Something he might not have given a second thought to ten minutes ago. Now, the vehicle holding fifteen or so people, all seemingly looking his way through the grimy windows, made him consider how many modern-day slaves were being bused around his county right under his nose.

He followed the chief inspector inside the tented area and was met by a milling crowd: some officers, some immigrants and some other officials who were trying to record as many details as possible. Some of those standing beside officers he understood to be interpreters, all helping to establish who everyone was.

'We've been here for hours,' his senior officer said to him over her shoulder as she led him to the rear of the tent, Tom and Sophia keeping up as best they could. 'It's not nearly as manic as it was when we first arrived, and this raid is not the first or the last we'll be doing in the area. This is an epidemic.'

At the very rear of the fifteen-by-fifteen-metre area, they reached what could only be described as a larder made out of fabric. Jean ushered them inside.

'As I mentioned on the phone,' she said, 'this raid may shed some light on what you're dealing with at Kitchener Street and the depths these people will sink to when taking advantage of migrant workers.'

She looked behind him at the two detectives. 'Come in and get as close as you can. What I have to tell you isn't necessarily sensitive information, and most of the people likely to overhear us can't speak English anyway. That's why they've been trafficked. Still, it's best if I don't shout it about.

'We got a tip-off from a British lorry driver who made a delivery here a few days ago. A young woman – gaunt and dirty, he described her as – tried to give him money, a handful of euros, he thought. She was foreign and only said one word to him – *Help*. He contacted us and we're here as a result. We don't think we've found her yet. Hope to God we do, but we've got the cadaver dog on standby.'

She gave another smile she didn't mean and said, 'There are some very sick people here, but they simply won't ask for our help. They're frightened, in pain, and this wasn't what they signed up for. It's best if you see if for yourself so you'll understand what you're up against.'

The three detectives looked from one to the other, the two lowest-ranking waiting for the senior one to speak.

When Harry did, it was a slow, reluctant, 'Go on.'

'Follow me,' Jean said, and took them back into the centre of the registration area. She spoke to a uniformed police sergeant who then pointed them towards one of the larger police vans parked about six metres from another entrance.

She marched them briskly across the pathway, shingle crunching under the soles of her Magnum boots, until they got to the van.

Jean Patterson put one hand on the door and raised the other as if about to knock. She turned to Sophia and said, 'There's a young man in here called Denis Boros. It's better that Harry and your other colleague go in for Denis's sake. We should leave them to it.'

She rapped on the side of the van then stepped back to stand beside Sophia.

The two men exchanged an apprehensive glance and slowly entered.

Chapter 12

Things with John Kersley hadn't started well, and certainly didn't seem to be getting any better. Pierre had tried everything to get him talking, and usually, even with the most reluctant, he had a knack of getting people onside. After twenty-six years of policing, Pierre thought he'd finally met his match.

He was trying not to let the frustration show: it wasn't just that John didn't want to say what he clearly knew, it was that he was giving Pierre the impression that he had an idea who had shot at his window.

People lying Pierre was used to, those who fell the wrong side of the law denying they knew anything, but this was someone who was clearly petrified, yet simply couldn't stop himself from saying the wrong thing.

'When I looked out of the window—' Kersley froze as soon as he realized what he'd said.

'Go on,' said Pierre, nodding his head, pen poised.

'No, no, I don't mean when I *looked* out of the window, I meant to say, when I was *sitting* by the window.' He bit his lip and rested his head against the pillow, seemingly satisfied that what he was saying was now making sense.

Pierre had been told to take it easy on the man. He was prepared to do that, yet he couldn't help feeling frustrated, wanting him to tell the truth. He decided he would bide his time and wait for the right moment.

'Tell me as much as you can remember about when you were sitting by the window.'

He watched Kersley swallow, rub his forehead and then give the smallest of shrugs.

'What is there to say about sitting by a window?'

'At three o'clock in the morning.' Pierre left his words hanging, neither a question nor a judgement. No tone of disbelief.

'I couldn't sleep. I sometimes have difficulty.'

'We really want to find who did this,' said Pierre as he moved his chair closer to the hospital bed. He lowered his voice. 'It's important that no one else gets hurt. You've been extremely lucky ... this time.'

Pierre watched Kersley struggle to sit up a little straighter in the bed, fiddle with the name band around his left wrist, smooth the cotton sheet over his chest.

'If you find out who tried to kill me, what'll happen to them?'

The officer kept his features neutral. 'They'll get arrested, charged and go to court.'

'Yeah, yeah, I know, but after that? What happens if they don't go to prison, or they go to prison and get, I dunno, six months for shooting at my window?'

'Firstly, John, firearms offences are taken very

seriously, so any court, on conviction, will hand out the maximum sentence. Secondly, you've just said that someone tried to kill you. Attempted murder carries the same sentence as murder – life with a hefty minimum custodial.'

He watched as Kersley put his hand up to his forehead, tapped his fingertips against his pasty skin and said, 'They'll come after me.'

'Who will?' said Pierre, inching forward in his wipe-down NHS seat.

Kersley opened his mouth to say something as the rustle of scrubs and the gentle footsteps of a Croc-wearing nurse made them both look towards the door.

'Hi, John,' said the nurse. 'The doctor will be in to see you in a bit and then you can go home.'

Pierre faced Kersley who had once again turned whiter than the sheet he was clutching.

'Carry on with what you were saying,' said Pierre as soon as the nurse was out of earshot.

'No, it was nothing,' he said. 'If I'm going home, it really was nothing. You can't help me, no one can.'

This time, the tears came.

Chapter 13

At last, the grubby minibus reached its first designated stop. From the route they'd taken, Anna guessed that her stop was about another ten minutes away. She would have liked to get out here, having being bounced around for over an hour already down narrow country lanes. They had passed what looked like another farm, with police cars and all sorts of people wandering around. She'd seen it through a break in the hedgerows as they had rounded a bend.

The driver and his right-hand man had seen it too.

She'd watched them whisper something, unable to hear them over the noise of the engine and the crunch of the gears.

She looked back out of the window at the rolling fields and gentle hills. Looking but not really seeing. Parts of the countryside might have struck her as beautiful and green had she not had so many other things to think about – getting some food, for a start.

She had overheard hushed conversations between the other women who had arrived in their damp, draughty bedroom a couple of weeks ago. They had spoken of being moved on whenever police turned up at nearby farms and factories unexpectedly. One even spoke about being taken off and asked questions, a Hungarian interpreter present.

'Why didn't you tell them?' Anna had wanted to yell at her. Except she already knew the answer.

They had to stick to the script.

It was ingrained in them all: they were happy to be here, working and sending money home, and they certainly didn't want any help. Along with the script had come warnings about the corrupt British police. Officers who would demand more money than any boss or controller, would beat and even rape the women in dark, damp police cells.

With every miserable day that passed, she became more desperate to get word home to her family not to send her beautiful, sweet, eight-year-old daughter out to join her. Yet she had no way to contact them. It hurt to think about it.

Instead, she had simply turned over on her mattress and tried to sleep, ignoring the gnawing hunger in her belly.

Snapping back to the miserable present, she sat up straighter in her seat as the two men from her house prepared to get out at the next stop.

'I've got used to the gut-wrenching stench now,' she heard Tamas mutter to the other.

'How much longer do you think we'll have to run all over the place catching chickens?' whispered the other.

'No idea. At least we've learned how to pick up two in each hand now. It's incredible how fast they can run when they want to.'

'Better shoes wouldn't be a bad thing either,' she heard the other say. 'My trainers have ripped laces and holes in the soles.'

She heard feet shuffling behind her, wanted to look round to sympathize, yet knew how this would be met.

'I know what you're thinking,' came the reply from behind her. 'If you want another pair, add six months of being pecked and scratched by chickens. For something like decent boots, add another two years to your debt.'

'*Two years*?' came the panicked reply as the minibus turned up a smaller single-lane track.

'Got to be,' she heard one of them say. She strained to hear, so hushed were the words. 'Think about it: the trip over was 110 euros each: compare that with what we're supposed to get paid, minus the fix-up fee for finding us work, less the rent we pay, minus the daily drop-off and pick-up in the minibus, and what are we left with? I've been doing this crap for six weeks now, and I haven't even paid off the trip from Budapest, let alone the 2,000 euros my family owe for getting me out of Hungary for a better life.'

'You call this a better life?'

'No, no, I don't. I call this a dog's life, but it's better than being *fed* to the dogs, which is what happened to the last person who decided they weren't going to work off their debt, so let's keep our heads down and hope that we eventually get out of here alive.'

As the two got up, the side door was wrenched open from the outside. Anna put her hand over her mouth and nose to avoid the pungent odour of poultry, and at that moment one of the alighting slaves slammed their elbow into the back of her head. She was so used to being beaten, it didn't even register with her.

She watched them as the door slid shut, standing in the morning chill beside their minder, dressed in jeans, trainers, T-shirts and tracksuit tops, and certainly no sign of gloves.

She couldn't help but stare at their hands as they turned them over to look at one another's palms, reddened and cut from ten hours' work the previous day.

It paid more than the work she did, but even if it took her another year to pay off her debt, it would surely be worth it to avoid being pecked, scratched and torn, over and over every single day.

The minibus continued on its miserable way, only herself, Lili, two other women and the driver now remaining.

If her luck was really with her today, she might use a flushing toilet, wash herself in warm water and be given a full day of packing salad rather than removing dirt from carrots and putting them in plastic bags. She might even get to eat a tomato or two.

That would be a good day.

Chapter 14

Harry Powell, a police officer for the best part of three decades, a career detective, a detective sergeant then a detective inspector, used to the worst of human misery and depravity, thought he was past being shocked.

Of course, some of the scenarios he had encountered still tugged at his heartstrings and made him wonder if the planet really was worth saving. He frequently found himself watching apocalyptic films and rooting for the natural disaster. He had always fancied joining Greenpeace, except his oath to the Queen prevented all that.

But as he stood in the makeshift doctor's surgery inside the police van, fighting to keep his breakfast down, he wanted to do what any normal person would do in this situation: grimace and run away.

It had taken a couple of minutes of persuasion between the Salvation Army volunteer and the interpreter to get Denis Boros to speak to Harry and the very silent and pale Tom.

Denis's reluctance was becoming more evident by the minute.

'It took us ages to get him to take his shoes off,' said the clean-cut SA volunteer, *Julian James*, according to the identification on his badge.

'What's wrong with his feet?' asked Harry, not entirely sure he hadn't spoken an octave or two higher than his usual pitch.

Julian gave him an empty smile. 'They've started to rot. He's been sleeping here in one of the shipping containers and working for months in a roadside car wash. He only had training shoes, none of the proper protective equipment. The flesh is coming away from his bones.'

'Then where the fuck is the doctor?' said Harry, following his outburst up quickly with, 'Sorry for my language.'

'Well,' said Julian, nodding in Denis's direction, 'there are a few cases worse than this one. There are a number of paramedics on hand here too, but it was ages before Denis would take his shoes off.'

'I'm not surprised,' muttered Tom, the first time he'd spoken since they'd shut the door behind them, closing off one room of horrors to step inside another. 'He was probably worried that both his feet would come off with them.'

Harry glanced down at Tom. Anything to distract him from the look on the young Hungarian's face as he sat in a chair, flesh-rotted feet resting lightly on a cushion covered with a thin cotton sheet. It seemed to Harry that Denis was keeping his eyes firmly shut and concentrating on his breathing, possibly a tactic to avoid catching sight of his condition.

'Who's in a worse state than this poor sod, then?' said Harry as the interpreter put his hand on Denis's shoulder, said something no one else understood and held a bottle of water out to the wretched young man. His eyes flickered open; he nodded and took the drink before closing his eyes again.

Julian folded his arms, shifted his weight from one foot to the other, stole a look at the trafficked young slave.

'We've not got him to take off all his clothes yet, as you can see.'

Both Harry and Tom chanced a look at the exploited worker's jeans and short-sleeved T-shirt.

'Don't tell me this is going to get worse,' said Tom.

'It's not only their feet that get wet with no hope of drying out,' said Julian. 'It's their legs, and particularly their groin area.'

The two detectives took a minuscule step backwards. Harry was glad that Denis still had his eyes closed, so he couldn't notice their repulsion and the penalty line-out pose they'd both adopted.

Even if Denis couldn't speak English, the way they had reacted at the mere mention of potentially damaged testicles still smacked of unprofessionalism.

'So you're saying that his ... er ... you know, nuts and stuff, are going to be in the same condition?' said Harry, now fighting the urge to put his hands in his trouser pockets.

His question was met with a small shrug from Julian. 'Ideally, we'd like to cut their clothes off. They're no good, really, and we have clothing from charity bins and shops to give them. Problem is, they have so few possessions, they don't like us to.

'In answer to your question, there have been two already this morning with a certain amount of rotting flesh in that region.'

'Rotting in that region?' asked Harry, not really wanting to know the answer, but unable to stop himself.

'Where they've got wet from the car wash and not dried out, and then slept in a cold shipping container. We find that, once we get them to remove their under-wear, maggots fall out from under their scrotum. I think that's what's behind Denis's reluctance to get undressed.'

There were several seconds of silence before Julian said, 'To give him some privacy and a sense of decency, would you both mind leaving us to it?'

'Of course, of course,' said Harry, one hand already on the door handle.

Once outside neither knew what to say. They walked past the immigrants, police and volunteers to Harry's unmarked car, got in, and sat side by side in silence for some minutes before a rapping on the passenger window brought them back to reality.

Tom opened the window to Sophia.

'What's the matter with you two?' she asked.

They responded with a slow shake of the head.

'I'm not sure you'd want to know, Soph,' said Tom. 'I know I don't.'

Chapter 15

On one of Detective Constable Hazel Hamilton's rare days off without Harry Powell, she started the morning by making a list of all the things she needed to do. It was quite a list, and it took her until her second cup of green tea to finish it.

For a start there were the phone calls and emails, and she needed to drive into East Rise to pick up a present for Harry. Every now and again, she liked to buy him something to wear, or something for his home. Harry hadn't realized how much his life would be enriched by an eight-litre glass drinks dispenser, or a vertical toilet-roll holder for the cupboard under the stairs.

Hazel smiled to herself as she thought of the expression on his face whenever he opened one of her household gifts. She had meant the very first of them to be a joke. She had lost count of the times they had been in the kitchen, Harry dashing from pot to pot, tasting each dish as he went, grabbing spoons from the drawer, draining board, dishwasher, then discarding them. Hazel would gather them up, wash them and wipe up the mess. So she'd bought him a spoon rest.

What she had been expecting was laughter and him to say something like, 'What the fuck's this, Haze?' Instead, he had gazed at the spoon rest in wonder, turned it over and over and said, 'That's bloody brilliant. You're the most thoughtful person I've ever met.'

She had been rendered speechless, unable to admit it had been intended as some sort of spoof offering. He wasn't meant to take it seriously, but she had felt obliged to humour him and not blow her cover.

'Just saw it and thought it might come in useful,' she'd said as he'd got up to rinse the spoon rest under the hot tap.

Harry had wiped it with the dishcloth, squirted some washing-up liquid onto it, rinsed it again and dried it before giving it pride of place in the centre of the worktop.

Even more astonishingly, he had continued to use it. Things had gone too far past the point of her letting on her gift had been a joke.

She knew exactly what she was going to buy him today.

Harry had complained often enough about the continual mess the seagulls made of his car and how it was costing him a fortune having to make frequent visits to the car wash on the local A-road.

Hazel picked up her handbag and found her car keys. She was going to buy him a portable car wash set.

Now that really was a thoughtful gift, plus she

wouldn't have to listen to his regular moan that not only did the car wash charge a tenner, but everyone working there always pretended they couldn't speak English.

Chapter 16

Hurrying from the minibus towards the farm buildings, Anna knew exactly what to do: smile at the English workers, try to look a little less miserable than she felt, and not stop if spoken to. Not that she would have been able to converse with them, even if she hadn't been petrified by the very thought of being seen talking to them.

A few days ago, there had been some posters in different languages in the toilets, some of them in Hungarian, giving helpline numbers in case workers thought they were being exploited. Her hands had shaken as she'd stood at the sink washing them, daring herself to read the words, memorize the telephone numbers. Not that she could get to a phone.

The posters had promised the police would help, but she knew the stories only too well – the women raped and the men beaten and tortured in police cells, messages passed back home about betrayal. She couldn't risk anything happening before her daughter was safe. Now it might be too late to stop it.

Head down against the biting wind as she hurried

across the yard, she'd failed to notice someone falling into step beside her. She felt a hand grip her arm, realized she was being pushed towards a barn and tried to dig her heels into the ground. A completely useless gesture.

'Come with me,' she heard Pock-mark hiss in her ear.

'No, let me go,' she yelled as she tried to turn towards him, fists balled.

'I'll punch you in the throat if you don't come with me and listen.'

They covered the short distance to the barn door in record time; he pushed her inside, threw his head back and laughed at her attempt at a boxer's stance.

'Don't flatter yourself,' he sneered. 'I need you to sign some papers.'

'Papers?'

'Yes, papers, you deaf bitch. Here.'

He produced a clutch of paperwork from his inside jacket pocket along with a pen.

'Sign these,' he said, thrusting them towards her. 'We'd have done it this morning if it wasn't for that mess with the bathroom. You people really know how to ruin a schedule.'

She scanned the words in front of her. They were in a language she couldn't read, all except her daughter's name.

Anna's breath caught in her throat; her heart was in her mouth.

'What is this?'

Her question was met with a shrug.

'It's so we can register her, get you some extra money to look after her, that kind of thing.'

'But I can't read any of this. I don't know what I'm signing.'

He glanced over his shoulder through the open door to where the rest of the retreating workforce was headed. The gesture wasn't lost on her: in a few seconds they'd be alone again.

'Remember that time you were taken to a couple of different banks to open accounts? They refused to give you an account, didn't they?'

She gave a small sad nod.

'Well, let's try not to fuck this up too. You want money for your kid, sign it.'

Miserably, she scratched a signature next to the crosses, unsure of what else she could have done.

Chapter 17

When Pierre phoned Harry, he had no idea that his DI was sitting stock-still in his car, traumatized by what he had witnessed, beside a much younger, but equally shell-shocked DC.

'Hi, P,' was all he heard when his call was answered.

'You okay, boss?' asked Pierre as he stood in the main A & E area, around the corner from John Kersley's room. There was a pause that Pierre felt obliged to fill. 'You sound very quiet. What's up?'

'Mate,' said his DI, 'just now, I don't think I can bring myself to tell you. It's too hideous for words.'

'Anything I can help you with?'

'That's extremely unlikely, but thanks anyway. How's it going at the hospital?'

Pierre ran an eye over the staff and patients passing by, some in more of a hurry than others.

'John Kersley is one very scared man,' said Pierre as he made sure that no one was lingering close enough to hear. 'From what I've gleaned from him – from what Gabrielle has told us about the Eastern Europeans he seems to be friendly with – I'd say with confidence that he's the opposite of a people trafficker. I think he was giving them somewhere safe to stay. For what reason, I can't yet say. If we want to get anything out of him, we'll have to take him away from here, get him somewhere safe.'

There was a slight pause as Pierre steeled himself to say what he needed to next.

'Thing is, as much as I hate to admit it, he'll probably respond better to you than he will to a mere lowly DC.' He waited a beat then said, 'What do you reckon?'

'I'll be right there,' said Harry, then he hung up.

Phone in hand, Pierre wondered exactly what had propelled his superior officer to drop everything and rush to A & E. He could only guess that he was desperate to get John Kersley onside.

After running his hands over the ginger stubble on his chin, Harry sat in his car, stared straight ahead and said to the young DC beside him, 'Sorry, Tom, but I'm going to have to leave you and Sophia here. Pierre needs me at the hospital. Call me if anything changes.'

'What?' said Tom, snapping his head in Harry's direction. 'What are we supposed to do?'

Harry met Tom's stare. He took in his expression of bewilderment.

'Go back to see that chief inspector and find out what you can about any links to Kitchener Street, such as firearms, paperwork with addresses, any intel. I'm on the phone if you need me. Look, there's Sophia talking to one of the paramedics.'

Truth be told, Harry felt bad leaving Tom and Sophia floundering in some sort of refugee triage centre, but the whole maggot episode had really got to him.

He waited as Tom slammed the car door shut with a little more force than was strictly necessary, and then watched as he stomped in the direction of Sophia. Harry could tell by the way Tom moved through the cars, boy-band hair bobbing up and down with each step, that he was less than pleased with this turn of events.

Harry couldn't blame him: there had been so many occasions, especially of late, where the wrong people were getting promoted for embarking on pointless projects rather than for simply being coppers, while he had seen for himself the rank and file being left in the dark, unsupported. Often it was because managers didn't have enough time for their staff, sometimes it was because they didn't care, but, worst of all, sometimes it was simply because they didn't know what to do themselves.

He had always, since the day he joined the police, aimed to be much better than that, but then he had never, until now, heard of anyone's scrotum rotting away to the point of being full of maggots.

Shaking his head, he turned the engine over and set off for the hospital.

Chapter 18

Feeling ever so slightly guilty about abandoning Tom and Sophia at the farm, Harry Powell pulled his car over in the Queen Elizabeth the Queen Mother Hospital car park. He drew up beside Pierre's unmarked car, fished around in the glovebox for an *On official police business* card and made his way past the smokers and wheelchairs to his favourite member of the team.

Of course, he didn't ever let on to the others that he preferred Detective Constable Pierre Rainer to anyone else in his incident room, including his girlfriend, Hazel. He didn't prefer him as a person, obviously, merely as a member of the workforce. Pierre was someone he could trust within an inch of his life. The man never gossiped, rarely had a bad word to say about anyone, and took his work very seriously. To himself at least, Harry could admit that Pierre was his 'go-to guy'. Hazel had probably guessed as much, but never questioned who he allocated work to, even in the confines of his home, off-duty with no one to overhear their conversation.

Harry walked past the scattering of people waiting

for appointments, news of loved ones or emergency treatment that clearly wasn't too much of an emergency if they had time to stand in the doorway smoking and complaining about a National Health Service they had probably never made a single financial contribution towards.

He had only taken a few strides across the A & E department when he spotted Pierre. He was side-on and chatting to a young blonde nurse. It amused Harry that she seemed to be flirting with Pierre.

As Harry approached, Pierre glanced at him and thanked the nurse for her help. She smiled and moved away to see to a patient in a curtained-off cubicle.

'Looked like you were doing okay there, P,' said Harry, nodding in the direction of what he couldn't fail to notice was a pert bottom, despite the attempt by the blue scrubs to cover all femininity.

'Whatever happened to old-fashioned nurses' uniforms?' he added, failing, for once, to embrace the modern era.

'I'd guess that they're mostly for sale in Ann Summers, not to mention that they were probably uncomfortable, impractical and women were fed up with being perved over by old men like you.'

'Watch it,' replied Harry, 'I'm only a few years older than you.'

'Physically,' said Pierre, 'but how about mentally and in attitude. *Carry On Doctor* is a very old film.'

'It's still funny though.'

Pierre raised an eyebrow at him.

'So what shall we do with John Kersley?' said Harry, remembering he was a detective inspector with an uncooperative, petrified victim of a shooting to deal with.

Pierre put out a hand and guided his boss towards the wall, away from anyone who might overhear. Keeping his voice as quiet as he could manage, Pierre said, 'The only realistic chance we have of getting him onside is to put him somewhere safe. He's genuinely terrified.'

He watched Harry run a hand across his chin before he nodded in agreement. 'I don't disagree with what you're saying, but ...'

'Let me guess,' said Pierre with a sigh. 'It's all about money at the end of the day, and we can't afford to house him indefinitely.'

'That's about right. The government with their "do more with less" bollocks. Fucking cretins. We should do away with armed police guarding some of those imbeciles for a start, that'd save a few quid ... Anyway, my point is, it's all well and good reassuring him with a friendly pat on the shoulder, then taking him somewhere safe and getting his evidence. But after that we'll be leaving him to fend for himself for the next six months, or longer, while we try to put a case together that'll actually get past the Crown Prosecution Service and to court. We just can't fund keeping him somewhere, fed and watered, for an indeterminate period of time.'

'I don't think he's going to tell us much without some sort of reassurance,' said Pierre, frown creasing his forehead.

'Yeah, I know. Let me speak to him and we'll take it from there. It's not as if he's the first victim of a shooting who's refusing to co-operate, is it?'

'That's very true,' said Pierre as he led the way to John's room. 'The difference with those is they refuse to tell us what happened because they've been dealing drugs on someone else's patch, not because they've been helping illegal immigrants hide from their captors.'

If Harry didn't know better, he could have sworn he detected a hint of annoyance in Pierre's tone, not to mention a tension in his face.

He followed his colleague towards the man who, for the next twenty minutes, he was going to try his best to persuade to reveal everything he knew about people trafficking in the area, all the while reassuring him that he wouldn't get himself killed for coming forward.

He hoped that he would come across as convincing, because right at that moment Harry wasn't at all sure he could guarantee the terrified young man's safety.

Chapter 19

Alexa enjoyed driving her Audi, especially after being in such close proximity to the workhorses. She was glad to get away from them and their complaining.

She had taken a particular dislike to the one called Anna. The daft bitch really got Alexa down. Her only saving grace was her eight-year-old daughter who was about to be dispatched. Children were where the real money was.

It was fair to say that eight was a little young, but Alexa herself had been around the same age when she was sold to a Russian syndicate, so why not?

Having paid little attention to the drive after leaving her slaves in the seedier part of town, Alexa turned into her road.

She pulled up on the driveway, got out of the car, and walked up the path to her detached four-bedroom house.

As she neared the front door, something caught her eye. She stopped, frowned.

The living-room curtains were closed. Despite a

ridiculously early start, she had paused to open the curtains, something she did every day without fail. She lived alone, having disposed of her 'home help' a few weeks previously.

For just a few seconds, she considered calling one of her underlings, but she decided against it, unlocking the front door and stepping inside.

Leaving the door ajar, she tiptoed to the kitchen, removed a vegetable knife from the rack and went from room to room.

Downstairs revealed neither missing objects nor any intruders in danger of getting knifed in the gut. She ran an annoyed eye over the wall unit's drawers, pulled open in haste and left to flaunt the messy search of her hard-earned possessions.

Satisfied that there was no one on the ground floor, she paused momentarily on her way to the stairs to check that the padlock was still in place at the top of the cellar door.

It wasn't.

The lock had been crudely prised from the door. Whoever had been in her home wouldn't have gone down there if they'd known what she kept in the darkness.

The cellar would have to wait until she'd searched the whole house. She wasn't going to risk getting trapped in her own dungeon by a stranger lurking in the shadows. Besides, her real worry was whether tomorrow's shipment was still safely stored in the loft.

She took her time getting to the top of the staircase,

two closed doors to her left, two to her right, bathroom door open straight ahead.

Empty.

Each bedroom door she approached with the knife clasped in her fist, her hand low and close to her body. One thing Alexa excelled at was the fast-blade punch.

She pushed open the doors, one by one, creeping across the plush carpet on her tiptoes.

Her own bedroom was empty of intruders, not to mention her jewellery, laptop and cash.

The missing couple of hundred pounds she had put in her bedside cabinet drawer was of no concern. Heart pounding, hands shaking, Alexa reached up to release the loft hatch, pulled down the ladder and, trying to keep a lid on her panic, slowly climbed. She took a deep breath, put a hand out into the darkness and felt around for the two holdalls of cash that were being collected in less than twenty-four hours.

Gone.

She grabbed the ladder with both hands, feeling her knees give a little.

Where was she going to get 400,000 euros by tomorrow morning?

Chapter 20

'You did a brave thing,' said Harry, seated in a chair opposite John Kersley, Pierre beside the bed, 'a very brave thing.'

Harry Powell gave his captive audience a hint of a smile; an expression that he hoped conveyed the message: *I know where you're coming from.*

A scratch of his chin, a loosening of his tie, a conspiratorial wink. Harry continued, 'How about you tell us everything that's happened and we'll see about getting you somewhere safe to stay, away from here.'

Harry watched the young man: haggard face, shadows under his bloodshot eyes licking his chapped lips. He stared at John as he struggled to decide what to do, his Adam's apple bobbing up and down as he swallowed.

The DI was forced to lean across the gap between him and the hospital bed to make out the next words.

'You won't be able to guarantee my safety,' rasped John.

Harry knew that he probably couldn't make such

a promise. The department had run out of biros last week and the staff had been asked to write smaller or buy their own pens until the new financial year. How could he begin to finance round-the-clock protection for a man who might not, evidentially, be of any use?

Nevertheless, it gave Harry a bad feeling when he failed someone. In this instance, he was letting the man down before they'd even begun. His mind flew to his warrant card in his back trouser pocket, nestled in the standard black leather wallet complete with the photograph of him looking sombre – he'd been told by the headquarters photographer not to smile, as the public mustn't think the police enjoyed themselves at work. Next to his official identification was his job-registered credit card.

Sod it, he'd book Kersley into a hotel if need be. Finance wouldn't even know what he'd done for a couple of weeks. He'd face the bollocking when it came his way, as it no doubt would.

He tried again.

'John, you're absolutely right, I can't make any open-ended promises about the rest of your life. However, what I *can* do is move you somewhere safe for the time being. Pierre and I can take you to a hotel. We can speak to you elsewhere on the way, and if you're able to tell us what happened last night, everything you can about who you think is behind this, we'll find you somewhere safe to stay.'

He searched the witness's face for any sign that he had got through to him and he would tell them what they needed to know.

The only sounds came from the scuttling staff in the corridor outside, paramedics bringing in new patients, visitors rushing to see loved ones.

A nod, a small nod.

Then, 'Okay . . . You're right, completely right. They shouldn't be doing what they're doing. These people are human beings.'

Satisfied that today was turning into a much better day than expected, Harry glanced over at Pierre, who had a look of concern on his face.

'We need to confirm that he can be released from the hospital,' he said. 'I'll go and speak to the nurse.'

John waited until Pierre had left the room, looked back towards Harry and said, 'Thank you for taking me seriously. Not that Pierre wasn't. It's just . . . well, if the two of you are so bothered about me and what I've got to say, it makes a difference, you know.'

'We all take shootings very seriously, and if you've been targeted for what you know about criminal activity, it's everyone's business to protect you.'

'Can I go home and get some stuff before we go to the hotel?'

'It's still a crime scene at the moment, but we can sort that out for you.'

'What about clothes? The paramedics cut my shirt off.'

'Leave it with us, John. We'll get you some half-decent clobber too. Okay?'

Harry noted a slight relaxing of John's facial muscles at this suggestion. He couldn't help but feel a little sorry for him, even if he was a touch aggravating. After all, this was a man who had been shot at for protecting someone else, for seemingly no personal gain.

'Right,' said Pierre from the doorway, 'the doctor will be in to see you soon, then you can go.'

'I'll leave you to get some rest, then,' said Harry as he stood up and made his way over to Pierre. 'Quick word with you again, P.'

The pair strode past the armed officer outside in the corridor and made their way back to the spot where they had whispered their updates to each other a little earlier.

'I see what you mean,' said Harry, 'he's a bit of a whingey bastard.'

'That's not exactly what I said.'

'Well, I can't say that I warmed to him. Anyway, get yourselves a hotel nearby with rooms – adjoining rooms would be best, but next door at the very least. I'll ring the techies and get a panic alarm for him to wear around his neck during the night, and we'll get someone to drop by with recording equipment for an interview. It's best if we do this on DVD. Any other thoughts?'

'What about his clothes?'

'I'll get someone to see if we can borrow some jogging bottoms, a top and plimsolls from custody. We can get him some stuff from the shops later.'

'Who are you asking to help me with the interview?'

'I think Tom. Is that all right with you? He's currently out with Sophia, but Hazel's off today, Gabrielle is completely unsuitable as she knows Kersley, and I could go on with who's got urgent stuff, Crown Court and so on.'

'Tom's a good bloke,' said Pierre. 'There's one other thing ...'

Pierre held his hand out to Harry, whose face made it clear he was at a loss to know what Pierre was waiting for.

'I think Frank'll get over the fact that I've booked myself and another man into a hotel if it's for work, but he won't be too impressed that police budgets are so non-existent that I've got to pay for it myself.'

'Oh, sorry, P,' said Harry as he reached into his pocket to get the card. 'How's Frank? Long time no see.'

'Good, very good. Listen ...' Pierre took the proffered card and leaned in closer. 'Keep it to yourself for now, if you don't mind: Frank and I are getting married later this year.'

'That's wonderful news! Congratulations.'

'You're invited, of course, and Hazel, only we're not making a big thing of it.'

Harry beamed at Pierre. He'd always liked him, admired him, and wondered exactly how a gay man had fared at the mercy of the police service. He would never admit it out loud, but there'd been a time it had made him uncomfortable, for reasons he hadn't been able to fathom. Good old-fashioned prejudice.

'We'd love to come along,' said Harry, smile still on his face.

'It's only family and a few close friends.'

This comment was met with Harry rubbing his hands together. To stop himself from hopping from foot to foot, as he feared he might at any second, he held out a hand and grasped one of Pierre's, before leaning in to slap him on the back with his free hand.

Aware that he was possibly making a bit of a scene by almost engulfing Pierre in his arms, he eventually let go and said, 'That's bloody marvellous, bloody marvellous. Well, I'm going to leave you be. Now, go and do some work.'

He made his way back to his car, glad that today was turning into a much better day.

Chapter 21

These days, Anna was grateful for small mercies. Cleaning carrots and putting them into plastic bags was fairly appealing compared to the other work she could have found herself doing.

Bent over the mound of carrots, she estimated that there was enough work to keep her going for at least a couple more shifts, possibly longer if there was more to harvest. She looked down at her hands: broken nails, dirt etched into the grooves of the skin. She picked up a carrot, studied it and the fingers holding it. Fingers that looked as though they belonged to someone with at least a decade on her.

Her dream had been to become a receptionist in a smart office somewhere. Legal, medical, it didn't matter. But she knew now that dream was out of reach.

As she brought herself back to reality, mind no longer fantasizing about answering a telephone and writing on message pads, she saw the door leading to the toilets open in the far corner of the open-sided shed.

Anna was sitting with her back to the yard, so she

hadn't noticed who was in the packing area with her. She had assumed that Lili was still crouched down behind her, picking over her own heap of vegetables.

She was wrong.

It was always noisy with the sounds of the workers moving goods, either by hand or with machinery. So noisy that she hadn't heard any of the conversation that had taken place behind her, where Lili had must have been persuaded to take an unscheduled break the same time their minibus driver decided to visit the gents' toilets.

Anna froze.

She was powerless to help Lili, and not entirely sure she should, anyway. Why put her neck on the line for a foolish young girl who ought to know better? Not two hours ago, Anna had warned her that nobody paid their debt off that easily, so what she hoped ten minutes in the grotty toilets was going to achieve was anyone's guess.

The plan was most definitely for Anna to keep her own head down and pray that, somehow, she was able to find her daughter, get them somewhere safe and as far away from this terrible new life as she could, using Lili, or in fact anyone else in the process if she had to.

The minutes passed by, but without a watch or clock, Anna could only gauge how many by the number of bags of carrots she had managed to sort. Sealing them at the end was the trickiest part, especially with cold fingers from the draught behind her and the cold of the crops freshly pulled from the ground. Frequently she had to stop, stretch the cramp from her hands.

She estimated that Lili and Pock-mark had been gone for about fifteen minutes. It seemed a long time, far too long for anyone to be that close to him. He had cold eyes. Cold, staring eyes.

He had been staring at Lili that morning, now she thought back to their journey. Anna's ribs had been hurting so much, and the attitude from the others on the bus hadn't helped.

Lili had stood up for her. She had spoken up against three men.

And what did Anna now find herself doing? Trembling in front of a pile of carrots.

On unsteady legs, hunger pangs gnawing her insides, Anna got up. At first, no one else noticed. Then one of the Controller's supervisors shouted to her. She could barely make out what he was saying, although she didn't need to hear him to know he was asking her where the fuck she thought she was going.

As Anna turned in the direction of the door tucked into the far corner, she saw a growing sliver of darkness as it opened, followed swiftly by Pock-mark as he made short work of the twenty-five metre gap separating them.

'What's your problem?' he spat at her as he got within touching distance.

Instinctively, she averted her gaze, unwittingly towards his open flies.

He stepped closer, rancid breath assaulting her senses.

He grabbed his own crotch.

'Want some too?' he taunted in her ear.

She shook her head in reply, grateful to move her nose from his mouth, her eyes now squeezed shut.

If Anna stood really still, she could hold her own breath and not inhale his stench. When she thought she couldn't risk standing rooted to the spot for a second longer in case she got another beating, she stole a look in her tormentor's direction. She caught the back of him as he walked away, laughing and doing his flies up.

Lili's entrance was a lot slower than her abuser's. Her hand crept around the door frame, followed by her arm. Her face gave everything away: pained by the stark reality of where she was and what she had just sunk to. Her unsteady gait was the bit that worried Anna the most.

Then Lili looked across and saw Anna staring at her, separated from her housemate by an enormous heap of carrots.

A lopsided smile crept across the young woman's face. It was probably supposed to reassure them both. It failed spectacularly.

By the time Lili reached Anna, she had at last put the carrot she had been clutching in her claw-like hand back on the pile.

'It's not what you think,' insisted Lili, her mouth closer to Anna's ear than Pock-mark's had been. Disturbingly, now the same rancid stench emanated from her.

'How do you know what I think?'

'The look on your face. Don't judge me, Anna. I'm trying to make the most of this and get myself out of here. I need a plan. We need a plan.'

'I've got a plan and it doesn't include having sex with that ugly bastard.'

'How dare you!' Lili grabbed Anna's wrist, now limp and by her side, her hand devoid of vegetables, forcing her to turn and look her in the eye.

'How dare I what?' said Anna. 'How dare I try to *survive*?' You go down this route, there's no hope for you. Stop being so naive.'

'Naive? That's incredible coming from you. I haven't had sex with him. I'm not stupid. I need to meet his friends and then I'll have my debt cleared once I've done what they ask. The driver only wanted to ...'

She avoided Anna's eye, looked down and added, 'Well, you know ... stuff.'

Everything in Anna's being told her not to get involved, to look after herself. This foolish young girl wasn't her problem, and risking her own safety was dangerous. She had enough of her own issues. Besides, the Controller and Pock-mark already had their hooks into Anna and life wasn't about to get any easier. To help out someone else, who was clearly only ever going to be a liability, was not only foolish but probably fatal.

Yet she didn't want to walk away and leave her to her own devices. The last thing she wanted was to have Lili's death on her conscience. One murder was enough.

It wouldn't end with sex – it never did.

'"Stuff"?' repeated Anna. 'I really don't want to

know what kind of "stuff". It's none of my business. I want no part of this yet you've made me a part of it by telling me.'

Seeing the hurt expression on Lili's face might have been the moment Anna told her about her daughter, had it not been for the blood-curdling scream that came from the open side of the shed.

Chapter 22

Once again, Pierre found himself waiting around for someone else so that he could get on with his job. He had already waited over an hour for a doctor to examine John Kersley and discharge him from the hospital, then another half-hour for Tom to arrive with the plimsolls, jogging bottoms and sweatshirt, begged from a not-so-impressed custody sergeant. He then had to listen to John complain for five minutes about how he shouldn't be made to wear someone else's cast-offs, then wait another twenty for him to actually get dressed and use the bathroom, on more than one occasion.

When, at last, they were ready to leave the hospital, Pierre spoke to the firearms officer still on guard outside John's room.

'Are you following from here?' he asked.

This was met by a smirk and a shake of the officer's head.

'No, we're needed elsewhere. Besides, the rationale was that if he's eventually going to an undisclosed location, there's little point in us turning up in a marked car with weapons. It's a bit of a giveaway.'

'Fair enough,' said Pierre with a shrug. 'I have to say, right at the moment, they seem to be taking this very seriously. I know someone tried to shoot him, but he's not exactly given us much information.'

'It's because someone mentioned people trafficking. It's the newest and latest thing the government have to pretend to give a shit about. It keeps the lefties happy, something being done to help the most vulnerable, while at the same time keeping the right wing quiet, thinking a load of foreigners are getting kicked out of the country. It's a win-win.'

'Unless you're John Kersley and you get shot at for trying to do the right thing.'

'I have to say, I admire him for trying to help them. We found out who they were yet?'

'No,' said Pierre, giving a glance towards the closed hospital side-room door. 'If we ever get out of here, I hope he's going to tell me.'

Since he was a child, Pierre had wanted to join the police. He'd wanted to help people and make a difference in any way he could. But after twenty-six years in the job, he was ashamed to admit that John Kersley was truly trying his patience. And Pierre had a lot of it. Or so he used to think.

'So it's *not* decaf tea?' he asked the detective for the second time, staring into the mug.

'No, John,' Pierre said, literally biting his lip. 'And

before you ask again, we don't have white tea, green tea or peppermint tea. If I'm honest, I'm amazed we've got tea at all, and the milk only being one day out of date is, in police terms, a right result.'

Pierre paused, tried to rid his tone of any hint of hostility. He reminded himself that he was dealing with a victim here.

'We really need to get your interview under way. As soon as Tom gets back, we'll start. Is that okay?'

John nodded.

'You're all right here? Happy with where we are?'

John nodded again.

'This house is one of the few police-owned houses left in the county. The idea was to keep witnesses and those who've suffered violent or sexual assaults away from police stations. This is only one of three remaining.'

He could have gone on a tirade of how budget cuts and short-sighted management thought it was a good idea to sell off the force's assets to make a few quid, but thought that his traumatized witness could probably do without it, and wasn't likely to be on his side under the circumstances.

'Yeah, you said,' replied John as he looked around the front room. There was a large red crate of children's toys in one corner, a twenty-year-old television set in another and a coffee table in the centre of the room strewn with magazines older than Pierre's car.

The sound of a car pulling onto the driveway was a welcome distraction for Pierre and he almost leaped from the sofa to open the front door.

One look at him made Tom's face break into a wide grin.

'You okay, P?' he asked with a head tilt towards the front room where John Kersley sat.

'Not too bad, thanks,' he replied before mouthing, *Help me.*

Tom grinned at him again and said, 'I managed to get cold drinks, milk and something to eat.'

'Thanks, Tom. Come in, we'll get started.'

Once in the living room, Tom asked John whether he wanted another drink and showed him the bag of sandwiches, crisps, fruit and biscuits.

'So what would you like?' he asked.

John pointed into the bag and said, 'Are those gluten-free?'

'I'm not entirely sure, John,' Tom replied, with a now forced smile on his face. 'I'm no expert, but I'd say with a reasonable amount of certainty that Jaffa Cakes probably aren't gluten-free. How about an apple instead?'

By the time he'd finished rustling the carrier bag, he looked up to see that Pierre had left the room.

Chapter 23

The scream had pierced the air, reverberating off the metal sides of the open shed. All thoughts of sifting and packing root vegetables gone from the minds of those hunched over their respective piles. Even those in charge of the immigrants and the English farm workers were momentarily stunned.

Then there was chaos.

Anna grabbed Lili's arm, pulled her into the farm-yard. Two men were standing beside the body of a young woman, face down, limbs sprawled out like a rag doll's. Only this body was mutilated, cut almost in two by a piece of farming equipment.

A metal blade was sticking out of the young woman's back, fifteen or so centimetres clear of her denim jacket, directly in the centre of her shoulder blades and stopping just shy of her waist.

Anna felt the bile rise, grateful for once that she hadn't eaten today. She felt Lili shudder beside her, aware she still had hold of the younger woman's arm.

Instinctively, Anna pulled her closer, turning her face from what was left of the former worker.

Unable to keep her own curiosity in check, Anna continued to stare in both wonder and horror.

Most of them gathered round, looking at the body of a woman they hadn't taken the time to get to know while she was alive. There would have been little point; no one stayed put for long.

A few of those who had stopped doing what they were supposed to be getting paid for realized that they didn't even know her name. Not that it was important now. But what they did know – what mattered – was that this was bound to bring the authorities running.

Pock-mark had been staring at the dead woman. He muttered something to one of the other supervisors that sounded to Anna like, 'Silly bitch.'

She caught his eye.

'You two, go and get in the minibus.'

'We can't just leave,' said Anna.

Surely this was her chance to get away, she thought. Now she was desperate to speak to someone about her daughter and the papers she'd been forced to sign. The police would come and she would tell them what had been happening. Nothing could be worse than this. Perhaps she would even get to go home and stop her daughter from leaving Hungary.

The thought made her feel light-headed. Though that could have been the lack of food.

It didn't take long for Pock-mark to cover the distance between them. Rancid breath once again in her face. She pulled Lili to the other side of her, an arm's length away from their tormentor.

'That daft bitch was told not to climb the ladder to go up there. If she'd used her brains and remembered she didn't have a head for heights, she wouldn't have fallen and impaled herself on the bloody blade, would she?'

Anna and Lili winced, not only at his choice of words, but at the odour emanating from his mouth.

'Go. And. Get. In. The. Minibus.'

They took a step backwards, Anna unable to resist one more glance at the young woman. A different day, a different job, it could have been her body lying there. She was weak from the lack of food. Accidents on farms weren't that uncommon. If nothing else, she could use this one to her advantage.

As soon as she was out of sight, she could try to make a run for it, hide in a hayloft or wherever she could find. It was a farm, at the end of the day; there were dozens of outbuildings in its curtilage. Then, once she was hidden, all she had to do was wait until the police arrived, and she could explain their situation.

The worst that could happen was that they wouldn't believe her and would send her back to Hungary.

There was only one problem – Lili.

She was now sobbing and drawing attention from both the English supervisors and the other Eastern Europeans.

She had to decide whether to ditch Lili or try to take her with her. She knew which one she preferred.

'Come on,' she said to Lili, eyes locked on Pock-mark.

'He's right, let's do as he tells us. We need to get away from here.'

A smile, perhaps a sneer, followed by a dropping of his eyes towards Anna's breasts, their outline clear through her thin T-shirt.

Fortunately, it was something that Lili didn't notice or else it might have set her off again. There was no way Anna had time for that. She knew it was now or never.

They crossed back into the open-sided sorting shed, more food than she could eat in a lifetime spread across the floor. Some of it was sorted and bagged, most of it lying in heaps.

Hidden from view, Anna whispered to Lili, 'When you went in there with the driver . . .' She pointed over to the toilets. 'Was there any other way out? A door? Somewhere out of sight?'

Incredulous, Lili turned, her red-rimmed eyes as wide as saucers.

'You want to escape? Are you mad?'

'No, Lili, listen to me.' Anna knew that she didn't have much time: she had to convince Lili now or leave her behind, and that raised the separate problem of whether Lili would run straight to Pock-mark and tell him. She'd have valuable minutes otherwise.

'I've checked this place out over the few weeks I've been here. I know how we can get to the main road and then ask for help. I hate to put my own family in danger, but we can't stay here. We're both dead if we do. We can do this, but together and now.'

She glanced back across to where there was a

reasonable crowd gathering, a few of them with mobile phones clamped to their ears.

'If we get in the minibus, then this is over. Her death was horrible, tragic, but let's at least make something good come of it. We'll use it as a diversion.'

Anna was at the point of giving up, the seconds ticking away, when a barely perceptible nod of the head was all she needed.

'Through there …' Lili pointed towards the toilet door in the far corner. 'There's another door that leads out towards the dirt track where the minibus is usually parked.'

'Good, good.'

Another nervous glance from Anna in the direction of the onlookers. It would only be a matter of seconds before someone came to see what they were doing and why they hadn't got back on the bus.

'Show me where,' she said, aware her fingers were now gripping the younger woman's arms.

They started to move across the concrete floor, huddled together in their misery. Almost at the door now, Anna steadied her breathing, barely able to believe that she might be about to taste freedom.

She waited for the shout from behind, the tug on her sleeve yanking her away from the door. Neither came.

Perhaps they'd been forgotten about after all.

'So you say it leads directly outside?' she breathed into Lili's ear.

'Yes,' she whispered back. 'The driver opened it at one point to flick his cigarette end out there.'

Anna was about to reach out and grab the handle when the door opened towards them.

The sight of one of their tormentors stopped them both in their tracks. Anna could feel the blood pumping in her ears. She willed herself to stay calm.

He towered over them, muscles testing the fabric of his short-sleeved T-shirt, jaw clenching and unclenching.

'Where the fuck do you think you two are going?'

'To ... to the toilet,' said Anna. She glanced at Lili, gave her what she prayed was a sympathetic smile and holding her nerve as steadily as she could she added, 'The woman in the accident. They were friends. Please ... let us have two minutes. We only need to clean up in the toilets then we're heading for the minibus.'

He took a step closer, steel toe-capped boots sounding on the concrete floor.

He peered down at them.

'Okay, two minutes. I'll be waiting.'

Unable to speak, fear taking over, Anna nodded and pulled Lili around the colossal heavy blocking their escape.

She reached out to the door, grabbed the handle and then stood rooted to the spot once more as she heard him take another step in their direction, place his hand on the door a couple of centimetres from hers. Anna stared without really seeing the tattoos that adorned his knuckles.

'What was her name?' he said, arm brushing the back of Anna's head as he leaned against the door.

'What?' said Anna as she tried to look up to meet his gaze, knowing that doing so would be worse than staring a wild animal in the eye, challenging it, causing it to attack.

'This friend of hers. What was her name?'

Anna couldn't get her mouth to move and her brain certainly didn't want to join in. She felt a scream forming somewhere. They were going to die now, her only hope being that one decent English person on the farm would come and help them. Why she thought this, it was impossible to say. No one had even looked at them since they arrived. They were an invisible workforce, forgotten people.

'Hanna,' said a tiny voice, then louder, 'Hanna.'

Anna stared at Lili. She hadn't expected Lili to have spoken to the woman, let alone known her name.

'Don't forget, two minutes.'

He pushed himself off the door. Anna felt the relief of pressure both from his bulk against the metal door and from her shoulders.

She bundled Lili through the entrance, not daring to hope they could get free from this hell on earth.

Chapter 24

Still reeling from the loss of 400,000 euros, Alexa heard her mobile phone ring from her discarded handbag. She steadied herself to sound serene, smoothed down her skirt with one hand and picked up the phone with the other.

'Yes,' she answered, then listened, eyes closed, fingers rubbing at her temples as the frantic voice at the end of the line rattled off at her about that morning's catastrophe.

'You know what to do,' she said. 'We're prepared for this. It isn't the first time, and certainly won't be the last. It's a farm; accidents happen. If you remember, we've lost workers in Cambridgeshire, Norfolk, Lincoln ... I could go on, but I've run out of fingers. So, get the ones out that you can before the police turn up and start causing problems. Those you can't get out, leave them there. Unless they fancy their chances in a cage fight, they'll never tell the truth.'

A text message alert on her phone caused her to stop and frown.

She opened the attachment, took a huge intake of breath at its contents, deleted it and wondered what other shit was coming her way today.

Chapter 25

Around the time their eight-hour shift was due to finish, Pierre and Tom had only just begun interviewing John Kersley.

Once they were all settled, Tom operating the camera and Pierre in a chair facing John, they finally got going.

Three questions in and John said, 'I'm not sure I can do this.'

Pierre tried to hide his frustration. 'Why's that?'

'What if they come after me?'

'We've been through all of—'

'I know we have. Still doesn't stop me getting killed, though, does it?'

'We can't talk about where you're going to go and what's going to happen to you all the time we're recording, John. I've made some calls and things are in place. Now, let's get this done. I'll know more after; my boss is making sure that you're going to be safe.'

Pierre allowed the information to sink in and then

asked, 'Tell me about the two men who were staying with you in your flat.'

Fidgeting, followed by a heavy sigh, a licking of the lips. Then at last John said, 'They were Hungarian. Starved, scared and hurt Hungarians. They'd been beaten – well, *tortured*, really. I can't imagine doing that to another human being. What's wrong with people? I felt I had to do something, help them, get them off the streets and somewhere safe. You'd have done the same if you'd seen their injuries: mostly bruising, but with a few cuts thrown in. One of them, the older of the two, had cigarette burns on his back. There were about eight or nine of them. How sick do you have to be?'

He paused, looked down at his lap.

'Know where I met them?' he said with a frown.

Pierre gave a minuscule shake of his head.

'Bins at the back of Sainsbury's. I was taking a short cut home when I saw someone in the bin. The store shuts at five on a Sunday evening and the staff start chucking out unsold items at about six o'clock or so. I think they get first dibs on it, but according to the two I met foraging though the waste, there was still a lot of grub going spare.

'Word spread, of course, so there were often fights and threats made, especially between different nationalities. That was how Marton got his face slashed.'

This piece of information jolted Pierre.

'Yeah, one of the Romanians sliced him across the cheek with a jagged piece of tin from a beer can, left a great wound. He couldn't even go to hospital, not that he knew where it was. He couldn't risk being found out, and could barely speak any English anyway. We only managed to get by using Google Translate. They had a go at cleaning his face up themselves, although they did a very crude job. He needed stitches, really.'

Pierre watched Kersley as he picked at a loose piece of nail.

He waited.

'Managed to get my hands on some antiseptic, bandages, that sort of thing. In the end, I took him to A&E. They asked questions, of course – we lied, of course. He was so scared that the people who had kept him prisoner would find out where he was.'

'So who was keeping him prisoner?' asked Pierre.

'That was the thing, he didn't know who they were. When they arrive here, they're moved around all the time: different houses, different counties, different controllers and heavies. They never know real names and identities. It's all part of the control.'

'We'll need to speak to these men,' said Pierre, 'the ones you were helping.'

What little colour was left in Kersley's face disappeared without trace.

'They won't.' He breathed the words rather than said them.

'Won't what? Speak to us? Are they scared of the police?'

'They're more scared of their controller.'

Kersley paused again, swallowed and ran a hand over his face.

'There's more,' he said to Pierre, this time with a tremble to his lip. 'I couldn't let them go once I'd heard why Marton tried to escape, despite the risk to his own family back home.'

Pierre let the silence hang between them, willed John to continue, understanding now his earlier reluctance to relay this diabolical story.

'He was looking for someone,' he said after a minute ticked by. 'His sister came over with him. She was only thirteen. He was told they'd start a new life together, except she was taken from him. He had no idea where she was, although he'd heard the rumours.'

'Rumours?' asked Pierre.

'Children sold into the sex trade. That's where the money is, apparently. Have you ever heard anything so depraved and barbaric? There was a rumour that this controller took them home, put them in a cellar and brought them out for parties.'

Pierre pushed a box of tissues across the table towards his witness. He had far from warmed to him, but here was an unexpected tale of bravery from a man who had nothing at all to gain from helping others.

'Translating online was hard going,' continued John through sniffs and dabbing at his eyes, 'but they told me what happened to people who tried to get help, escape.'

'What happened to them?'

Kersley chewed the inside of his mouth.

'Marton told me that if anyone stepped out of line, pissed the Controller off, they were made to fight each other. How could I have lived with myself if I didn't help them?'

His words were barely audible now.

'It's how they were kept under control, made to stay and work. If they stepped out of line, they were put in a cage. Marton won. It's the only reason he's still alive. Only the winner got to live.'

Chapter 26

By four o'clock that afternoon, Harry'd had enough. He was feeling tired to the core and wasn't sure how much longer he could sustain being woken up in the early hours and expected to keep working throughout the day. The novelty of being alerted to some sort of disaster in the county that required his urgent attention had long since worn off. And prising himself from his warm bed to spend the next twelve to sixteen hours working was not a prospect he relished with his fiftieth birthday on the horizon. The hours he didn't mind, the lack of sleep he was struggling with.

Perhaps all Harry needed was a holiday. When he was married, he, his wife and the kids often took two weeks away somewhere. They'd had some good trips. Perhaps he'd mention it to Hazel when he got home, if he ever got home.

As he sat at his desk in his office next to the main incident room, bereft of people like the majority of police departments, and indeed stations, up and down the country, his phone rang.

'What have you got for me, P?' he asked.

'More than I expected,' said Pierre, giving Harry the run-down on everything he'd just learned from John Kersley. 'We couldn't get any names of the people holding them, but he did tell us that one of the blokes he helped – a Hungarian – was called Marton.' A pause. 'And he's probably on his way back to Hungary by now. Only, the other one's dead.'

'What makes him think that?'

'Because Marton told him who killed him.'

'What?' Harry almost shouted into the earpiece. 'What happened? Where is this Marton guy now?'

'Okay, so they left his flat one night with John. He took them to the docks to put them on a ferry to France. He dropped them off, never expecting to see them again. Except one came back – Marton – mostly, it appears, to look for his thirteen-year-old sister.'

'What sister?' said Harry.

'It would seem that, on top of everything else, if you want to make it big-style dealing in human misery, kids are the way forward. Both for benefits and for selling into prostitution.'

'Have I told you today how much I fucking hate people?' said Harry, headache forming.

'At this moment in time, I couldn't agree more. I have a sneaking suspicion this Marton fella is how the traffickers knew where John Kersley lived and where the other runaways were staying.'

'We're guessing they either followed Marton or, more likely, beat it out of him?' asked Harry as he wondered how much money he could ask for at the next meeting of the bigwigs.

'You're probably not going to be overly fond of what I'm about to say.'

Pierre took his time continuing, about one second short of Harry telling him to 'hurry the fuck up'.

'When Marton came back, covered in claret from what Kersley told me, his words to him were, "If you don't help me, I'm a dead man. It was me or him." At least, words to that effect, given that Kersley doesn't speak any Hungarian and they don't speak much English. That's part of the fundamentals of modern slavery: the traffickers deliberately choose the ones that they know won't be able to talk their way out of trouble or ask for help when they're having seven bells kicked out of them.'

'So, what did he say about how this other bloke died?' said Harry.

'He said that he killed him. They were forced into a cage fight organized by the Controller.'

'Well, this controller's a fucking charmer,' said Harry, mentally analysing how his funding bid would go and whether the Home Office would spare any more cash to deal with modern-day slavery.

'Marton didn't get a name, unsurprisingly,' replied Pierre. 'But he had quite a description.'

'Really? What did he look like?'

'Oh no,' said Pierre, 'that was my assumption too. The Controller was a woman.'

Chapter 27

Alexa Gabor had come a long way since arriving in England six years ago and she wasn't about to see things go wrong now.

The weekly cash run through the ports always added to her stress, and it wasn't a simple matter of doubling up next week's shipment. It was far too risky to smuggle so much in one minibus. Besides, they were expecting the money at the other end when the transport arrived to pick up her new workhorses.

Apart from the pressing matter of having lost 400,000 euros, the business was growing, putting her under increasing pressure. Not to mention the fact that there had been two raids on places she was sending workers to. The last few weeks had caused her a financial dip, especially taking into account the three slaves who had got away without wiping their 23,000-euro debt.

It was fortunate that she was such an astute entrepreneur, her financial security taken care of. If it weren't for the children she regularly brought into the country, who knew what her financial situation would be.

Running through the mental arithmetic with regard to her child benefit scams and the money she made from selling children into prostitution, she was relieved to work out she would be all right. She shook her head at the prospect of wiping out a chunk of her savings, plus the takings from this evening's activities.

Thinking hard about how she would have to move her own cash around meant she didn't notice the Nissan Qashqai that pulled up opposite her driveway.

Chapter 28

The two Hungarian women huddled together, partly for warmth, but mainly for physical support. Unable to believe her luck, Anna pushed open the fire door next to the toilets and peeked through the entrance to the deserted frontage of the farm. At any moment, she expected a delayed fire alarm to ring or someone to come after them.

For a second, she considered running upstairs and finding someone from the farm who might help them. Someone must have put up the posters she had seen in the toilets, so surely would care. Without the henchmen or Pock-mark, she might be able to make herself understood and help would come to them.

She hesitated in the doorway, stealing a glance towards the bare concrete stairs.

Almost five weeks she'd been working on the farm and the English had all looked through her. No one had ever spoken to her. She had never needed to go into 'script mode'. Why should she think that this would be any different? All that would happen was that they would shout for a Hungarian interpreter. And who would they shout to? Pock-mark, no doubt.

'What are we waiting for?' whispered Lili. 'We do this now or turn back.'

That was the jolt she needed.

''Course, let's go.'

Not wanting to alert anyone to their flight, Anna pushed the door to with as little noise as possible.

Lili took a step forward.

'No,' said Anna. 'Haven't you noticed there are windows up there? They look out from the offices to the front of the farm. I don't know who'll be up there.'

She felt Lili's body begin to shake as they clutched one another's arms.

'It'll be all right, Lili, I promise you.'

Anna bit her lip at her own words. She was deceiving herself, and now she was filling a younger, more impressionable woman's head with a ridiculous notion that salvation was only a short trek away.

False hope was very cruel, even if given in kindness.

'We need to keep to the side of the building. There's what looks like a pathway over there and that will lead to the road. As long as we stick to the ditches and keep out of sight of traffic, we'll be okay.'

The first hundred metres or so of their journey met with no resistance from Lili. Then suddenly she stood stock-still.

'What's wrong?' said Anna, unable to keep the panic from her voice.

'It's not too late to go back, is it?' said the deathly

pale Lili. 'I'm not sure I can do this. I can write off my debt. One night, he said, and then I'll be free.'

Anna stepped in front of Lili. She gripped the other woman's arms.

'Listen to me. You need to wake up. If you come with me now, we'll try to get help, possibly even get word home to warn our families, but we'll definitely escape this horrendous existence. I've only been here for five weeks, yet it feels like five years. How am I going to feel when it's actually *been* five years? Like I've been here fifty, that's how.'

'But we can do it together,' said Lili. 'We'll look out for each other and then we'll—'

Anna shook Lili's arms, forced her to look up and meet her eyes. 'Please don't tell me you were going to say, "And then we'll be free." We won't be free. I have a daughter on her way to this miserable country, and I won't let her become a part of this, especially not when I've seen what happens to girls her age.'

She stooped down to Lili's level, their eyes locked on one another's. 'Even if you don't care about my child, think about this: in just five weeks, I've seen three different girls like you arrive full of promise and annoying optimism. They were all offered the "write off your debt in one night" deal. Want to know what happened to them? Do you?'

She shook Lili's arms, making her whole body rock backwards and forwards, her face turned away from Anna's.

'One of them now takes heroin to block out the pain

from being fucked nightly by up to six or seven men – so she can pay for more heroin. Another drinks so much cheap vodka – for the same reason – that she's a danger around a match. The third is the worst—'

A noise from the building caught Anna's attention.

Momentarily distracted, she turned her focus back to her fellow escapee. 'Either come with me now and hear the rest of the story from me, or go back in there and find out first-hand how it ends.'

She saw what looked like understanding in Lili's eyes, as well as something she herself had become well acquainted with over the last five weeks – fear.

Unsure why she was offering reassurance to someone she owed little to, Anna found herself saying, 'Come with me and I'll get you home.'

'I don't want to go home,' said Lili.

'What?'

'I don't want to go home. I came here looking for someone. I came to England because that's where my boyfriend was headed. I came here to find him.'

'Are you insane? We don't even know what part of the country we're in. How are you supposed to find someone when you don't even know where you are?'

Lili smiled, a beautiful beam of a smile that lit up her delicate doll-like face. 'He managed to get a message to me that he was living not far from the ferry that brought him from France. He doesn't know where he is, but he can hear seagulls when he's at work at the car wash.'

'Car wash?'

'Somehow,' said Lili, 'I'm going to find him; Denis and I will be reunited. You see, I have to believe that everything will be all right. All I have to do is find him and this nightmare is over.'

Chapter 29

Evening of Monday 12 February

The atmosphere in the dilapidated factory was charged. The guests were locked in, all doors and windows shuttered to keep in the light, not to mention a few of the people. Doormen stood guard at all the entrances, checking invitations and ensuring the clientele weren't carrying more weapons than their hosts.

A lot of money was at stake, and a lot besides money. The stench of sweat and blood permeated the run-down building, mingled with the smell of cigar smoke and alcohol.

The crowd of two hundred or so was mainly made up of men – less than twenty per cent were women – all there to network, drink impossibly cheap vodka and watch someone get the beating of a lifetime.

Some people were privileged enough to be part of the paying audience, others unlucky enough to be part of the performance.

A raised area away from the action was roped off

and marked *VIPs Only*. It was hardly salubrious, but under the circumstances it would suffice, especially as its elevated position meant that select guests had a bird's-eye view of every single fight. And all without getting their hands dirty.

Alexa Gabor stood at the makeshift bar, glass of champagne in her hand, scanning the packed area around her, while trying to appear as though she was having the best night of her life.

Truth be told, she was expecting it to be the night she finally met her boss face to face.

A venue full of people there for illegal fights, in an isolated area. It's where she would have taken out someone who owed her 400,000 euros.

The reason she had lasted this long was because she had thought like them. Kept herself ahead of the game and, most importantly, alive.

A Turkish man – superb English, bad teeth – was talking to her. Something about cocaine, if she wasn't mistaken. She had grown tired of listening to him when it became obvious he was boasting about his drugs empire. There was no business to be done here, nothing she could gain from him, so she excused herself and moved away, untouched champagne still in her hand.

It wouldn't be long now until the first fight started, so Alexa had something to look forward to. While she hated to lose her workhorses when they ran away, there was always a silver lining; there were always plenty of ways to recoup her money.

If *they* didn't feel the need to bite the hand that fed them, *she* wouldn't need to make them fight to the death.

They only had themselves to blame.

Despite the other odours assaulting her nostrils, she smelled the sour breath of one of her drivers – the pockmarked one – before she saw him.

She said over her shoulder, 'What do you want?'

'There's a bit of a problem.'

She turned in her black silk dress, material swishing around her knees as she did so. 'I fucking pay you to sort the problems. What's wrong now?'

He looked down. 'Do you want to know about the problem earlier today at the farm, or the one here this evening?'

She tilted her head back, gazed up at the filthy ceiling, anything to avoid seeing his ugly face.

'Well, you moron, let's start with this evening and then later, when you've sewn your balls back on, you can tell me about the farm.'

Now she was staring him straight in the face. 'And?' she prompted.

She watched him swallow, run a hand through his thinning hair. 'There's a problem with one of the fighters,' he muttered.

'What?'

'There's a problem with one of the fighters.'

'I heard you the first time. I'm simply not able to believe what I'm hearing. I pay you to sort the problems so, once more, why are you fucking bothering me?'

'He said he wasn't going to fight again, so he's done something.'

Her face was a mask, given away by the tapping of her fingers against the glass she was clutching.

'Done something?'

Pock-mark moved his mighty weight from foot to foot. 'He's managed to find some glass and cut himself. He's lost so much blood, I think he's going to die.'

Even though she knew the breath-stench would be incredible, Alexa stepped towards him.

'Just so you understand, there will be a full programme of fights this evening. These people have spent an awful lot of money on coming out here, looking nice and placing bets. If whoever thought it was a good idea to self-harm on my cage-fighting night has any modicum of decency, he'll die before his allotted spot. And to be perfectly clear, if he dies, you're taking his place. Now fucking get on with it.'

Chapter 30

Pleased to be putting this horrendous day behind him, Harry pulled into his driveway, turned off the engine and sat in the car for a couple of minutes. He listened to the noises of the engine as it cooled, took a couple of deep breaths and thought about what he was going to tell Hazel about his day.

Not once had he ever burdened his ex-wife with the trials and tribulations of police work. Maybe that was why their marriage had failed: his inability to let her know how he spent most of his waking hours. Chances were it was more likely the fact they made each other bloody miserable, whatever he might have said to her.

Hazel was different. She was used to the grief of the job and, working in the same incident room, often knew the finer points of an investigation before Harry did.

His big decision of the evening was whether or not to tell her about Denis Boros and his maggot-infested testicles.

He'd see how the evening went.

By the time Harry was out of the car, through the front door and in the kitchen, Hazel had the fridge door open and their dinner in her hands.

'Hi,' she said as she held out the meal. 'I was about to call you, see how long you'd be. I made meatballs. Is that okay with you?'

He'd leave out the part about the young Hungarian's privates.

'I got some of that lovely fluffy white rice you like to go with them.'

'Thanks, Haze,' he said. 'Do you mind if I grab a beer and have a bath before we eat? First night off from being on call, I could do with half an hour to myself.'

He saw a flash of concern cross her face, something that he would have taken for annoyance from the former Mrs Powell.

'Besides,' he added, 'I've been on the go for something like sixteen hours and I probably could do with putting this suit in the cleaner's and freshening up.'

'I'll be the judge of that,' said Hazel as she put the dish on the table and stepped into Harry's arms.

'Er, actually, Harry,' she said a few seconds later, 'I've no idea where you've been today, but you're spot on about the clean clothes and a bath.'

Holding her tighter so she couldn't wriggle free, he said, 'Another ten minutes or so of cuddling and I think I'll go and get changed.'

She giggled into his chest and then said, 'Seriously, let me go. You smell.'

Releasing her, Harry made his way to the fridge.

'Luckily for you, I know there are some cold bottles of Tiger beer in here, or I'd have shown you no armpit mercy.'

He held one out to her as she opened the drawer to get the opener.

'A wall-mounted bottle opener,' he muttered more to himself than Hazel, 'I really must get one of those.'

'That reminds me,' said Hazel, chinking her bottle against Harry's, 'I'll sort the food out while you go upstairs and open your present.'

Meatballs aside, Harry felt like the luckiest man in the world. He took a long drink of his beer, winked at her and said, 'What have I done to deserve a present?'

'Just being all-round fantastic. Dinner will be in half an hour.'

He took the stairs two at a time, keen to see what his thoughtful girlfriend had done for him this time. How she knew he wanted these gifts he couldn't make out. It was as if she read his mind sometimes.

Harry pushed open the bedroom door.

He assumed from the size of the box lying on their double bed that Hazel would have struggled to hide her purchase from him. That meant she had been shopping that day, possibly around the same time he had been at the police raid, talking to the young man who worked at a roadside car wash.

Beer still in hand, he plonked himself down on the edge of the bed, kicked his shoes off and practised looking pleased with the new jet washer for his car.

Chapter 31

Acclimatized as they were to Hungarian winters, neither Lili nor Anna were used to sleeping outside in their thin clothes. They had spent a couple of hours wandering across footpaths, through farmers' fields and climbing over stiles, never discussing the fact that, once the daylight had completely faded, they were going to have to lie down on the ground and do their best to keep warm.

Even though Anna didn't really know where they were, she had spent the last five weeks being driven to and from work, traversing the area and getting a feel for the kind of place they now found themselves in. Although most of that time spent on the minibus was either before the sun had come up or after it had gone down, she had worked out from the lights in the distance that nowhere really seemed that isolated.

Now on foot, they had to try hard to avoid pockets of houses and shops; even a castle had appeared in the distance. It was important they stay away from people until they had decided what to do.

They needed a plan. That was something Anna had realized as soon as they'd got away, seemingly undiscovered. Her focus had been escaping from the Controller, something that, if she were honest with herself, she never thought would happen. It took only an instant for her to recognize that that was probably the easiest bit: the next was definitely uncharted territory.

At night, she had lain awake, listening to the whispers of the other girls in the damp, draughty bedroom. On occasion, she had picked up on mutterings from others at the salad-packing farm she had worked on before being moved to vegetables. They all spoke of one thing and one thing only – escape.

'I have to rest,' said Lili, breaking into Anna's thoughts, as she leaned against a tree trunk. 'Please give me a minute. I'd be all right if we'd had some food.'

Anna paced backwards and forwards, unwilling to stop and unable to rest, the ache in her ribcage a constant reminder of what was waiting for her if she was caught. She wanted to put as much distance between her and the farm as possible.

She had an uneasy feeling about where they'd ended up. They had passed a couple of other farm buildings, some with shipping containers. For all she knew, they could be walking right into another farm being operated by the Controller. Not only would they end up where they started, but both of them would get a beating for their troubles.

Or worse.

There was no way Anna could go back now, even without a good hiding waiting for her.

She stopped pacing to look at Lili. She was doubled over at the waist, face still pale.

'You okay to go on?' Anna asked.

'I am, as long as we've got a plan.'

'Of course I've got a plan.' Breaking eye contact, Anna said, 'We can't go back and we can't get home on our own. They've got our passports. The only thing for it is to go to the police.'

Lili launched herself off the tree trunk, almost ran to the other woman's side.

'Police? That's crazy. They can't help us.'

'Didn't you see the police cars this morning? The ones on that other farm we drove past on our way to work?'

Her question was met with a blank look.

'We must have been something like fifteen minutes from getting off the bus. I looked out of the window and saw lots of police, all sorts of flashing lights. Perhaps they were there to help people like us.'

'People like us are scum to them. We've been warned what the police will do to the likes of us. The only ones we can rely on are ourselves.'

Lili reached out and took Anna's hand in her own.

'If I had to get stuck out here with anyone, I'm glad it's you. I knew when I arrived two weeks ago that you'd be the one to help me. If you help me find Denis, then we'll go to the police. Okay?'

Once again it was impossible for Anna to hold Lili's gaze. She didn't have the heart to tell her that she had only wanted to escape and go to the police so she could make sure her daughter was safe. Right at that exact moment, tired, scared and lost, she really didn't care what happened to Lili.

Besides, Anna knew full well what had happened to Denis. That a few weeks ago he had passed through their miserable house and was now no doubt living his own pitiful existence.

She wasn't sure if it was kinder to tell Lili or leave her guessing.

Chapter 32

The crowd were expecting a show: anything less would result in violence from more than just the scheduled events.

Alexa worked the room, which took extra effort as it was more of a hangar than a room. Initially, she had tried to stay in the VIP area, glass of champagne in her hand, smiling sweetly and paying compliments to the fat, sweaty businessmen who leered at her. Their tobacco-smelling breath corrupted the air, made her flesh crawl. Twice she had wiped vodka spittle from her cheek, twice the Russian millionaire from whose mouth it had come pretended not to notice. Try as she might, she failed to hide a shudder when, the second time she brushed her hand across her face, she felt peanut on her skin.

'Do excuse me,' she said. 'I have to go and make sure my staff are doing as they're supposed to. You know how people seize any chance to neglect their work.'

Glad to be away from him and his putrid breath, Alexa took a step towards the edge of the VIP area. A hand on her arm stopped her in her tracks.

Always on show, no matter how crowded the venue, she smiled without turning back towards him. Her manicured fingers tightened on the champagne glass.

He lunged at her and said in her ear, 'I've got a large bet on one of the fighters not making it through to the end of the show. I assume you can help me with that?'

'Of course,' she replied, slight tilt of her head towards him. 'Leave it with me.'

She felt the intensity of the grip on her arm, fingertips digging into her flesh. Still she smiled. In a room this busy, someone would be monitoring her reaction.

The second his hand left her arm, she made her way through the crowd to a metal door tucked into the corner of the main bar area. It would probably have gone unnoticed by the hundred or so punters drinking and gambling, had it not been for the two enormous men standing guard in front of it.

Without a word, they parted to let her through, one grasping the handle and opening the door for her.

The noise from the excited crowd was reduced to a dull hum of delirium once the door was slammed shut behind her. The smell didn't lessen any; in fact, it was decidedly worse. This side of the barrier, the odour of excitement was replaced by fear. Not to mention blood.

She walked along the narrow, dark corridor, heels clipping the concrete floor with every step. There were three rooms on each side, every door flanked by a minder as gargantuan as those at the main entrance.

A flicker of annoyance crossed her face as she noticed that her champagne glass was almost empty.

For a second, Alexa paused at the first cell to her left, hesitated, shook her head at the expectant doorman, and continued on her way to the next.

This one would be more likely to listen and co-operate. His name wasn't important, but his reason for being there was.

This time, she stopped and waved the doorman away before stepping inside.

The room, about three metres by two, had once been used as a dry storage area, like its five counterparts. Now it housed nervous, expectant fighters.

The sight of her in the doorway made the clammy-skinned young man recoil towards the back of the wooden bench he was sitting on; his white bandaged knuckles as they gripped the edge of the seat a stark contrast to the rest of the holding area.

'Confident?' she asked as she watched him swallow.

He couldn't have been more than twenty-five, and if her own well-being wasn't on the line, she might have actually felt sorry for him.

A half-hearted shrug met her question.

'Listen,' she said, glancing over her shoulder, 'there's a way to increase your chances.'

Then came her favourite part: panic and confusion. For a second, he dreamed there was a way out. Taking it away was definitely the ultimate power play for Alexa.

She crouched down in front of him.

'See this?'

She raised the champagne glass, a centimetre or two of now flat and warm liquid in the bottom.

'Well, it's yours.'

Again, her heart soared as she witnessed the total bewilderment that took hold of him.

'I don't mean the champagne, though you can have that too.'

She held out the glass to him, her diamond bracelet catching in the stark light from the bare overhead bulb.

Unsure what to do, he lessened his grip on the wooden bench and put out a hesitant hand.

Alexa couldn't remember his name, and wasn't interested. All she knew was that this loser owed her 3,400 euros and had two sisters at home in Hungary, both with fatherless children. If she were a gambling woman – and quite frankly, she thought it was a mug's game – she would have risked a hefty wager on this one being the most likely to take the bait.

Always go for the one with the most to gain.

'Your opponent' – she indicated over her shoulder the opposite cell – 'I happen to know has a weak left knee. A couple of good kicks to that, followed by a jab to the neck with this' – she waved the glass – 'and you're home and free.'

Something shone in the young man's eyes. It was probably hope – usually the cruellest part.

She set the glass on the ground and stood up to leave, completely undecided as to whether or not he was going to make it out alive.

Chapter 33

Neither Anna nor Lili had any chance of getting a refreshing night's sleep. All they had managed so far was a couple of hours' broken rest underneath hedges, as close to the road as they could risk without being seen.

When Anna thought her bladder couldn't take any more, she managed to sneak off behind a tree for a minute's privacy.

It was at least better than the bucket in the Controller's house. It had always been how Anna had thought of it: the Controller's house. She probably didn't own it, but she certainly ruled it. Anna had hated it there, they all had. Most of them hadn't been kicked in the ribs repeatedly, yet no one had tried to escape either.

Anna went about her business, staring into the black of the night, shivering in the bracing air. If she had been feeling less than certain that they had done the right thing by slipping away from the farm, the dull ache in her side reminded her that this was surely a better existence than the one they had been enduring.

Standing once more, trousers back in place, Anna allowed herself the luxury of tears. With her eyes screwed shut and the sleeve of her jacket stuffed into her mouth so Lili wouldn't hear, she felt her whole body convulse. What she really wanted to do was throw herself on the ground, pound on the earth with her fists until they bled, and scream into the darkness.

What she did though was get a hold of herself, putting an end to the self-indulgent and silent sobbing, and reminding herself that no one was about to rescue them. No one could help them. They were alone. And yet . . .

She had a feeling that if people knew about the way they had been treated, someone would help them. It wasn't what they'd been led to expect when they were sold the one-way trip to England. As far as they'd been told they would be earning several hundred euros a week. Board and lodging would be deducted, only not on the scale it had been. Certainly, no one had mentioned the level of fear and control they would experience.

If someone knew, they would get help. Shouldn't the world work that way?

Then she remembered how her life had been before she'd accepted the chance to go to England and start a new life.

Anna wiped her hands across her face, momentarily forgetting that, minutes ago, she had been squatting behind a tree. Even in her small family home in Hungary, she'd had the means to keep herself clean.

She heard a movement in the bushes, not far from where she was standing. She held her breath, unsure whether it was the sound of an animal or a person. If it was an animal, it was a large one. Then she heard Lili whisper her name.

'I didn't want to startle you. Are you okay?' she said a little louder.

'I'm fine,' said Anna, 'and I doubt there's any need to speak so softly. I don't think there's anyone else around.'

'What are we going to do? It's pretty cold and I'm hungry.'

In response, Anna shook her head, a pointless action since she could barely see her hand in front of her face.

'The best idea I've come up with so far is the one I've told you about – we go to the police.'

From the sigh that emanated from her fellow escapee's lips, Anna guessed that Lili was now standing closer.

'And I've told you it's insane. What are they going to do?'

Anna reached out, felt the fabric of Lili's jacket, and placed her hands on the young woman's shoulders.

'I know how huge a deal this is. No one, I mean *no one,* in our position goes to the authorities. But I really believe the police will help us, otherwise I wouldn't be suggesting it.'

'What makes you so sure?'

'You remember the farm I told you about? The one we drove past on our way to work this morning?'

She felt movement from Lili's shoulders and took it as a nod.

'There were police there, lots of police. What else would they be doing if they weren't freeing people like us?'

'Locking them up perhaps? Beating them? Taking bribes? I thought I was the young, naive and trusting one. What you're suggesting is that we give ourselves up to the police, who we know only bad things about, and hope for the best. What if they put us in prison for being here without the correct work permits?'

Now Anna was grateful for the cover of night. It hid her tears, along with the expression on her face that would surely have given her away.

'You can tell them about Denis and they might even help you find him. Then you can go home together.'

Not being able to see seemed to heighten Anna's other senses, including her hearing. The tiniest of gasps escaped Lili's lips at the prospect of seeing the one person she had been prepared to face hell on earth for.

Anna would deal with her own personal hell for the lie she had told to get what she wanted.

The thought that she was probably as worthless a human being as the Controller didn't pass her by.

Chapter 34

Tuesday 13 February

Alexa Gabor reached out a manicured hand to switch off her alarm clock. The cage fighting had gone well, attendance had increased for the last event and she was several thousand pounds richer. Not a bad thought to start the day with.

She lay in her bed, duvet wrapped around her, duck-down pillows beneath her head, and let out a slow sigh.

She threw back the covers and sat on the edge of her bed, feet sinking into the carpet. She went to the bathroom and, shower at the correct temperature, she stepped around the two-metre-long glass screen and allowed the water to wash over her.

The combination of the sound of water hitting the anti-slip porcelain tiles and the hum of the extractor fan meant that it was several moments before she heard the noise.

In fact, it was possibly the slight breeze on her skin her senses registered first. It was hard to tell.

The water still running, she stepped from the shower and turned her head to the door, which she had left ajar. She wrapped a towel around herself as she heard a floorboard creak in the hallway.

Rather than leave anything to chance, she took a couple of steps back towards the glass shelves holding her toiletries and other bathroom clutter. A can of hairspray clutched in one hand and a pair of nail scissors in the other, she crept towards the door.

Then she heard a light tapping.

'Boss?' said a voice she recognized. 'Boss, you okay?'

She snatched at the door handle with the hand holding the hairspray, making sure she kept the can out of sight.

With as much authority as she could muster, dripping wet hair and only a towel covering her modesty, she demanded, 'What are you doing in my house?'

The gormless face of her pock-marked driver stared back at her.

His eyes flitted to her hand grasping the scissors.

'What?' she said. 'Can't I even cut my toenails without a fucking minute's peace?'

For several seconds they stared at one another, until Alexa felt the satisfaction of victory as he looked down at the floor.

She was about to ask her driver why he hadn't thought to remove his boots at the front door when he muttered something.

'What?' she said again. 'I can't hear you over the noise of the shower.'

'I said, I wouldn't have come in, but your front door was wide open.'

The hairs on the back of her neck weren't capable of standing up, not with the mass of bedraggled locks hanging over her shoulders, but it didn't stop the goose bumps on her arms.

'How about you go downstairs and make us both a coffee while I get dried and dressed,' she said, attempting something resembling a smile.

His ugly face lit up as he risked looking directly at her again. With an overenthusiastic nod, he bounded down the stairs.

'Hey,' she called out as he got to the bottom, about to turn into the hallway, hand still grasping the end of the banister.

He stared back up at his boss, dressed in only a towel, hand on one hip, her head tilted to the side.

'What are you doing here at this time of the morning anyway?'

'I ... I was worried. Well, not worried, but checking you were okay.' He ran a hand through his thinning hair, the knuckles of the other hand tightening their grip on the banister.

'Why would you be worried? Or checking?'

'No particular reason.' He gave a shrug and dropped his hands to his sides. Now he had stopped squeezing the life out of the handrail, he looked as awkward as he no doubt felt. He began to smooth down the legs of his jeans, grease stains and all, before realizing what he was doing.

She took a step towards the top of the stairs.

'Are you telling me you knew something was likely to happen?'

'No, boss, no.' He shook his head, jowls wobbling. 'Only, after last night, you seemed jumpy, and when I dropped you off, you ran in and slammed the door. I took a drive by to be on the safe side after your break-in and the door was open. That was all.'

She felt slightly guilty that she had shouted and sworn at him so often.

It didn't last long.

'Don't make a mess with the coffee. And hurry up. You've made me late now.'

He gave her a smile that made her flesh itch and, thankfully, disappeared from her view.

As if she didn't have enough to worry about, her ugliest heavy seemed to have an unwelcome crush on her.

Chapter 35

John Kersley had trouble sleeping.

The hotel bed was comfortable enough; he simply couldn't relax.

He knew he should have walked away from the bins at the back of Sainsbury's that day, yet he felt he had to help, had to right some wrongs.

He had always tried to do his bit for charity – a donation, a raffle – but that had all been done from the safety of his own home. The home he was no longer safe in.

Try as he might to get comfortable, rearranging the pillows, moving to the centre of the bed, he knew he wasn't going to get back to sleep.

Pierre would probably be awake by now. John felt they had really hit it off and he had been able to talk to the officer in a way he usually struggled with.

If he knocked on his door and the officer was dressed, perhaps they could go to breakfast a little earlier than they had planned. It would be the right time for John to tell him the reason he had risked his own safety for a few illegal trafficked workers.

John pictured them sitting at the table over pots of tea, waiting for their food while he shared with Pierre the uncomfortable story of his old classmate, an Albanian called Dibron. He was bound to understand that John had tried to befriend the boy, despite him being foreign, not in an exotic way, but in a weird way that was unacceptable to the rest of the class. No one was capable of spelling his surname and few wanted to talk to the newcomer, yet John had tried to make an effort.

His effort had lasted as long as the class bullies had left Dibron alone. He winced when he thought of Dibron's first week and how he had sat with him at break times, shown him the quickest routes around the school corridors. By Thursday of that week, John had given in to the snide comments. Already so close to the bottom of the pecking order, he simply hadn't had the backbone to defend himself, let alone others.

And that was before he knew how bad it was really going to get.

Helping Marton and the others was supposed to be John's defining moment, when he made up for his past actions. Only he had failed this time too.

John knew he needed to pull himself together. The least he could do was to get up, shower and dress, then speak to Pierre.

As soon as he was ready to leave his room, the self-doubts started again: maybe Pierre wouldn't get it, wouldn't understand.

He sat back down on the edge of his bed, unsure whether he was ready to share the untold story of what had kept him awake at night for the last twenty years.

No, he would stay in his room, watch television and wait for Pierre.

Chapter 36

Pierre's eyes snapped open. For a second, he couldn't remember where he was, and then he let out a sigh. A hotel room, in bed on his own, witness next door.

Except he had the distinct impression that John Kersley was not, in fact, next door, but was the source of the noise that had woken him.

A light tapping on the door. Then he heard it again. He pushed the duvet to one side and padded over.

'Pierre,' said John in what sounded to the detective constable very much like a stage whisper.

Then slightly louder, 'Pierre, are you awake?'

Holding back another sigh, Pierre opened the door wide enough to show his face, yet shield his witness from the sight of his striped pyjamas.

'I am now, John. What's the matter?'

'I wondered if you wanted to go for breakfast ...'

The officer glanced at his wristwatch, a present from his fiancé and something he hardly ever took off.

'It's 6.30 in the morning, John. We didn't finish until

late last night, then we had to drive here, and we agreed we'd meet for breakfast at half eight.'

'Well, you're up now,' said John. 'So, how long do you need? Twenty minutes?'

'Go back to your room and I'll call you when I'm ready.'

The temptation to slam the door shut and go back to bed was strong, but John was in his care.

The trouble was, John simply stood there, no hint of movement.

'Go and watch telly, or something,' said Pierre. 'I want to make sure you get back to your room safely.'

'My remote's not working.'

'What?'

'The remote, it won't work. I think it's the batteries.'

Pierre rarely swore. Some occasions called for it – this was definitely one of those – but, ever the professional, he scanned the room in search of his remote.

He reached around the door to where it lay on the dresser and held it out to his annoying visitor. 'Here,' he said, 'use mine.'

'No, don't be daft, I've called the front desk and they're sending someone up with new batteries.'

At the sound of the lift doors opening, they both turned their heads to the far end of the corridor, Pierre hoping that whoever had risked shooting at John's window wouldn't choose this exact moment to take them both out. He could think of better endings than being gunned down in his pyjamas, remote control in his hand and with only John Kersley for company.

His heart rate was climbing a little too high considering he hadn't even had a chance to brush his teeth.

Still uselessly holding aloft the remote control, he considered grabbing John with his free hand and pulling him inside the room. He stalled for two reasons: firstly, no one apart from a couple of police officers knew where they were, and secondly, the only things Pierre had to defend them with were his PAVA spray and his ASP extendable metal baton. Both useless against a gun.

Fortunately, all the lift doors revealed was a young woman from housekeeping who smiled as she walked towards them.

'Have you brought batteries for room 378?' said John.

'Yes,' she said. 'Is 378 your room?'

'Yes, I called down. That's a lovely accent you've got. Where are you from?'

Pierre shook his head at the messy beginning to his day. 'John,' he warned, 'how about you take the batteries and I'll see you as soon as I'm dressed. No more small talk now.'

By this stage, the young employee had reached John's door.

'I'm Polish,' she said, 'and I'm supposed to deliver them to the room. Do you have your room key, please?'

'Yes, yes, of course,' said John as he fished in his pocket for the plastic card. 'Have you been in the UK for long?'

Pierre stopped himself from rolling his eyes, biting his bottom lip instead. It was obvious where his witness was heading with this.

'John, seriously, stop with the chat. Open the door, take your batteries and go and watch the television until I'm showered and dressed.'

The annoyance must have been all over Pierre's face, not to mention in his tone. The Polish woman looked from Pierre to John and back again, held out her hand and said, 'Here, on second thoughts, take them. It doesn't really matter.'

Suitably admonished, John took the batteries and without another word opened the door to his room. He paused to look at Pierre and the retreating figure of the housekeeper before he went inside.

Closing his own door, Pierre couldn't help but look longingly at his bed. It was probably still warm. He could sneak back under the duvet, perhaps even drop off for ten minutes.

Pierre knew he was the one with the issue: John was scared, people were trying to kill him, yet he was still trying to identify and help exploited immigrants.

All he needed was a warm shower, clean clothes and a good breakfast, and then he'd get on with the business of investigating an attempted murder.

Chapter 37

Hazel left Harry snoring away and got ready for work, well aware he'd started work the previous morning before most people had even begun to think about getting out of bed.

She made him a cup of coffee before waking him and then making her way to the incident room.

As soon as she parked her car in East Rise Police Station's car park, she texted Pierre to ask him how it was going. By the time she had walked the few metres or so from her car to the rear security door, her phone alerted her to a text message:

It's like pulling teeth. He's petrified to tell me any-thing. It's going to be a long couple of days!!! Call when you get five. X

Smiling to herself at the thought that someone had finally broken Pierre's patience, she waved her pass at the reader, entered the building and headed towards the Major Crime offices.

Once inside, she dialled her friend's number.

'Hi, Haze,' said Pierre. 'How are you?'

'Better than you, by the sound of it. I take it you're free to speak?'

'Yeah. I'm about to knock and escort him to breakfast. Not too sure what I'll do if anyone tries to take him out over the cornflakes. Maybe throw a bread roll at them and run like hell.'

She gave a snort of laughter and said, 'Listen, Harry told me the good news about you and Frank. That's wonderful.'

'Sorry I didn't get a chance to tell you myself,' he said, 'only, what with the hospital, interview and now the hotel, I haven't had a chance to speak to Frank, let alone anyone else.'

'Honestly, P, don't worry about that. And if you need to get away to make plans and stuff, I can always swap with you, do a bit of witness-sitting.'

There was a short hesitation, a sigh, and then he said, 'That's really good of you, but I'll finish what I've started. He may even begin to trust me, give me more details.'

'As long as you're all right. I really don't mind.'

'Be careful with your helpful attitude or I might take you up on it.'

'I can think of more depressing weeks at work,' said Hazel as she finally came to a stop at her desk, piled high with files and strewn with paperwork.

'For starters,' said Pierre, 'there's talk of taking him to a safe house for a few days. Fancy that?'

'Not really,' she admitted, 'though they must be worried if they're prepared to go that far.'

'Well, it's all got political so – oh, I've got to go. He's banging on the door again.'

'You sure it's him?'

'Definitely. He's already texted to tell me he's on his way. He's only bloody next door.'

'Just make sure you stay safe,' said Hazel before she turned to give the mound of paperwork her full attention.

Chapter 38

Some of the others considered his driving job to be an easy number. That wasn't how Marko saw it. Not only did he have to be the first at work in the morning, to get the crappy, run-down minibus up and ready, he had to drive the miserable bastards round all day to and from their jobs, and silence their whining. He was also the one who had to deal with the police if they stopped the bus.

It had happened a couple of times now.

Once was his own fault for not checking the vehicle properly and failing to notice that a light was out. A small bribe back in Hungary often took care of that, but here in England he got let off with a warning. How pathetic was that? What was the point of the British police and their woeful warnings to motorists? The downside was that some young girl, barely out of school, had insisted on checking the entire bus over and speaking to the three remaining workers inside. Fortunately, they spoke little English and knew what to say in any case.

Today, top of his to-do list was body disposal.

Even if it wasn't one of his favourite tasks, he would have done almost anything for Alexa Gabor. She was the most beautiful woman he had ever seen, and he would put good money on her being an incredible fuck. He reckoned she was dirty – a by-product of her past as a prostitute. He would have drifted off on one of his fantasies about her if he didn't have a bloodied corpse wrapped in tarpaulin three metres behind him.

He glanced at the satnav on the dashboard. He still had fifteen kilometres to go until he reached the drop-off point. Driving a body around was a risk, a big one. Nevertheless, it was one he got paid well for and it didn't hurt to ingratiate himself into the boss's good books.

Worrying about what women thought was a new one for him: what they liked didn't come into it. It had never mattered much.

The little blonde bitch yesterday at the farm had been about to give in. That always made it more fun, when they were begging him to have sex with them for favours and food.

The satnav told him to turn left. He indicated and turned into a narrower country road than he had been expecting. The left-hand side of the minibus caught on the brambles of the steep bank. The sound of paint-work being scored was loud and clear above the roar of the engine.

Marko swore under his breath. Yet another bloody thing he was going to have to make someone else pay for.

It was that runaway slag's fault he had damaged the bus. If he hadn't been thinking about the blowjob she'd given him, he wouldn't have driven against the bank. The only thing he had to be grateful for was that he didn't have to deliver the food he had promised her. Even if she hadn't fucked off, had she really expected him to hand over groceries?

Another stupid bitch.

Without fully taking in which way he was going, Marko followed the directions from the small grey box attached to the windscreen and realized with a great deal of satisfaction that he was within metres of his destination.

The sign at the top of the driveway welcomed him to *Kiddemere Abattoir*, the home of locally sourced meat, and the friendliest place to dispose of dead cage fighters.

Chapter 39

Pierre received a text message from Harry during breakfast. He was at least grateful it gave him an excuse to get up and leave the table: he'd told John he had to make an urgent phone call to his boss. He hated to be so negative about the man when he'd been through so much, but he needed some space.

He sat in the hotel lobby, out of John's view, and gathered his thoughts. The last thing he wanted was to spend days with someone so draining, yet he couldn't quite bring himself to take Hazel up on her offer. Pierre and Frank had been together a good while, had made a lot of the plans for their upcoming wedding and even booked a month off so that they could spend as much time together as they could possibly stand. Hazel and Harry's relationship was still in its infancy, and besides, he knew that with the amount of overtime they did they struggled for any hours off.

He would see this through to the bitter end and then reap the benefits of the overtime.

Perhaps he could make Frank a really romantic gesture and upgrade their honeymoon.

This happy thought in mind, he called his detective inspector.

'P,' said Harry, 'thought my text said not to bother ringing.'

'It did, it did . . .'

'Ah, I see. He's doing your fucking head in.'

'That's a bit harsh, boss. He's a traumatized victim of a crime.'

'Look, take care of him today and then I'll get someone else to take over tomorrow. It's not fair on you

'No, no, it's all right,' said Pierre. 'Every cloud, and all that. The way I see it is, every minute I spend with him over and above my scheduled eight hours means more money towards the wedding and honeymoon fund. I'll brave it out unless anyone else particularly wants the overtime.'

He heard one of Harry's laughs, a sound that made most people smile.

'Hazel told me that she offered to take over from you,' said Harry. 'Don't tell her that I told you this, but she was pretty relieved you turned her down. She'd have done it if you'd had enough, but it's only that she's expecting another of the dogs she fosters to arrive any day. Some arsehole went to stab his wife and her Labrador jumped between them. As soon as the vet's given him the all-clear, he's coming to us for a while.'

'She's a keeper, that one, Harry.'

Pierre heard the pride in his boss's voice as he said,

'Don't I just know it. Anyway, you've got the address we're meeting at? It's all very cloak and dagger: I'll meet you at that RV point and an unmarked firearms car will take us to where we need to go from there. There's another unmarked firearms team at the destination where you'll be staying with John.'

'Yeah,' said Pierre, 'I've got that so far. It's what happens after I'm a bit vague on.'

'Well . . . there's a reason you're vague on details.'

The pride had been replaced by another tone to Harry's voice. Pierre recognized it as the usual annoyance all police officers failed to mask on a permanent basis.

'I've tried,' said Harry, 'believe me, I've tried. There simply isn't enough money to have firearms officers in situ for the entire time he's with us. Quite honestly, I'm amazed we've got any at all. I'm sorry, P, it's the best I can do.'

'If anyone's tried, Harry, it's you. Leave it with me. I'll take one for the team.'

Chapter 40

'I'm not sure if it's the cold making my head pound,' said Lili, 'or my head only hurts because I'm freezing.'

It was the first time either of them had spoken for some minutes, largely because they hadn't the energy to talk, but also because they had run out of things to say.

'We should be near a road soon,' said Anna.

They had trudged on through the trees until the landscape had given way to scrubland, then finally marshland. Their cheap shoes doing little to prevent them sliding on the boggy ground, their concentration was taken up with watching every cautious step. Animal droppings added to their perilous journey. Twice Anna slipped on sheep muck.

There were sheep all around them. When they drew close, the sheep scattered, moving with more energy than either of them had.

Anna eyed the sheep, the ridiculous idea of slaughtering one crossing her mind. Her belly had stopped growling some hours ago. Now, it was gnarling at her.

She was so thirsty even the animals' water trough

looked appealing. A thought that made her want to both laugh and cry. When had her life become so desperate? Sharing water with dumb sheep.

'What are you laughing at?' said Lili, keeping in step beside Anna. She continued to glance over her shoulder, expecting someone to come running up behind them at any moment, as she had ever since they'd hit open ground.

'I guess I'm delirious,' said Anna. 'I was thinking about food and water. You know, the basics. That, and keeping warm.'

'Where are we heading?' said Lili, as she slid on sheep dung, hands out to steady herself.

Anna grabbed her arm, more to stop her knocking them both over than in an effort to help Lili.

'There's a road down there . . .' She pointed ahead. 'I've seen traffic coming from that direction.' Again she pointed, this time to their left. 'I figured that if we see someone we think we can trust, we ask for the police. Even better, we see the police themselves.'

She carried on walking, feet alternately sliding in the wet and sticking in the mud, shoes and lower legs now caked in dirt. It didn't take Anna long to realize that Lili was no longer panting and stomping along beside her.

It was Anna's turn to glance over her shoulder.

'We agreed!' Anna called out. 'Remember? We tell them what's happened to us and about Denis. They have to help. It can't be any worse.'

They stood for a few seconds, staring at one another.

Each a ridiculous sight, splattered in mud, jeans turned brown up to the knees, each out of breath.

Then it started to rain.

Torrential pounding rain across the marsh.

It came straight at them as they tried their best to hurry towards their unseen destination. It lashed at them, hitting them in the face, soaking their thin layers straight through to their skin within seconds.

If they had been anywhere near to a farm building, Anna might have risked taking shelter. With a vast, open expanse between them and the edge of the marsh, they took to running as fast as they could. But their fast wasn't actually that quick, hindered by the now treacherous condition of the ground, plus the fact they hadn't eaten in two days.

It took them several minutes and many falls, one of which would have made Anna scream had the pain from her ribs as she tumbled to the ground not already been so intense that, for a couple of seconds, all she could see was a white flash in front of her eyes.

Tired, lost and wretched, they reached the edge of the marsh and slid to a stop at the hedgerow. Lili peered through a gap.

'This is the best place to get out,' she said. 'It's a bit of a steep bank, but further along is a wire fence. I could see signs on the top of it as we were running.'

For the first time, Anna felt some admiration for Lili: perhaps she was more useful than she had initially thought.

In answer, Anna looked into the distance and

nodded. 'I saw those too,' she said. 'The fence is electrified. You're right, this is the best place to get onto the road. And look, there's a bus shelter. We can stay there until the rain stops.'

Lili lowered herself to the soggy ground, inched herself forward and grabbed one of the firmer hedgerow roots. With a shove from Anna, she wiggled forward until she was able to squeeze her arms, and then her head, through the gap. Her denim jacket snagged and tore on the coarse branches, cutting her arms and slicing into her stomach as her cotton shirt rode up. Still, Anna pushed at her legs from behind until her mud-crusted training shoes disappeared from view.

Rain still lashing down, Anna tried to follow Lili. She knew that lying on her stomach was out, so she opted for scooting herself along on her left side, eyes shut to avoid being blinded by a thorn. She felt Lili reach through the gap, grab her by the shoulders.

Lili seemed oblivious to the sound of an approaching car as she yanked Anna by the top of her sodden jacket, both women grunting at the effort.

Finally, she was through. The new danger of falling head first into oncoming traffic hit her at about the same time as the thought that the Controller would have people out looking for them on the roads.

She had no time to contemplate whether this route had been a mistake. They needed to get clear of passing vehicles. The sheltered bus stop she had spotted earlier was about two hundred metres away on the opposite side of the road.

Anna stood up with a little help from Lili and said, 'Let's go over there and get under cover.'

They made it to the small wooden shelter, closed on three sides, open to the road, roof taking a battering from the downpour. The relief of stepping out of the wet didn't escape them before they made for the far corner, wrapping their arms around themselves in a vain attempt to warm up. Shivering, they huddled together for warmth.

Over the sound of the rain hammering on the shelter, the noise as it cascaded down onto the tarmac in front of them, and no doubt the pounding of her own heart, Anna didn't hear the reverberation of a vehicle's engine as it pulled up.

She had screwed her eyes up tight, willing her blood to warm and take away the chill from her very core. It was probably the bus door opening and a raised voice that finally forced her eyelids to snap open and made her try to sit upright.

The movement jolted Lili to full alert and she gave a small gasp at the sudden appearance of a grey-haired man.

He said something that neither of them understood. He waved his hand in the direction of the bus behind him, and was met with bewildered stares from the two women cowering in the bus shelter.

Again he said something incomprehensible, got no response and gave a shrug to the bus driver who closed the door and drove off.

He took a step towards the girls as they shrank back

as far as they could. Unable to get any response to his questions, he reached into his pocket and pulled out a handful of coins. They watched him warily as he walked up to their bench and put the money down beside them.

The stranger then pulled up the hood of his raincoat and went out of the shelter and disappeared from view.

'Why did he give us money?' said Lili.

'I've no idea, but perhaps it's enough to catch a bus. We can go as far as the nearest town and ask for help.'

'And listen,' said Lili, 'I think the rain's stopping. Our luck must be changing. I can hear another bus.'

She was up and away from the bench before Anna could stop her. She reached out a hand to pull Lili back inside the shelter. Buses in the remote countryside didn't come along every few minutes.

But it was too late – Lili had already made herself known to the oncoming vehicle.

A tatty white minibus with a pock-marked driver.

Chapter 41

The van pulled up outside Alexa's front door. The signage down the side read *Fitzhubert-Bring Security Systems*. She had done her homework, and not only was the firm highly reputable, it was based a distance away in Riverstone. The last thing she needed was someone too close to home.

The person she had spoken to on the phone had sounded ideal and had promised, in his well-educated tones, 'to send his brother along right away'.

Alexa looked out at the small silver van, words emblazoned in blue along its panels, and saw a gangly middle-aged man unfold himself from the passenger seat. He stood facing her, she mostly hidden behind the drawn curtains, he rubbing his genitals through his jogging bottoms.

From her vantage point she watched the driver get out, a much younger version of the passenger, and heard him say something. She wasn't entirely sure it was English, although she had got used to that over the years. The words spoken by these people didn't always resemble their language.

Bored of peeking out at them from behind a curtain as if she had done something wrong, she marched to the front door and yanked it open.

Both men turned to face her, and the older of the two let go of his crotch, a grin taking over his features. Even from that distance, she saw that he had a number of gaps in his teeth.

'All right, love?' he shouted, adjusting his joggers as he approached. Without waiting for her to speak, he said, 'I'm Joe and this is my boy.' He made no indication towards 'the boy' whom she took to be the driver.

'Once we're inside and you've made us a cuppa, we'll go over exactly what it is you want us to fit. My bruv's gone over most of it, but ...' He gave her a conspiratorial wink and added, 'He's not exactly the expert, if you know what I mean, darling.'

As much as she wanted to recoil from this baggy-trousered idiot, she needed him to do the work. Most importantly, she needed him to do it fast and without too many people getting wind of it. Her pock-marked driver for a start. There was definitely something about him she didn't trust, and he had let himself into her house without her realizing that the front door had even been left open.

Or so he'd told her.

'So,' said the man in front of her, 'kettle on and we'll discuss the final details.'

She didn't move.

'Three sugars for me and a splash of milk for the boy.'

Joe took another step forward and said, 'Before I come in and make it myself, I have got the right drum, haven't I?'

Reluctantly, she stood back and gestured them in. Still not entirely sure about this strange man, she shoved a smile to her lips and heard herself say, 'I'll make the tea as we talk.'

Within a minute or so, the three of them were in Alexa's impressive kitchen waiting for the kettle to boil, as Joe pointed out to her the myriad ways the house could be broken into. He seemed to take delight in each and every one, from the windows to the garage and their weaknesses.

'I mean,' said Joe, 'take a look at this back door, 'ere.' He stopped to tap the glass window about three quarters of the way up. 'Beautiful idea, one of these stable-type doors, so you can leave the top half open, allow some air in and all that. In reality, what are you doing?'

He looked at her. She stared back.

'I'll tell you, shall I? Quick tap on the pane here, they can put their arms through, unlock the door and Bob's your uncle.'

She was on the cusp of telling him she didn't have an uncle Bob, when it occurred to her that it was another stupid expression these fucking imbeciles had, but most importantly, she was paying them to work and not talk nonsense.

'Okay,' she said. 'You can stop talking bollocks. I'm

very busy. Let's leave it there. The basement is out of bounds and I'll be upstairs so don't disturb me unless you have to.'

With that, she left the kitchen and sauntered to the staircase, not failing to miss the looks exchanged between Joe and his boy.

Chapter 42

The scream that escaped Lili's mouth would have alerted anyone in a generous radius. Unfortunately, the closest houses were ten minutes' walk away and the road was completely empty of traffic. The only bus for an hour had just departed, and the recent atrocious weather made the chances of a rambler or dog walker ambling by extremely unlikely.

Pock-mark screeched the minibus to a halt, skidding for some distance in the wet. It gave Anna and Lili several seconds before he was out of the bus, shouting and swearing at the 'pair of whores' to 'get the fuck back here'.

Lili took full advantage of a slight head start on Anna, having been that bit closer to the road when their tormentor had loomed into view. Not to mention, her ribs hadn't recently received a good kicking.

Anna sprang from the bench, arm still outstretched in her now-forgotten attempt to grab hold of the other woman and stop her reckless appearance outside the bus shelter. The movement sent a pain slicing through her insides, momentarily knocking the wind out of her.

She heard the minibus door slam, yet didn't dare waste another precious second looking behind her at the person who would surely kill them both.

Her tired, aching legs wouldn't move fast enough, not helped by the muddy training shoes failing to get any purchase on the wet tarmac. Her breath now came in laboured wheezes. Up ahead, she saw Lili frantically scanning the banks either side of the road and failing to locate a single break in the dense vegetation. Anna doubted she would have the strength to pull herself a metre or so over the bank anyway. Long before then she would be caught. Her petrified mind told her that much.

The scraping noise of his boots was getting closer. She was sure she could smell him, sense his fingertips reaching out to grab her as he got nearer and nearer.

Then, a searing pain to the back of her scalp.

At first she thought she'd been hit on the head. And then she fell. An almost perfect view of fluffy clouds in the now-blue English sky was Anna's to witness as she smacked to the ground, as if her feet had been pulled from under her.

This misperception hit her almost as hard as the road when Pock-mark's ugly face peered down at her. He threw a handful of something at her face. She flinched in preparation for more pain. Instead, something soft and wispy floated to her cheek. She put her hand up, took hold of fistfuls of her own hair.

Then the stinging started, as if needles were being jabbed into the follicles, whereas it was more likely to be grit and dirt.

The crunch of his boots, centimetres from her left ear as he came to a halt beside her, made Anna screw up her eyes in anticipation of the kick. Why would he waste energy bending down to punch her when he could stamp on her face? She didn't want to die on a greasy, wet back road in a country she hated.

Powerless, she kept her eyes closed and silently prayed it would be quick.

The gravelly sole of his toe-capped boot pressed down on her throat. Instinctively, she brought both hands up to push it off, trying and failing to sit up. The constraint on her breathing brought forth her desire to live, to go home to Hungary and hold her little girl once more. The child she had failed to protect.

Her struggle was futile.

'Fucking keep still,' he spat at her.

Then she heard him shout to Lili, 'If you don't come back, I'll crush her windpipe.'

He ground his foot into her throat. Anna heard the sound of gagging and gasping, panic coursing through every part of her when the horror hit her that she really was about to die.

Through her tears, deprived of oxygen and flailing in the road, she convinced herself that she could see Lili, her silhouette getting closer. Most importantly, she was coming back to save her.

Tricks of the mind were so very cruel.

After what seemed to Anna like minutes, the driver shouted, 'I fucking mean it. Come back now and you'll save her life. You run, I'll kill her, then I'll find you and kill you too.'

The pressure on her throat must have been about to crush her windpipe, her effort to push his foot away futile.

Anna could only see blackness now, even with her eyes open. Her hands had dropped to the tarmac. She hadn't given up, had merely been beaten.

She felt a surge of unrestricted air and an arm dragging her off the road, hauling her up.

For a moment, she had a complete view of where she'd been lying. Clumps of her hair still on the road convinced her that the blow to her skull as she'd hit the ground hadn't entirely eradicated her memory.

Then she heard the sound of the minibus door sliding back, and she was thrown to the floor.

Hurled into a world of black.

Calais–Dover Ferry
Five weeks earlier

Truth be told, Anna had no idea if she would feel seasick. As she stood clutching the handrail, watching France fade from view, the swirling might of the waves beneath her, it was only the thought of her beautiful daughter that stopped her from leaping over the side.

It would have been less suicide attempt, more cry for help.

But it was too late now, she was crossing the Rubicon.

Her hands gripped the rail so tightly her knuckles turned white. The roll of the waves was weirdly comforting; she felt no nausea, except for when she thought of the cheese sandwich she had eaten on the minibus. She had made it last six hours or so, trying to hide the nibbles she took, purely so that the ugly driver wouldn't see her eating it.

She fought down the bile she knew wasn't a result of the motion of the ferry, rather the memory of him leaning over to give her the food then snatching it away as she reached for it.

The feel of his hand against her breast as he pulled

her towards him, the other hand holding the sandwich he let go of only to maul at her.

All the troubles in her life had been brought about because of men. She was determined to give her daughter a better start in life than she had had.

At first, Anna thought that the sea spray was dampening her one good set of clothes. However, it quickly became obvious that it was starting to rain, dark clouds gathering above.

She hurried inside, desperate to use the toilet and get a drink of water while she had the chance. She hadn't washed or changed her clothes since Thursday morning. By the time they got to the hotel where she would be working, she would have been wearing the same underwear for something like sixty hours. It wouldn't give the best first impression, to arrive looking so dishevelled and possibly smelling a little, too.

On her way up from the vehicle deck, she had seen signs for the toilets. For the first time since leaving home, she felt as though she had five minutes of freedom. No one had followed her, told her to hurry. Earlier, the driver had mumbled something about being back at the minibus on time or he would go without them.

That wouldn't be a bad thing either, except she had no idea where the hotel she was going to be working in was.

Lost in thought as she descended the stairway, she saw Dominik come out of the men's toilets before pausing, wincing and then turning one hundred and eighty degrees and going straight back inside.

When she looked back on the next five minutes of her life, she blamed herself for not having her wits about her. After all she had been through in her twenty-four years, she had taken her eye off the ball.

As she drew level with the disabled toilet, the pock-marked driver appeared at her side, flanking her escape route. One arm across her waist, the other grabbing for the toilet door. Before she knew what was happening, she was bundled inside. Those who only seconds ago had been swarming around her to get their breakfast, reduced-price alcohol and cigarettes, 7 a.m. pint of beer, were completely oblivious – or unconcerned – about what was happening to a frightened young woman.

She tried to lash out, to defend herself. The last thing she wanted was him touching her, thinking he had the God-given right to do as he pleased.

'No,' she said. 'No, let me go. Stop. Please stop.'

But he didn't.

She weighed less than forty-five kilos and was a full head and shoulders shorter than the man tearing at her zipper, pulling her trousers down.

Anna would always remember that she'd tried to scream, but he'd clamped his hand across her mouth, and when that hadn't worked, he'd punched her in the throat.

That was how her mind replayed it, again and again and again.

When the second most horrific thing that had ever happened to her was over, he pissed into the toilet and stepped over her, heading for the door.

On shaky legs, she gathered herself up, tried to wash the disgrace from her skin, and when she'd finished trying to pull herself together, she opened the door and walked out.

The pretence that everything was all right might have worked, had it not been for Dominik standing near the toilet door.

He couldn't bring himself to look at her.

Chapter 43

Two middle-aged men sat in the centre of a modern café, just off one of the city's squares. Office workers drifted in for late lunches, shoppers stopped by for a coffee. For all intents and purposes, the two might have been locals, or tourists.

The best way to describe them was nondescript.

The waitress buzzed around with drinks and food, paying them no attention.

'So,' said the slightly older and more senior of the two, 'things appear to be going wrong overseas at the moment. A couple of them bolting is one thing, losing a few through natural wastage, acceptable. But organized walk-outs? I'm far from happy about the situation.'

'Me neither,' said the other, taking a sip of his coffee. 'We've gone for damage limitation for the moment. You know we sent a warning to the English fool to stop him interfering in other people's business.'

'Yes, but do you think he will listen?'

He glanced up at the waitress as she cleared the table beside them, wiped his mouth with his serviette and, once she was safely out of earshot again, said, 'If he's talking, I want to know who to. If he's being kept someplace, I want to know where. We need to stop this now. And someone should take care of Alexa. I'm sure she's due an ... appraisal.'

'Good idea, I'll get the Russians to do it.'

Chapter 44

'Well,' said Harry as he stood in the kitchen, John Kersley seated at the green-tiled six-seater table, Pierre checking both of the radiators for heat, 'this is a pretty nice drum.'

Pierre Rainer, professional through and through, wasn't entirely sure who Detective Inspector Harry Powell was trying to convince, although he would keep that thought to himself.

'The heating seems to have been on for a while,' said Pierre to no one in particular. 'At least we won't freeze in our beds.'

Harry gave a laugh, probably a little too loud to be genuine, and said, 'Take a look around, you two. It's going to be your home for the next few days, anyway, so you may as well be familiar with it.'

'Hmm,' said John, 'that's electric, isn't it? I don't like cooking with electric. Gas is better.'

'Unfortunately, mate,' said Harry, 'we don't have time to get a gas-fitter in to change it. There should be a load of food in the fridge-freezer and cupboards.

Besides, it's only for a few days. Not to mention, old Pierre here is a real dab hand when it comes to a Pot Noodle.'

The look of total disgust on John's face matched Pierre's, although the officer turned his attention to the thermostat at the doorway leading to the open-plan living room.

'Good,' he said, again to no one in particular, 'it's only on eighteen degrees, but it seems to be very efficient, which is especially handy being out here in the middle of nowhere.'

'Talking of being in the middle of nowhere,' said Harry as he picked up the kettle to fill it from the tap, 'I'll go over the panic alarms with you and firearms will be here for the rest of the day to make sure everything's okay. Once they've gone, you've got the security system that'll tell you if anyone's nearby. But only a handful of us know where you are anyway. You'll be fine, absolutely fine.'

Pierre noticed that Kersley had wandered off to take a look at the television, leaving him, Harry and one of the firearms officers in the room. Behind Harry's back as he was opening cupboards looking for tea and coffee, Pierre made some unsubtle gestures to his armed counterpart, who took the hint and left them to it.

'Now, who wants ...' Harry turned round with a box of PG Tips in his hand, paused and said, 'Where did everyone go?'

'I have a bad feeling about this,' said Pierre, with a glance towards the living room. He took another step closer to his DI. 'We'd be safer in a town centre or London. At least they have a few more resources than we do.'

'Pierre, I wouldn't do anything to risk your safety or the safety of a member of the public. It was a hard enough job getting him here, but if you want to head the seventy or so miles back towards East Rise, that's what we'll do.'

He listened to his boss, saw the worry etched onto his face and leaned back against the sink, arms crossed.

'Sorry, Harry. I know I'm being a bit highly strung about it. It'll be fine. I know you wouldn't send us here if there was any chance something could happen. It's just, I've never really liked the quiet of the countryside; always preferred towns, even the beach. Anything but woodlands and open fields. They make me jittery.'

'Funny, that. I love the countryside. It's the peace and quiet that does it for me every time. By the way, I'm making a pot.' He waved the box of tea bags to reiterate his point.

For a couple of minutes, Pierre watched Harry as he added tea bags and water to the stainless-steel teapot, removed cups and saucers, packets of biscuits and plates from the kitchen cupboards and chattered away about how he'd love to live miles away from anyone else.

'That's the problem with the world, P,' Harry said as he turned his back on the brewing pot of tea. 'People. By and large, they're horrible bastards.'

'Do you really think that or has this job made you cynical?'

'Bloody hell, yeah.'

'Well, which is it?'

Harry opened his mouth to speak but stopped short of replying as John Kersley appeared in the kitchen doorway, remote control in his hand.

'There's no Sky,' he said. 'Football's on tomorrow.'

Not for the first time, Pierre wondered if the overtime was really worth it.

Chapter 45

If it were possible, the pounding in Anna's head worsened when she opened her eyes. Immediately, she felt the urge to vomit. Unable to sit up, the thought flitted through her mind that she might choke to death. Then it occurred to her that the cold floor was shuddering, and she was no longer on the road.

She was alive.

That was a good start. Although she doubted it would be for very much longer.

'Hey,' someone whispered. Anna couldn't see who was with her on what she now realized was the floor of the minibus, beneath the worn tatty seats.

'Can you hear me?'

With a growing sense of dread, Anna realized that the whispering voice belonged to Lili. The only chance either of them had had of living to see another day had rested upon Lili. All she'd had to do was keep running until she found them help.

Now they were rattling along on the sick-flecked,

dog-crap-smelling plastic mats of a minibus driven by a psychopath.

Anna wasn't sure if her body was shaking because of the vehicle's mechanical failings, or because she was crying. It was hard to tell where one ended and the other began. She hadn't expected, when she first climbed aboard the minibus headed out of Hungary, life to be this cruel. All the time she had stayed in the Controller's house, gone to work and kept her head down, at the back of her mind she was secretly hoping that she would escape and go home.

Now that hope was lost for ever. Or for however long she had left on earth. She figured it was probably hours.

'Please, Anna, stop crying. You're frightening me.'

With some effort, Anna turned herself over, went to put a hand up to the back of her head. Thought better of it.

'Here,' said Lili, 'let me help you up.'

She knew that, if anything, the damage to her ribs must have increased. Perhaps it was the distraction of seeing a pool of congealed blood under the seat next to her that helped take her mind off the pain, plus the surfacing of a recent memory.

'You . . . you know why he picked me up when he did, don't you?' said Anna through cracked and bloodied lips, another injury she didn't remember getting.

She worked out that resting against the seat cushion with only one side of her head, the spot behind her ear, in contact with the plastic material caused her the least discomfort.

Lili's mouth tried to form the word 'No'. It gave up on the second attempt.

'Someone was coming,' said Anna. 'I could hear a car or van or something in the distance. Even a thug like him wouldn't have risked beating up a woman in front of other people.'

She broke off to wipe her eye. It wasn't a tear – those were getting her nowhere. This was pure and simple grit from her ordeal, now invading her vision.

'He's going to kill us,' said Anna. 'You do know that, don't you? Any chance you had of seeing your boyfriend again, any possibility of going home, any idea of having a normal life, they're all gone now. They'll probably bury us in a farm somewhere or feed our bodies to the pigs.'

'I'm sorry,' murmured Lili.

'What?' said Anna.

'I said, I'm sorry. It's all my fault. But I can fix it.'

Lili sat up straight on the floor of the minibus, back against the side panel, her crown barely visible to the outside world. Only visible if anyone should happen to look in and see two wretched modern-day slaves on their way to their execution.

Up until now, no one had given them much of a second glance, except the elderly man who had got off the bus and handed them some coins. That was all the attention their lost lives had attracted in the weeks they had been in this country – a handful of loose change and a sad smile.

'What are you going to do?' said Anna, shifting on

the floor to find a position that only meant ninety per cent of her body protested.

With some difficulty, she moved to follow Lili's eyeline.

'That won't work,' said Anna, guessing at what was in her companion's mind. 'He'll have locked the doors and we know from other journeys we can't open them from the inside.'

There was a look on Lili's face that Anna might have taken as determination, had she not known how scared she was. The last twenty-four hours had truly brought home to the young woman how much danger they were in. A spark had gone from her, although it might simply have been because they were both so very hungry and exhausted.

'Just get ready,' said Lili. She moved her legs so she was kneeling, palms of her hands on the floor.

'Get ready for what?'

'To escape out of the door.'

'The door that's locked? What's the matter with you? I've said it won't open.'

'It will if I unlock it.'

Lili leaned across and kissed Anna very gently on the cheek.

'This is my fault for coming back to the minibus and not going for help. I thought he was going to kill you, that's why I came back. When I looked round, he had his boot on your throat. This should make up for it. Try and move closer to the sliding door.'

Anna wasn't convinced she would make it to the

door. The arm's distance might as well have been a kilometre away. Still, she wasn't dead yet.

Anna saw Lili's legs and filthy footwear as she clambered onto the seat. Her head jolted as her feet hit the chair, and then again as she catapulted herself up and over the back, on towards the driver.

Because of the throb of the engine, crunching of gears and general rattling of the vehicle, Anna, from two rows of seats away from the action, could only hear shouts from the driver and a yell from Lili.

Nevertheless, Anna inched her way to the door. With all the strength she could muster, she crawled to her only chance of escape, raising one fragile hand to the catch.

The minibus swerved. She banged her outstretched fingers on the metal panel.

The driver hit the brakes. Anna shot forward, her hand grabbing the black plastic handle, clinging on to her lifeline. The engine was still running, but it felt to her as if they'd stopped. About to pull on the handle, hoping that this was at last their lucky break and Pockmark had died at the wheel, she became aware that the struggle at the front of the minibus hadn't come to an end.

She looked along the minibus's floor and saw Lili's already fragile body fall between the first and second row of seats.

South-east England
Five weeks earlier

Somehow, Anna had found her way back to the minibus from the ferry toilets and had waited until her tormentor returned to let them all back in.

Since climbing across to her seat, she hadn't lifted her eyes from the grey chewing gum stuck to the floor in front of her feet. She couldn't risk catching his eye, or look anyone else in the face, in case they guessed.

They had only been travelling for about twenty minutes from their slow roll onto land when she felt the bus slowing. Fear gripped her as she saw they were pulling into a service station.

Her panic subsided as she saw they were coming to a stop at a hotel. A few of the others exchanged comments about why they were stopping, but Anna used the time to calm herself and get her breathing under control.

This might be the hotel where she'd be working. It didn't look like much, but it was a start.

Just as the thought occurred to her that she was on the point of being free, the driver called out, 'Keep quiet, all of you. We've got another pick-up to make.'

Anna wiped the window with her sleeve and watched

the driver walk towards the front of the building, more of a motel than a hotel. Standing waiting for him was a haggard woman, probably around the same age as Anna, except time hadn't been kind to her: rings under her heavily made-up eyes, lank hair hanging over her shoulders, miniskirt showing bruised and mottled legs. However, the most frightening thing wasn't the dejected woman, but the young child standing beside her. She was dressed in a similar outfit, the same spiritless air about her.

At first what Anna was seeing didn't register. Then it hit her.

The little girl, hardly much older than Anna's daughter, was being brought over to the minibus. The woman was too busy taking a drag from her cigarette to even watch the child as she was led away, her tiny hand encased in the filthy fingers of the minibus driver.

Anna frantically rubbed at the window pane to make sure her eyes weren't deceiving her, but the bastard driver was giving the child the same perverted look she'd seen only hours ago when he raped her in the toilets.

The driver slid open the door, picked the child up and pushed her inside.

Anna's gaze was drawn firstly to the driver's hand as it lingered on the child's bottom, and then to the delicate green and blue silk scarf tied loosely around her neck. It crossed her mind that it was a strange thing for the little girl, otherwise dressed so provocatively, to wear.

Strange only until she saw the bruises it was put there to hide.

Chapter 46

Ready as ever for the afternoon shift ahead, public counter supervisor Ian Davis peered through the glass front doors of East Rise Police Station. One glimpse told him that the coast wasn't going to escape the storm he had driven through on his way into work.

The sky was the colour of ash, the seagulls making more noise than they had any business to. He glanced out at the small, empty car park, before he retreated to the counter to mentally prepare himself for whoever would walk in on this cold and miserable February afternoon.

He heard the doors open, looked up and ran a well-practised eye over the man, aged about seventy years old, white, medium build, dry jacket yet rain-sodden trousers and footwear.

'Afternoon,' said Ian.

'Afternoon,' he said as he approached the counter, body language suggesting he was unsure whether to lean against it or not. 'This is a bit odd, and I'm not sure where to start. It may be nothing . . .'

He decided upon leaning his elbow on the wooden

ledge between himself and Ian, and then ran a hand around his jaw, all the while glancing back towards the doors.

'The thing is,' he continued, 'I was at a friend's last night over in Edgemount Grove and we had a few drinks, so I left the car and went back this morning to collect it.'

'Right . . .' said Ian, more to show he was listening than to make comment.

'Well, I got off the bus to walk the ten minutes to my friend's house and there were two distraught-looking young women at the bus stop.'

He stopped and studied Ian's face.

'I feel a bit daft now, talking to you like this, I just, I—'

'No,' said Ian, 'please go on. If it's important enough for you to think you should tell the police, it may be something we need to look into.'

'They looked so frightened, you see,' he said. 'Perhaps I shouldn't have, but I gave them all the spare change I had. They didn't ask me for money; in fact, they looked scared witless at the idea of taking it. The thing was, not more than fifteen minutes later, I drove back along the road, after I'd collected my car, and the women were gone.'

Now was the moment Ian's poker face came into its own: two women, who had been waiting at a bus stop, were no longer there fifteen minutes later.

'I know they could have got on a bus,' he blurted out, as if able to read Ian's thoughts, 'except, the buses are only every hour at that time of day.'

'Oh, I see,' said Ian, drawing a pad and pen towards him.

'That's not all,' the man added, 'I was that worried about their whole demeanour, I pulled over by the bus stop and got out of my car. It could have been anything, anything at all, I suppose. A cat, a fox . . .'

Ian waited, pen poised.

'I'm pretty sure there was blood on the road by the bus shelter. I could be wrong, only that's what it looked like. I feel terrible I didn't do more at the time.'

'Okay,' said Ian, 'I'll take some more details from you, and about the two women, descriptions, that kind of thing. Then I'll make sure this gets passed on to our control room and we'll get the nearest patrol out to take a look in the area for them. I doubt they've gone far. We'll make sure these two ladies are safe and well.'

When they had finished and the good citizen had made his way out of the police station, Ian set about passing the information on. He wasn't too confident that it would be treated as a high priority, but that wasn't going to stop him from trying.

Ian need not have worried.

Before he'd even begun typing the information, a flash call appeared on the screen in front of him.

999 call – female informant on her way to Edgemount Grove witnessed what looked like a white male dragging an unconscious female into a white minibus. Possible abduction in process from the bus stop in Farleigh Lane. All available patrols to make their way – silent approach.

Chapter 47

That was the rest of Harry's day taken care of. A crime in action – in this case, a kidnap – cancelled out everything else. The hum went around the incident room, some officers curious, some keen to avoid additional drains on their time, all aware that the saving of a life was paramount, and the very reason they all got out of bed in the morning.

DI Harry Powell made his way back to his office, taking DC Tom Delayhoyde and DS Sandra Beckinsale along with him.

He couldn't help but notice the look of relief on Sophia's face as he walked past her desk, paperwork still stacked high on every available part of its cheap Formica surface.

'Shut the door,' he said to Tom when they were all inside his modest office. 'Not that anyone's likely to want to overhear. They show an interest, I'll take that as wanting to get involved.'

All three sat at the small, round table pushed into the corner, mismatched chairs so close together that their knees became acquainted. Tom and Sandra opened brand-new investigator's notebooks, Harry took out his twenty-first century electronic equivalent.

He was aware that two members of his team were sitting watching his enormous fingers stab awkwardly at the on-screen keyboard, all the time wishing he could return to using a pen and paper instead of following orders to modernize. He was getting too old to keep up, something he would never admit out loud.

'Bear with me,' he said. 'I'll let you know what I know in a minute, which isn't a lot. And it's called Operation Kilo.'

Out of the corner of his eye, he saw movement as they scrawled the name on the front of their notebooks, all the while cursing the touch-screen technology and muttering, 'Fucking *Minority Report* has got a lot to answer for. Bastard Tom Cruise. We'll all be thrashing around in bathtubs in the incident room next.'

'What, sir?' said Tom.

'Nothing, nothing. Oh, here it is. Why does this screen keep moving?'

'Because you're touching it, sir. Move your hand off it and just use one finger.'

Sandra Beckinsale made no attempt to hide a yawn.

'Want me to print the CAD off?' she asked.

'No thanks, Sandy,' said Harry, 'I've got it now.'

'It's not Sandy, it's Sandra.'

'I know. You've told me dozens of times but this iPad is getting on my tits, so I'm taking it out on you.'

He cleared his throat and started to read the briefing

document. The other two scribbled away with their scratchy biros.

'Two separate reports today from members of the public. One was from a young woman who phoned 999 to say, on Farleigh Lane she had seen what looked like an unconscious white female, approximately twenty years old, being dragged into a dirty white minibus by a stocky white male, aged about thirty. The white minibus had windows along both sides and to the rear, and the woman was being dragged towards what appeared to be a side door. Unclear whether it was a side sliding door or the front passenger door. The informant was returning home with her six-year-old son, whom she picked up from school after he fell ill. She felt it unsafe to stop. Partial registration was LV06.'

Harry glanced up. He waited for them to stop writing.

'The other report,' he continued, 'is from a man who came to the front counter this afternoon and spoke to Ian. He said he saw two women at the Farleigh Lane bus stop, but a short while later they'd disappeared. All that was left behind was what he thought looked like blood on the road. He thinks they might have been Eastern Europeans and said they looked frightened and exhausted.'

Harry looked straight at Tom as he said, 'After what we saw yesterday morning on the raid, who knows what living hell trafficked workers have gone through. I hate to think what these young girls have had to endure. Let's see about finding them, and fast.'

Tom nodded, remembering the horrors he had witnessed.

'Where do you want us to start?' replied Sandra.

'The ANPR team are already doing everything they can with the partial registration and local cameras, but Tom, I'd like you to go out and take a look for private CCTV, anyone's vehicles in the vicinity with dashcams, that sort of thing. I don't need to tell you how important it is to get the full registration, or even better, a sighting of this minibus.'

He paused and looked at his DC and DS in turn.

'I have no doubt that if we don't find these two soon we're going to be too late. I could be way off the mark, but I think these girls legged it or were hiding from something. Life's cheap to these trafficking shits. What's two more dead slaves to the bastards?'

'What are the priorities for me?' said Sandra. 'We've got no more staff.'

'This is the best bit,' said Harry as he closed his iPad. 'They're actually sparing me some staff from headquarters to work on both this and the shooting of John Kersley, so will you stay here and brief them when they arrive? I need to go out. I've got to get to yet another meeting with the chief about the progress, or lack thereof, on the shooting. I'm putting my money on both that and the kidnap being connected. If I'm right, and they're found safe and sound, I'll let you take all the credit for finding them alive.'

'Really?' she said, face contorting into an expression that was a far cry from its usual look of scorn.

'No,' he laughed, 'don't be stupid. We find them, the credit's all mine.'

Chapter 48

Harry finished handing over to Sandra and Tom, grabbed his car keys, reluctantly tucked his iPad under his arm and walked down to the rear yard.

For a couple of seconds, as he stood next to his car, door open, wondering where to secrete the iPad so he could pretend he'd left it behind, he glanced up and saw someone watching him. If he wasn't mistaken, peering through the security gate between the police station's car park and the street, was none other than reformed burglar Joe Bring.

Even at that distance, they stared at one another, an expression of instant recognition on their faces.

In a gesture that seemed to Harry both unnatural and impetuous, Joe waved his hand in the air, a strange jerky gesture.

From the look on his face, it was as if Joe couldn't quite believe what he was doing, as much as Harry couldn't quite believe what he was seeing.

Then Joe called his name and came towards him. Curious as much as anything, Harry found himself through the side gate, taking giant strides towards him.

'Well, how the devil are you?' said Harry.

Joe opened his mouth to reply. No words.

'You all right, Joe?' said Harry, peering into his eyes, aware he was checking for pupil dilation.

Harry glanced around, trying to guess what had brought the former world's worst burglar and drug addict to willingly come to a police station, albeit he had only made it as far as the pavement outside.

'What you doing in this neck of the woods?' asked Harry. 'Have you been assaulted? 'Someone twat you?'

Eventually, Joe found his voice. 'No, no. I'm, er, I . . .'

He watched Joe take a deep breath.

'I need to speak to someone, only I don't want anyone to know I've been talking to the police.'

Harry glanced at the five-storey building. He pointed to the sign over the door. 'Probably best you don't stand in front of East Rise nick talking to one of its DIs, then.'

'Congratulations,' said Joe. 'You were a sergeant, last I heard.'

'And you were doing a stretch. Good to see you looking so well.'

'Look on your face just then gave me the impression you were looking for signs I was back on the gear.'

Harry gave a short laugh and ran a hand over his chin. 'Too true, I was. Thought for a minute you were either smacked off your tits or suffering from a head injury.'

He had a meeting then a kidnap to get to, but Harry

knew Joe Bring of old and he wasn't a man to speak to the police unless he had something mammoth to get off his chest. Harry mulled over whether he could spare thirty minutes, having left one of his hard-working and tenacious, if miserable and sullen, detective sergeants temporarily in charge.

'Tell you what, mate,' Harry said, 'if you want to speak to me, how about we meet somewhere else. Any suggestions?'

'Yeah, see you in ten minutes in the Seagull Pickings? It's a bloody awful café so no one's likely to spot us there.'

Without waiting for an answer, Joe walked away at a speed Harry had never seen him move at before.

Exactly ten minutes later, Harry Powell walked into about the worst dining venue in the south-east of England. How it stayed open was anyone's guess, including the owner's.

Joe was seated at the back of the café at one of only two occupied tables. The two other customers sat at the table closest to the counter, presumably so they could enjoy the smell of rancid chip fat.

Harry ran an eye over the middle-aged man and woman as they tucked into the most unappetizing mixed grills he had ever clapped eyes on. Between the couple and Joe were four tables strewn with dirty cutlery and crockery, congealed food and ketchup stains.

Harry stood at the counter, made the 'Want a drink?' gesture to Joe, saw he was already holding an off-white mug, and quite frankly, not looking too overjoyed with his purchase, before he ordered himself a tea and made his way across the sticky floor.

He sat down on a lightweight silver chair, the type that would take off in a breeze.

'They've done it up in here,' said Joe as he cast an eye around the café.

'Christ, have they?'

'Yeah,' said Joe as he added sugar to his tea. 'I've checked under the tables, and they've definitely scraped the chewing gum off.'

An orange waitress with angry eyebrows approached the table, leaned over and put a mug of tea in front of Harry.

''Ere, De Niro,' said Joe, 'has this place had a makeover?'

'What?' she said, eyebrows on full attack mode.

'If I'm not very much mistaken,' said Joe, 'you've even emptied the dead bug tray under the insect zapper.'

'You're such a funny sod,' she said as she ambled back towards the counter.

'Firstly, Joe, good way to keep a low profile, and secondly, if you know her, why did you suggest coming here?' Harry leaned across the table and added, 'And is her name actually De Niro, or is it something to do with her eyebrows?'

'What about her eyebrows? And I know what you mean – De Niro's surely a boy's name. Anyway, this isn't what we came 'ere for, is it?'

'No, it's not the beverage either, so why don't you enlighten me?'

Harry watched Joe as he squirmed in his seat, drummed his fingers on the tacky tabletop.

'Look, Harry, you've known me for a while, and you know that, despite whatever's gone on in the past, I don't like the police. One or two of yous are okay, but on the whole, I wouldn't bother with ya.'

'Go on.'

Joe took a sip of his tea and winced.

'I went to this house today to fit some security alarms and stuff. Some snooty foreign woman out in Singletrack. There was something wrong with the house.'

He looked up from inspecting his nails to see Harry staring at him.

'Okay . . .' was all Harry said.

'You get that I don't mean there was something wrong with the house, like it needed underpinning or something?' Joe took the nod as a sign to continue. 'It wasn't only cos this woman was up herself – I get that from time to time. No, there was something off about the set up.'

He ran a broken thumbnail along the edge of the tabletop.

'It's really not easy for me to speak to you like this when I'm not in custody. I . . . er . . . . fuckin' 'ell. What I'm trying to tell you is that it looked as though, at some point, she'd had someone locked up in the cellar.'

'At some point?'

203

'See? This is why it's easier to go "no comment" in interviews with you lot. Question, question. I couldn't swear to it, no, but there was blood on the door handle and on the busted padlock. She also got very funny about us going anywhere near it.'

'I understand why you might be concerned, Joe, but I've not got much to go on here.'

Joe chewed his bottom lip, jammed his hands under his legs to stop himself from peeling the surface off the table with his hangnail, and said, 'I know what was in the cellar. Or to be precise, I know who.'

He couldn't look at Harry as he said, 'There was kiddie's clothing down there.'

Chapter 49

Anna wasn't sure waking up was an improvement. At least when she was unconscious, she wasn't aware of the pain she was in. She looked around her and tried to take in her surroundings, although that was pointless in the darkness. She concentrated on slowing her breathing, both to limit the expansion and contraction of her ribs, and to keep as quiet as possible.

Nothing. Not a whisper.

She waited.

Then she heard it. There was someone else in the dank basement with her.

'Lili,' she said, head turned towards the barely audible sound.

Perhaps it had been an echo of her own laboured gasps. And then she heard what she thought was movement.

'Anna,' came a whisper, 'I can't see a thing. Is it my eyes?'

'No, it's just dark, that's all. Can you move?'

'I think so,' said Lili, louder now. 'The back of

my head hurts. I think I hit it, that's why I thought I couldn't see.'

'You did hit your head,' said Anna as she tried to pull herself across the cold, hard floor towards her cellmate. 'Don't you remember trying to distract Pock-mark and him throwing you to the ground?'

'I know we were standing on the road, that bastard hit you and then forced you inside the minibus. I'm not too sure of the rest.'

Safe in the knowledge that Lili couldn't see her own hand in front of her face, Anna shook her head, kept her thoughts to herself. If Lili hadn't come back to the minibus, they would have stood a chance. The sound of the car coming along had, for one second, given Anna the cruellest of emotions: hope. They might, just *might* have been rescued. At best, they wouldn't be here in a clammy prison, whereabouts completely unknown to the outside world.

Although there were a few who knew exactly where they were, and that was the most terrifying thought of all.

Anna crawled towards the sound of Lili's muffled crying, wincing with the pain. She inched along the wall Lili was leaning against, felt the grimy fabric of the young woman's jacket. Tentatively, Anna reached an arm around Lili, hunched over her legs, face pressed against her thighs, hugging herself. The rocking motion was probably the most disconcerting part.

'Lili,' she said pressing herself to her side, 'we'll get

out of here, I promise. We'll look out for each other, won't let anything bad happen to each other, okay?'

'We're going to die. They won't let us out of here alive.'

Anna squeezed Lili's shoulder, fought down what she really wanted to tell her and said, 'It's important we stick together now. We can't let them turn us against each other.'

'I shouldn't have listened to you. I'd be debt-free now, not to mention far from this hell hole.'

Her words were slightly clearer now, her face turned towards Anna, warm breath on her cheek.

'I could be with Denis right now if I hadn't listened to you.'

Despite her hunger, raging thirst and searing pain, Anna could no longer control her temper.

'If it wasn't for me, you'd have been fucked by a dozen men, given cheap vodka and told to clean yourself up for the next dozen. That's what you'd have wanted?'

She made a move away from Lili, more slowly than she would have liked, but under the circumstances any distance she put between them was fine by her.

'No, of course not. What I want is to be with my boyfriend, preferably with a couple of cold beers in front of us, drinking to our good fortune beside the river. It was our dream to go to Budapest and see the city; instead, I ended up here. Where Denis is is anyone's guess.'

'The third woman,' said Anna. 'Remember, back at the farm, I was going to tell you about the third woman?'

She heard the loud silence and carried on.

'Not only was she used and fucked by hundreds, and I mean *hundreds* of men, she's now sporting a tattoo on her hand. It's the number four – she's the fourth girlfriend of her pimp and pregnant with his third kid. Ideal for benefits and a house.'

'That's not true, said Lili. 'You've made that up.'

The despair was there for Anna to hear, yet so was something else.

Someone was coming. The sound of footsteps was growing louder.

Both women sat still, apart from their shuddering from the cold, which was involuntary. Every movement or sound they had any control over – and there weren't many – was kept in check.

Although slightly delirious, Anna thought she imagined whoever was coming closer was wearing high heels.

For a fleeting moment, she couldn't fathom why anyone would be heading towards their pit of despair in anything other than boots.

Then she remembered – the Controller.

She wore stilettos. That beating: there'd been kicks to the ribs, some from designer footwear, some from the heavier-duty range of enforcer gear. As Anna's head had lolled to the side, the bright blue peep-toe high heels were the last thing she saw before losing consciousness.

Up until the moment the door swung open, neither Anna nor Lili had known which side of the basement it was positioned on. Not that it mattered.

What did matter was the person standing in the doorway, hand on hip, most of her face cast in shadow.

Anna squeezed her eyes shut against the harsh light thrown across the room, not to mention the sight of her tormentor.

It didn't prevent her from hearing what the Controller had to say.

'Don't get too cosy, you two. Being friendly won't help you one little bit. I'm not sure why I didn't think of it before: women cage fighters. There's such a gap in the market for women beating each other to death,' she said.

'Sleep well.'

Chapter 50

Evening of Tuesday 13 February

For want of anything else to do, and for a little privacy, Pierre took himself off to his room. As soon as Harry had left, any potential joy had gone. The only option he had to brighten the remainder of his miserable day was to ring his fiancé.

Frank answered on the third ring.

'How's it going?' said the man Pierre had shared the happiest years of his life with.

'Like pulling teeth,' replied Pierre. 'I don't think I've ever been so grateful for the cuts in police budgets. Harry said that this crappy set up is only likely to last another day or two.'

'Well, being broke does have its advantages. Miss you.'

Pierre smiled and said, 'Me too. I'll be home by the weekend, come what may. I feel bad that I don't want to spend any time with my witness. Besides, if the powers that be really are that worried about an attempt on John's life, it'll take more than me and my paltry collection of personal-issue protective gear to stop it.'

'It's about time they gave you all guns.'

'We've had this discussion before: I don't want to kill anyone, and I've my doubts that some of my colleagues should be trusted with a can of hairspray, let alone a gun.'

He heard Frank's laugh, pictured him at home, nightly mug of hot chocolate in his hand. He had never been one for drinking alcohol, something that had rubbed off on Pierre over time. Tonight, however, Pierre would have loved a couple of pints of the strongest lager he could get his hands on.

'What was that sigh for?' said Frank.

'Oh,' laughed Pierre, 'I wasn't aware I'd made any noise. I was thinking I could murder a pint right now. I'll save that thought for the weekend ... And I know I sighed a second time then. I've got a text coming through, I'd better go.'

'Keep out of trouble.'

'Love you.'

'Love you too. See you at the weekend.'

As soon as he ended the call, Pierre opened the text message sent from the nearby patrol. Only trouble was, according to the message, they were no longer the nearby patrol.

Even though the creeping gloom of the evening had made Pierre more alert to their isolated surroundings, he could only see so far. His vantage point from the bedroom window overlooked the rear of the house, but he couldn't see the road at the front. Not something that had bothered him too much when it was daylight, or when he knew he had an armed patrol not far away.

Now it was him, John Kersley and an extendable ASP.

The text had been brief, but told him all he needed to know:

Sorry, P, been called to a kidnap so have no choice but to go. Call if you need us. Our replacements will be on at 00.00 hours. Having a recce before we go. Stay safe.

Holding in a third sigh in as many minutes, Pierre put his phone back in his pocket. A whole night ahead, all alone except for his semi-hostile witness. He did have to admit, the man had rushed to the aid of strangers when most would have walked away, but he did still think John was keeping something from him.

Sitting on his bed, Pierre knew he should get up and knock on John's door. There were times when his attitude had got to the officer, yet his reluctance to talk was because he was scared, and Pierre understood that.

Over the last couple of days, they seemed to have reached an understanding that Pierre would back off whenever John seemed to be having an unsteady moment. For the time being, it was working. He wanted it to stay that way.

Pierre had given him long enough: he made up his mind to go to John's room and see if he wanted to talk. He owed him more than that for risking his life to save others.

He walked along the hallway, paused at the bedroom

door, hand ready to knock, when he heard the unmistakable sound of John's voice on the other side.

With a mixture of fear and annoyance, Pierre burst into the room to see John's face turn to panic as he dropped the mobile phone he had sworn to officers he didn't own.

The worst part was what Pierre had heard him say.

Whoever was at the other end of the line now knew their location.

Chapter 51

At some point, Anna must have fallen asleep again, or more likely passed out. When she woke up, for one blissful second she forgot where she was, until the physical and mental reminders kicked in.

Anna would have loved to see her daughter one last time, at least to know she was safe. She thought about praying for her parents to not let her out of their sight – the vision of the child with the dead eyes being led to the minibus by the ugly bastard driver was never far from Anna's thoughts. She had been as powerless to help the little girl then, five weeks ago, fresh off the ferry, as she was now to help her own flesh and blood.

She put a hand out in the darkness, felt to her right where Lili had been huddling. Nothing.

'Lili,' she said, 'Where are you?'

She tried to stay quiet, although she could hear herself panting, her breath more and more shallow. She knew enough to recognize that she was taking in less air than she had been previously. It didn't take medical training to know that she was in serious trouble.

Perhaps the kindest thing she could do for them both was to let Lili kill her. It might save her from a more painful death and could be mercifully quick. Her parting gift to the young woman would be her own life, in exchange for them letting her go.

She was no longer sure that Lili was in the confined space with her. It was difficult to work out the size of the room, but from what she had seen of it when the Controller had opened the door, it couldn't have been larger than two metres by three. 'Lili, are you all right? I can't find you.'

Anna didn't have to fight the urge to feel every centimetre of the floor; she simply wasn't up to it. All she could hang on to was that, if Lili had been taken somewhere, she was doing better than she herself was.

'So,' said the Controller, 'I'm not exactly sure why you two thought you had any chance of escape.'

Lili eyed the table in front of her. The bread smelled incredible. It had been so long since she had eaten, she was having trouble concentrating, although that could be down to a number of other factors, too.

The Controller lurched towards Lili's side of the table and banged her fists on the wooden surface.

'Listen to me when I'm talking,' she shouted, spittle landing on the sandwich, not that it was putting Lili off wanting to grab it with both hands and ram it into her mouth.

'Eat the food if it'll mean you focus.'

Lili's hands shot out and took hold of the food before

she realized what she was doing. She chewed off a piece, mouth working as fast as she could make it. Her only goal was to get some sustenance inside her before it was taken away. The woman sitting opposite had the power and the viciousness to do that.

For the first time since being summoned from her cell, Anna fitfully dozing beside her, Lili looked their captor in the eyes.

'You make a lot of noise when you eat,' the Controller said. She gave a careless shrug and added, 'I suppose you're hungry, although you wouldn't be if you hadn't run away.'

Lili tore off another bite and started to cough on the mammoth chunk she'd tried to fit into her mouth in one go. For an instant, she had a horrible thought that she was about to die from poisoning. She threw the sandwich on the table and her hands went instinctively to her throat.

'Oh, stop being so dramatic,' said the Controller. 'Do you think I'd waste good food to kill you? I'd snap your scrawny neck if I wanted you out of the way.'

She reached under the table and picked up a plastic bottle of water. She rolled it towards Lili and said, 'You're eating too fast. That's why you're choking.'

Aware that the older woman was watching her with a look of total indifference, Lili gulped at the water.

The taste was so incredible it made her want to cry.

'What's with the tears?' said the Controller. 'They won't help you. There's not much that *will* help you. Except me.'

Lili paused, bottle to her lips, free hand inching towards the abandoned sandwich.

The Controller looked with disdain at the young woman's fingers, nails encrusted with dirt, skin broken and raw.

'I can help you,' she said, 'but it comes at a price.'

Sandwich in her grasp again, Lili felt at the slightest of advantages with food in one hand and water in the other. And here was someone offering to come to her aid.

'You ready to hear more?' she said.

Lili nodded.

'That's if you can hear me over the noise of your own chewing ... Right, here's what's going to happen: people like to come and watch the entertainment, have a few drinks, let off steam. You know how it is.'

Despite the situation she found herself in, Lili couldn't stop herself from scowling. This too was met with mirth.

'Okay, so you don't know how it is, being a peasant girl, and a peasant girl with a criminal record, for that matter. You should be more cautious of your stablemates – not all of them have the odd conviction for violence and theft like you. Some of them are actually dangerous. Why do you think you're here? Why do you think any of you are here?'

The Controller leaned back in the chair and crossed her legs, blue satin dress shifting across her thighs as she did so. One long manicured fingernail tapped at the side of her head.

'Think about it: why would anyone be stupid enough to leave their own country and come to a foreign one, especially one as blind as this, to work and take it in shifts to sleep on a mattress, if they could have a better life in their homeland?'

Lili forced herself to stop eating long enough to say, 'How did you know I'd been arrested in Hungary?'

A shapely eyebrow shot up towards immaculate hair. 'Because your second cousin, or whoever he was, who recruited you for this fun-ride, told us. You see, you'd never have got a job in your home village, or even the closest town. Why would anyone in Budapest hire you when there are hundreds of people without a criminal record looking for work? This is information you've always had, but were too thick to process.'

The Controller gestured to the room they were in: it was twice the size of the cell where Lili and Anna had been kept, a little less damp with a bare overhead bulb and, despite the lighting, furniture and food, had the same feel of despair.

'Now you're here,' she said as she placed her hands on the table a short distance from Lili's. 'This could be behind you if you fight your friend in there and win.'

'When you say win, you mean kill Anna?'

A half-hearted shrug. 'If that's her name, then yes. Her ribs are damaged for starters. Pneumonia has probably taken a grip of her already, so you'd be doing her a favour. It's not a nice way to go, and besides, you'd have a second chance with me. Pay off your debt, get a new job. I see it as win-win.'

The Controller pushed her chair back and stood up.

'Once you've made up your mind, let Marko know. He'll make the arrangements if you decide you want to win, live to see another day and all that. If you don't value your life, I'm pretty sure that Anna won't turn down the chance to get out of here. I'm going to have to dose her up with some sort of medication or else the punters'll think it's a fix. They're quite a nasty bunch and I don't want them turning ugly. Some of them can be quite violent.' She paused. 'Well, you go ahead and make your decision. I can just as easily put her in a position to win, broken ribs aside.'

She pulled open the door and stepped outside.

Lili heard the bolt slide across, put her head in her hands and wept for what she was about to do to the only friend she had.

Chapter 52

Harry Powell had spent most of his afternoon and evening on the phone, attending various strategic planning meetings and either being briefed, or briefing other officers and staff in relation to the kidnap.

The preservation of life was everyone's number one priority, no exceptions.

CCTV was being downloaded and viewed, all ANPR cameras checked and extensive accounts and statements taken from everyone who had anything to tell the police about the two women seen that morning in Farleigh Lane.

The problem they had was that no one appeared to be missing.

Without a victim making contact about a hostage or even the hostage themselves being identified, there was only so much the officers of East Rise Police Station could do. But it didn't stop them trying everything they could think of, including visiting the registered owners of all the battered white minibuses in the area. Although the problem no doubt lay with the non-registered ones.

Harry wasn't a man to give up easily, and yet he was getting older and the rules were changing. He wasn't sure he had it in him any more to keep fighting the system. No one had specifically said he only had a limited time to find these young women and that before it was up there was every chance they would run out of resources, but he wasn't a fool. He knew the next major crime that came along would strip them bare and all his staff would have to move on. Him too.

Harry sat at his desk, untouched coffee in front of him, thinking about where this one was headed and how long he had before he was dealing with a body, or even two.

There was something about the information Joe Bring had given him that gave Harry his only glimmer of hope of finding these women alive. Even though he would always err on the side of caution over the word of an ex-junkie, Joe had proved reliable in the past. There was that at least. What Harry hated was feeling like Joe's word was the only thing he had to go on right now.

Harry tightened his tie, pushing the knot to his collar, straightened his jacket and smoothed down his hair.

Open and transparent – that was how modern policing was supposed to be. There was nothing open and transparent about Harry's next actions.

Ordinarily, it was something he would get one of his detective constables to do, except the problem was, he would either have to pass on half of the story or divulge his informant, and no self-respecting DC would trust the word of Joe Bring, former junkie, burglar and shoplifter. Quite why Harry was about to put his trust in a repeat offender, he couldn't himself fathom.

On the walk from his desk to his car, Harry thought about the mess of human misery he had witnessed first-hand at the raid on the farm. It had touched a nerve with him, got into his core. No one should have to exist that way, their lives lost and set adrift, not to mention being taken advantage of.

What exactly did it take to turn a vulnerable and destitute person into a slave? The only conclusion Harry could come up with as he drove the three miles from East Rise Police Station to the out-of-hours on-call magistrate's house, was that those people were not being protected by the law. Mainly because they didn't know that the law was on their side in the first place. Desperate people, out of sight and being abused, assuming they were forgotten and alone.

For the likes of Denis Boros to be protected, the only thing Harry could do was use the legal powers at his disposal. People were being enslaved by those using violence to entrap and harvest a workforce.

He pulled up outside the address, mind already made up, yet now convinced that he was not only doing the right thing, but the only thing he could.

Detective Inspector Harry Powell was about to swear out a warrant in a magistrate's living room, Bible in hand, and, while not exactly about to commit an act of perjury, he was prepared to embellish parts of Joe Bring's story.

If John Kersley could put his own life on the line to help some illegal immigrants, Harry could tell a few fibs under oath.

Chapter 53

Once again, Anna huddled on the floor, listening to the sounds of footsteps in the corridor outside. She guessed from the direction of the noise that she was at the far end of a narrow tunnel, possibly with stairs to the right-hand side of her cell. She couldn't be sure, although without anything else to do, and to take her mind off the pain, she had become attuned to what, or who, was nearby.

There was a sliver of light under the door now. And silence. Whoever it was had stopped outside the door.

Heavier boots, not the high heels of the Controller. That, at least, was an improvement.

She heard the bolt slide across and couldn't help but look towards the doorway, even though she knew that the stark light would temporarily blind her. At least she would get to see something. It had to be better than this vast emptiness.

Hand up to shield her eyes, Anna waited until she dared to risk peeking between her fingers.

The first thing she set eyes on after several hours

of nothingness was the ugly, pock-marked face of the minibus driver. She would have laughed if she'd had the energy. Instead, something resembling a snort came out.

'You look like a pig, so you may as well make noises like one,' said Pock-mark.

More accustomed now to the light, Anna stared directly at him. Perhaps it was the severity of the pain she was feeling, her brain unable to accept that she could possibly put herself in any more danger, only she couldn't remember why she had been so afraid of this pathetic excuse for a man.

'You say that now,' she said, shifting back against the wall, seizing the rare opportunity to examine the confines of her cell, 'only you had a different opinion a few weeks ago.'

He at least had the manners to look uncomfortable. He shifted from one black toe-capped boot to another, rubbed a hand over his forehead.

'A few weeks is a long time. Besides, your little friend is a better option, especially as she's the one more likely to make it to the end of the week.'

'So that's it, then, is it?' said Anna. 'I'm going to die, you'll get rid of my body and Lili will go on to bigger and better things?'

'Lili? That's her name, is it? It's nothing personal, just business. You happen to be expendable.'

He stepped inside, took a bread roll from one jacket pocket and a plastic bottle of water from the other.

'Here,' he said, 'we don't want you dying on us ahead of schedule.'

He put the water on the floor beside her, handed her the roll.

'At least do me a favour and stay for a bit,' she said, looking up into his face, unsure whether the expression she saw there was pity or repulsion. 'It's not as though I'm likely to overpower you: I can hardly move.'

'Good point,' he said, moving away to lean against the far wall. 'I suppose we'll have to give you something to overcome the pain or it won't be much of a show.'

'There's another way: you let me go.'

'Why would I do that? You know I have a good job and a good wage, but you have no idea who I work for. My boss – immediate boss – may be the scariest woman you've ever met, but have you ever stopped to think about who *her* boss is? And what they'd do to both her and me if we started letting people go?'

He shook his head, grotesque jowls wobbling. 'We'd all end up dead. At least this way I get to live, even if you don't. As I said, it's nothing personal.'

'What about your family?' she asked, moving to find a more comfortable position, feet out in front, legs bent.

'I'll probably go home one day, find myself a wife and settle down, or perhaps stay here in England. It's not so bad here – well, not for me it's not.'

'Children?'

'Why do you want to know all this?' he said, pushing himself away from the wall, taking a step towards the door. 'It's not going to make any difference to the outcome.'

'I thought you'd like to know,' she said, stopping him in his tracks.

'Know what?' he called over his shoulder.

'You're the only person I've had sex with since I left Hungary five weeks ago.'

He took another step towards his escape, albeit a tentative one. 'It means nothing,' he said.

'In fact, apart from you, there's been no one for a very long time. Not since my daughter's father was murdered.'

He turned one hundred and eighty degrees, forced himself to look at her. Anna prayed he was seeing her as a person, as someone's mother. It was probably futile, yet she had to try.

'That's how I know, you see,' she said.

'Know what?'

'That I'm pregnant. I knew straight away. I die, so does your baby.'

Chapter 54

Sweating more than someone his size and age should in the February weather, Harry left the magistrate's warm and cosy house, Bible still in hand.

He had only told a bit of a lie – well, it wasn't exactly a lie, more an embellishment of the truth. The important part was that the magistrate had granted the warrant. Now all Harry had to do was rally up some troops, organize a search team, and find the missing women before they were either killed or moved on to another part of the country.

Though that was, at least, better than picturing them in a shallow grave.

Realizing that mooning around in the street wasn't going to solve a kidnap, he got a grip of himself and got in the car. His mobile vibrated in his pocket, snapping him back to senior detective mode.

With a frown, he answered the call. 'If it isn't the wonderful Joanna Styles, Senior Crime Scene Investigator of East Rise town, calling me with good news.'

'Depends what you class as good news, Harry,' she said.

'Give me the worst of it,' said Harry.

'It's definitely blood on the tarmac in front of the bus stop where the two women were last seen. And it's got what looks like long dark hair caught up in it. That's the good news. The bad news is that the lab run will have to be now if we've any chance of getting a fast turnaround on it.'

Harry thought out loud as he connected her to the hands-free and started on the journey back.

'Problem we've got,' he said, aware he was telling Jo what she already knew, 'is running the DNA through the European databases. If our witness is correct about the women being Eastern European, that's any number of searches in various countries. This'll take far too long to identify whoever's blood that is.'

'Not to mention,' added Jo, 'that she may not even be on the database.'

'It's like looking for an immigrant in a county of immigrants. I don't like where this is heading.'

'We're still down at the scene, though, to be fair, I don't think it'll take us much longer. How are you getting on?'

'I need to sort out search teams now, Jo, so I'll let you go.'

'That sounds very much like you want me off the line.'

'That too. I need to get back to the office. See you later.'

*

A few minutes later, Harry was back at his near-empty incident room. Only Hazel Hamilton was left in the office.

He risked a wink in her direction: there was no one to catch him in his boyfriendly act.

He walked past her. He'd update her about what was going on as soon as he'd got on top of everything. At least, he'd tell her as much as he was allowed, especially when it came to the fact he'd lied to the magistrate under oath.

Harry emerged from his office some minutes later and found Hazel still tapping away at her computer.

'Thought you'd at least have made me a brew,' he said.

She shrugged and looked up at him. 'Didn't want to look as though I was sucking up to the boss.'

He gestured to the empty banks of desks.

'Exactly who were you worried about seeing this sycophantic act?'

With a smile she said, 'Just because we're alone, doesn't mean you can take liberties. Anyway, how's the kidnap going?'

He pulled over one of the stained cloth-covered chairs, loved by many other departments until finding its final resting place in Major Crime, and took a seat opposite her.

'I don't fancy these girls' chances at all. I've got teams in place about to do the necessary door knock for a warrant that needs executing tonight. Wondered if you'd go along to ensure everything goes smoothly?'

'Oh, you make it sound totally irresistible.'

'I've handpicked you.'

'I'm the only one here.'

'Would you believe that I orchestrated this exact scenario?'

'No.'

'Fair enough. Haze, I've got to go. The briefing document's in an email I sent you a couple of minutes ago, along with the warrant and the number of the search team sergeant you need to speak to.'

Harry was up and out of his seat before he had finished speaking. He reached his office door, turned and added, 'And don't forget your body armour. These people don't seem to care about dragging a woman out of a bus stop in broad daylight, so they won't lose much sleep if they stab a copper.'

'Okay,' she called. 'I'll get it from the store room. It's hanging next to Pierre's. I think he must have forgotten to take it.'

Something about Hazel's comment stopped Harry in his tracks.

'Grab Pierre's too, then, will you?' he shouted to Hazel's back as she disappeared into the store cupboard. 'I'll drop it off to him on the way out. Better to be safe than sorry.'

Chapter 55

One option Lili had seriously considered was breaking the furniture and using one of the legs to jab in the Controller's face when she came back. If she was really lucky, the next person through the door would be Pock-mark. Ramming the splintered wood straight into his neck would give her the most satisfaction she was ever likely to experience in her short nineteen years of life.

Anna had been right about one thing: these people would never let her go.

The best chance she had was to kill Anna, as they wanted, and then plead for her job back sorting vegetables.

Surely life was meant to be better than this?

Despair washed over her as she fought back another sob. If she didn't come up with something soon, they were both going to die.

The idea was creeping into her mind that it was probably too late for Anna. There wasn't much she could do – kill or be killed. It was, no doubt, all in a day's work for the Controller and Pock-mark, yet, to her, it was her life.

When it came down to it, Lili simply wasn't sure she would be up to it.

Shaking from fear and hunger and deprived of any sanitary facilities, Lili considered her options in terms of being bait.

It wasn't long before the door in front of her was flung open and Pock-mark was standing in the doorway.

'These are for you,' he said.

He flung something black and heavy into the corner behind her.

'Make sure you use them well. You know her weak points. Get her on the floor and you're home and dry.' He gave an empty laugh. 'When I say home, I mean a shitty, unforgiving part of England.'

Lili watched him walk out, slamming the door and leaving her shut in once again.

Without really wanting to, she couldn't help but examine what he'd thrown into the corner.

If she wasn't mistaken, he had tossed her steel toe-capped boots.

Chapter 56

It wasn't often that Hazel felt Harry had only told her half the story, but tonight was one of those occasions: she was being kept in the dark about the details of that evening's out-of-hours warrant.

She met the uniformed sergeant as per his instructions, took part in a hurried briefing in the police station car park, evening gloom settling in, before she followed the marked police van around the town centre's ring road towards the rural part of the division.

The traffic was heavy, making their progress a little slow. Hazel used the time to concentrate on what they were about to do.

At best, they were going to find two injured, scared women, who had, by the sound of it, been enslaved and possibly sexually abused. That in itself was going to be a difficult situation to deal with. The women would probably have their own mistrust of the police and authorities; after all, no one had come to help them so far. They might even deny anything bad had ever happened to them. It wouldn't be the first time, and most certainly not the last.

Hazel followed the van as it took the third turning at the roundabout, keeping it in her sights, fidgeting as she turned the steering wheel, the unfamiliar feel of her body armour digging into her side.

Harry had been specific in his email about the likely physical state of the women they were looking for. One had been dragged into a minibus, possibly with head injuries from being slammed into the road. It was anyone's guess what other abuse they might both have suffered.

The marked Sprinter van in front of her turned into a lane, too narrow in places for traffic to flow in both directions. It gave her the chance to look into vehicles as they slowed to pass one another, banks of shrubs and bushes on either side. She wasn't too familiar with the area, but her knowledge, backed up by the satnav, did tell her that they weren't too far from their destination.

Most of the cars that drew alongside her had their interior lights off, making it almost impossible to see inside. Now and again, she would catch a glimpse of a commuter on their way home from work or a parent ferrying their children to some activity or other.

One, however, did grab her attention.

A blue Nissan Qashqai, two up, window down on the driver's side giving her a good, if brief, view of both occupants.

They were laughing, something that wouldn't ordinarily have bothered Hazel. People were allowed to laugh. Perhaps having a long night ahead of her was making her begrudge other people's enjoyment.

She continued to watch them in her rear-view mirror after they'd gone past. There were two other cars between hers and the marked police van now, dying light making it difficult to make much out. And yet, if she wasn't mistaken, the passenger threw something from the window.

All she could say with any certainty was that it was a dark object and the passenger seemed to get rid of it with ease.

Normally her suspicious mind would have jumped to the conclusion that it must have been drugs. The problem with that though, Hazel realized, was that the driver seemed to find it funny, and the police van was heading in the opposite direction. Even the most stupid of drugs dealers didn't throw away their stash when the police were driving in the opposite direction, no hint of turning round and giving chase.

Whatever they had been up to, criminal or otherwise, she didn't have time to worry about it: little stood in the way of a live kidnap. She tried to catch a glimpse of the number plate as it retreated from her view, dialled up Pierre on the hands-free and, when he didn't answer, said, 'Hi, P. Hope everything's okay there. Would you please write down Golf Juliet One Eight, then Papa, I think? I didn't get it all. And Harry's heading over with your body armour in a bit. I'll call you later.'

Hazel focused on the rest of the journey and what she had to do next, with only a passing concern as to why Pierre, all alone in the middle of nowhere, just his witness for company, hadn't answered his phone. The only other method of communication he had with the outside world.

She remembered that not only was Harry heading over there, but firearms officers were stationed close to the safe house.

It wasn't as if Pierre was really on his own out there.

Chapter 57

'Seriously, John,' said Pierre, his own mobile phone clutched in his hand, 'you need to tell me who you were speaking to and why you told them where we are.'

A twisted, anxious face stared back at him. Pierre watched John's mouth open and shut, no words coming out at first, only the sound of someone in torment.

'I'm sorry,' he said eventually, 'I didn't think it would do any harm.'

Pierre took a step towards him. 'I need to call up and report this now,' he said as he tried to keep his voice calm. He felt as though he was approaching a scalded child about to bolt for the door. 'It's vital that no one knows where we are.'

He risked another step closer.

'Who were you speaking to?'

'Marton's cousin,' he said.

'Cousin?' said Pierre. 'You didn't tell me about a cousin.'

'I ... he ... well, he called me, said he'd found Marton in France and was taking him home. Knew all about how I'd helped and got him to the ferry. He said he was coming back and getting Marton's kid sister too.'

Unable to believe what he was hearing, Pierre got as far as dialling 99 on his phone when John took a giant stride towards him and all but took the mobile from his hand.

'You can't,' he said.

'Why not?' said Pierre.

'His cousin swore me to secrecy. That's why I didn't tell you I had the phone. I'm so sorry I lied, but I had to do it. I had to help Marton's little sister. You see that, don't you?'

'You've no idea that actually *was* his cousin,' said Pierre, grabbing ownership of his phone back from John's sweaty fingers. 'You should have told me.'

'I would have done,' said John, now raising his voice, 'but what's the harm when there are armed police sitting outside the door?'

'It's one of the things I came to tell you,' said Pierre. The look of panic on John's face would have been almost amusing if the situation hadn't been so frightening.

'They've gone, and they won't be replaced for hours.'

Chapter 58

With an air of boredom, Alexa looked out of her living-room window.

She wanted to tell the police that the blue lights and silent approach were unnecessary. She would give in without them needing to batter down the front door.

The fight had very much gone out of her.

Instead, she sat on her sofa with as much dignity as she could muster in her current state, facing the door, hands in her lap.

Her hands were holding her mobile phone.

She'd known her days were numbered from the moment the first text message arrived. And now a beating thrown in for good measure.

Blackmail was a very ugly thing and it sent an extremely strong message.

There was only one thing to do.

She stood up on weary and bruised legs and went to the kitchen.

Chapter 59

'You and whoever's bastard baby that is, get up,' said Pock-mark. 'It's about time you did something useful.'

His words were met with silence and a look of pure hatred.

'You could do with some fresh air. You stink.'

Without waiting for her response, he walked away from Anna's cell door.

It was the first time she had seen it open without someone barring her way to freedom. Only now, she hardly had the energy to walk through it, let alone make a run for it. Any thoughts of overpowering the ugly, despotic bastard had long since left her.

She could hear his retreating footsteps as she heaved herself to her feet, one hand against the wall for support.

Slowly, she walked to the door, stuck her head into the confined space of the dimly lit walkway and peered in the direction of Pock-mark's voice.

Anna could make out his squat, barrel-like physique, illuminated by the light coming from what she guessed was Lili's cell. It didn't escape her notice that he was speaking to Lili in softer tones, in an almost flirtatious pose as he reached one hand up and placed it on the door jamb, leaned against it, other hand on hip.

'Come on, then,' called Pock-mark to Lili. 'Trust me on this: you don't want your friend getting a head start on you.'

He sauntered in the direction of the short flight of stairs, his back to both of them. Anna saw Lili's head appear around her own cell door. Lili glanced in their captor's direction before turning to her former housemate.

The look of surprise was at least a reassurance to Anna. Somewhere along the way, she had realized that her own vulnerability had increased as soon as they had been separated. There had to be a reason to split them up. One's survival depended on the other's demise. Anna didn't think she was in any fit state to outmanoeuvre anyone else, although out*smarting* Lili was still a possibility. Her trump card had failed her, but she wasn't defeated yet.

Her feet felt as though they belonged to someone else. They reluctantly went in the direction of Lili. Feeling her heart rate increase as she moved for what seemed like the first time in days, yet was only several hours, she took tentative steps towards her fate.

By now, her breathing was so laboured it sounded more like panting. As she shuffled along in the depths of the earth, that was the only sound she could hear until she made out Lili whispering to her.

'There are two of us. He's on his own.'

Even in the gloom, Anna couldn't help but notice that Lili didn't want to meet her eye.

If their physical states were reversed, would Anna honestly care whether Lili made it out alive? They weren't related, not even really friends. Doing the right thing was a luxury for the free, not the enslaved.

Nothing was as precious as survival.

'I said come on, you two,' he shouted from the top of the brick staircase. 'The pair of you are pissing me off.'

'Lean against me,' said Lili as she pressed her shoulder to Anna's arm, braced as she took some of her weight. 'It's okay. We'll be okay.'

Anna knew they were supposed to be words of reassurance, yet, for some reason, she couldn't stop her tears. Crying wouldn't help, fighting would. She barely had energy for the former; there was no chance of the latter.

'It's very touching,' Pock-mark said from his vantage point of three metres above their heads at the top of the steps. 'But it won't help you. You women are all the same: you pretend to care for each other, but when the situation calls for it, you're the first to rip each other's throats out.'

'You're such a pig,' said Anna, determined to die with some dignity. Her body couldn't take much more pain before it simply gave up.

She looked up at him – the man who had the power to free them, make them kill each other, or kill them both and bury their bodies.

Anna felt the tears streaming down her face, though she continued to lock eyes with her tormentor. It was less a show of strength – that would have been impossible – more a show of her hatred for him.

'You know the thing that amazes me about all this?' she said. Despite the tightening of Lili's grip on her hand, Anna carried on.

'I could probably understand it more if we'd come to this country and been taken advantage of by English people.'

He threw his head back and laughed at her.

'Do you actually think this is about nationality?' he said. 'It's about making money and supplying a workforce. Where you come from is irrelevant. It's just handy that we speak the same language and you can't speak a word of English. Now, get up here and get on with it.'

He turned and pushed open the door behind him, stepping onto the harshly lit concrete floor of a disused factory.

The difference between this one and most other disused factories was that not only was it fitted out with a caged area the size of a boxing ring and surrounded by chairs, it also carried the stale stench of sweat mixed with the unmistakable metallic tang of blood.

Chapter 60

Heart pounding, Pierre went to press the third 9 on his mobile to summon help. He was silently cursing himself for leaving his police radio on his bed, its panic button the quickest way to alert the control room that their location had been compromised.

'Please understand something,' John said to him, his expression stopping Pierre from hitting the button.

For a moment, Pierre wanted to give John the benefit of the doubt, then he reminded himself he had been stupid enough to put them both in danger.

'You really think that was Marton's cousin?' said Pierre, barely able to conceal his rage. 'He probably doesn't even have a cousin.'

'If it wasn't his cousin, I wouldn't have told him where we were.'

The officer pressed the last 9.

As the call connected, he ran back along the hallway to his room to get his radio.

'You lied to me and kept a phone hidden,' he called over his shoulder, John following in his wake.

'I know all that,' John said, 'and I'm sorry. I tried to explain to you so many times why I wanted to help these people so badly. I'm not a brave man, certainly not someone who's used to making a stand, especially if it means there's a chance I'll end up getting shot and killed.'

As Pierre, phone held to his ear, started to ask for police attendance, John interrupted.

'I've heard you and the other officers talking,' he said. 'You've already told me that you've got nowhere in trying to find out who shot me, and I know you're not even close to having enough officers to protect me indefinitely.'

Frustrated, and scared for them both, Pierre handed John the phone. 'Here,' he said, 'you explain what's happened. I'll use the radio and hope for both our sakes the police get here first.'

He couldn't help but notice the shake in John's out-stretched hand as he took the mobile phone.

The officer turned away from him, making a pretence of needing to use his Airwaves radio out of earshot, all the time trying to conceal his own trembling hands.

Chapter 61

It hit Anna like a physical blow. The two shovels standing proud in the ground, a metre or so apart. She failed to form the words on her lips, though they were screaming inside her head. She heard a gasp from Lili, thought for a moment that the sound had come from her own mouth. Then she realized she was incapable of forming words.

'The shovels are exactly the same length,' said Pockmark. 'They're a little over a metre long.'

Anna watched him as he rubbed his hands together, shifted his weight from one foot to another. His grotesque features were backlit from the single spotlight, no doubt shining on their macabre challenge.

'You're enjoying this,' she croaked. 'You're actually enjoying this.'

Lili stepped forward, slightly blocking Anna's view of their tormentor. 'What is it you think we're going to do? Dig our own graves?'

'Yes,' he said, still rubbing his hands together, 'that's precisely what I think you're going to do.'

He took a step towards the two women, glee plastered across his face.

'It'll give you something to do while you're waiting for tomorrow night's fight. Sitting around won't do you any good.'

'You're completely mad,' said Lili. 'This is the most barbaric thing I've ever heard of. We're not doing it, and we're not fighting each other.'

Clearly buoyed by her brave words, Lili moved closer to Anna and put an arm around her in solidarity. Anna felt the tremble in the young woman's touch and put her own arm around her.

There was probably no hope for either of them now. At least one of them was going to die, likely both. Why would the Controller and her cronies leave any witnesses? It wasn't a mistake that Anna would make, and she was far from professional at killing people. She had only taken one life in her short time on earth, an act that had led to this very moment. Staying in Hungary hadn't been an option for her. She thought she'd been given the chance to start afresh, begin a new life with a job, roof over her head, steady income.

Her eyes flitted over the scene: one of the ugliest men she had ever had sex with, had ever been touched by, was standing before her with two shovels forced into the icy ground where their unmarked graves would lie, and the only person present who might have had an opportunity to make something of her life was wrapping her shivering limbs around her.

Anna risked putting her hand into Lili's pocket. Their only hope.

Anna sank to her knees, threw her head back and started to laugh. It was a soft laugh at first, more of a giggle. She had little energy for much else; besides, it hurt her too much when her sides expanded and contracted. Not that that would matter soon. She was going to die. If nothing else, she was a fighter, and that was how she would draw her last breath – fighting.

She was aware that Lili was attempting to crouch beside her. Pock-mark – she neither knew nor cared where he was. For the first time since coming to this horrendous country, she actually felt as though she was the one in control.

'Stop fucking laughing and get up,' said Pock-mark. 'I'll stop you acting like a fool if you don't get up and show me some respect.'

Anna would never know for sure, but that seemed to be the trigger that brought her back to reality, the stark reality of being on her knees, ribs broken, cold and starving, with nowhere to go. She had sunk to the depths of depravity.

And he wouldn't be the first man she had stabbed to death.

With her last reserve of strength, she pushed against the hardened earth, hands propelling her forward.

Her progress was rapid for a woman everyone thought was destroyed in more ways than one. Neither Lili nor Pock-mark saw the broken bottle until Anna, in one swift movement, pulled it from her jacket and swung it into his neck.

As much as the pain in her sides coursed through her, Anna knew she needed to sever as many veins and arteries in his throat before the element of surprise wore off. She drove the jagged edge further and further until the loss of blood kicked in.

He fell to the ground, one hand uselessly trying to push the blood back inside his neck, trajectory of red still pumping in an arc.

The two Hungarian women stood and watched him die.

All Lili had to say was, 'That was my broken bottle.'

Chapter 62

Alexa set the microwave to three minutes. It was probably too long ... still, it paid to be cautious.

Her bare feet took her back across the hallway to the front door.

She had decided to let the police in, prevent damage to her front door. This week had been expensive enough as it was.

With as much poise as she could muster, she opened the door and stared into the faces of a uniformed search team.

'You had better have a warrant,' she shouted to no one in particular.

'What happened to you?' the one in front asked.

'Mind your own business,' she said, throwing her head back in an attempt to toss her hair, a pointless habit given that she was now mostly bald. Patches of what had been her crowning glory remained, but in sad little clumps.

She stood in her doorway with as much ferocity as she could manage, a look of defiance on her face, and watched a woman in a cheap suit step forward.

'Alexa Gabor,' she said. 'My name's Detective Constable Hazel Hamilton. This is a warrant to search your home. Please step out of the way.'

They locked eyes for a few seconds, Alexa's head held high, chin pushed out, eyebrows raised in an angry arch on the way to her hairline. At least, where her hairline should have been had someone not crudely shaved her head.

She saw the group of officers about to push their way in, felt she had made her point and stood to one side.

The Hungarian slave master knew what a sight she looked and didn't need to read minds to know that the policewoman would have a thousand questions. The dried blood caked to both of her calves visible underneath her navy skirt, the torn front of her blouse revealing her bra and her swollen lip – all strong indicators of the beating she had endured only minutes ago.

'Anyone else here?' the woman asked.

Alexa snorted at her.

'Answer me, Miss Gabor,' said the detective.

'No, only me. Typical police, you're too late.'

She heard a shout from one of the officers flooding through her house.

'Why's there a mobile phone cooking in the microwave?' he called from the kitchen.

She shrugged and said, 'I fancied a snack.'

With every ounce of strength left, she was trying to hide her humiliation, soft wisps of remaining hair falling to her bruised cheeks and over one of her blackened eyes.

Alexa was determined to stand, one hip pushed forward, hand resting on her waist, a look of nonchalance.

'Who did this to you?' said the policewoman.

'No idea,' she said, accent thick, yet the strength of her voice belying the situation she was in. 'I was burgled last week, so I suppose they realized I lived alone and came back.'

When the police detective opened her mouth to say something else, Alexa flicked her words away with her manicured fingers, about the only part of her that didn't look pitiful.

She hadn't expected the grilling to stop there, but the detective was called away by one of the officers in uniform.

Alexa felt her stomach drop when she saw they were discussing the cellar door which was now wide open.

Losing 400,000 euros, losing two slaves, being blackmailed along with being beaten up – it all meant that Alexa had never got round to clearing the cellar.

The only thing she could do was stand and watch as they descended the steps, her heart pounding.

After what seemed like an eternity, one of the officers returned with a handful of children's clothing: a miniskirt, ripped T-shirt and a green and blue silk scarf.

Chapter 63

'They're on the way,' said Pierre as he moved away from the window. 'You need to hide somewhere.'

'Is this really necessary?' said John, voice trembling. 'I know you're worried he might not actually have been Marton's cousin, but it had to be: not only did he know so much about what had happened, he said he could help, said he knew where the little girl was.'

'Listen to me,' said Pierre, grabbing John by both arms, 'they've tried to shoot you once and that was before you'd even gone to the police. Why do you think we told you not to tell anyone where we were; made sure you didn't have a phone with you?'

'I'm sorry, Pierre, really I am. I was scared and he knew where I lived anyway, said he'd been there with Marton to find me, thank me for what I'd done for his family.'

Pierre watched as the penny dropped and fear ran riot across John's face.

The officer spoke slowly and clearly. 'Did you ever speak to Marton again after he came back that time from the ferry terminal after the cage fighting?'

John shook his head, tears forming in the corner of his eyes. 'Oh my God, I've been so stupid. I was so scared, running for my life. Marton's dead, isn't he? And now I've led them to us.'

Tightening his grip on John's arms, needing him to focus, Pierre said, 'Never mind that now. Officers are coming for us, but we don't know who else is. We need to get out of here. We'll hide in the woods until they get here. It's our only chance but we need to go now.'

'Pierre, I'm so, so—'

'We don't have time, let's go.'

Pausing only to grab his Airwaves radio and, for what it was worth, ASP and PAVA spray, Pierre dragged John Kersley from the room towards the top of the staircase.

He put up a hand to silence his witness, certain that he had heard a sound from downstairs.

Then he felt the draught from the front door. The front door that had been bolted from the inside and was now wide open.

For a few bleak seconds, Pierre stood where he was, unable to move, not sure what was going to save their lives and what was going to get them killed quickest.

The police officer turned to John and mouthed, '*On three,*' held up his hand to the man whose very survival now depended on him, recognized the petrified look on his face, and knew he would have to drag him down the stairs and out of the front door.

No time to think any further, Pierre grabbed the front of John's jumper and pulled him down the stairs to the open door.

Chapter 64

Harry Powell, a police officer for nearly three decades, didn't scare easily. He didn't get flustered over much either, but he did worry about his staff. More so, his friends.

He had made a couple of attempts to call Pierre after receiving no reply to his earlier text message. He tried to rationalize it by reminding himself how cheap and unreliable job phones could be, especially in a remote location. Despite telling himself it was a glitch and he shouldn't worry, Harry made a call to the control room.

His blood turned to ice when his call was put through and the control room inspector calmly informed him that firearms and all available patrols were already on their way.

'So long as someone is fucking taking my staff's welfare seriously, not just me,' he shouted before ending the call and slamming his foot down on the accelerator.

His driving was completely reckless, he would be the first to admit. As he took bend after bend, making his way through the rural outskirts of East Rise to the supposedly safe house, he cursed the day that John Kersley had blighted his incident room.

In all his time in the job, Harry had never lost a member of his staff; hadn't so much as had one seriously injured working on an investigation.

He'd be damned if he'd start now.

He jumped on the brakes as something ran across the road in front of him, its eyes momentarily lit up in his headlights.

'Fucking badgers,' he shouted, banging a fist against the steering wheel, then trying to regain his concentration. He was certainly no good to Pierre if he crashed. The way his luck was going, he was bound to hit a deer and really have one hell of a shit-cart. That thought made him reduce his speed to sixty and open the window, both to wake himself up with the brisk late-evening air and allow him to listen for oncoming traffic.

He doubted whether he would be able to hear a car approaching from the opposite direction, although it didn't stop him trying. It might give him the edge, prepare him for what he might find.

The thought was a hideous one. Pierre was simply one of the most decent people he knew, not to mention under his care. If Harry had been the sort to display any emotion, he might have allowed himself a couple of tears. But not only would it do nothing to help the situation, he didn't want to look like a total arsehole if he got to Pierre to find him sitting at the kitchen table with Kersley and the armed officers, drinking tea and asking Harry why he looked like he had hay fever in the middle of February.

He got closer to the house. The lights were on. That was a good sign. Or was it a bad sign?

Shouldn't they have gone to bed by now? Harry screeched his car to a halt, Pierre's car on the driveway where he had left it when they first arrived.

Perhaps he was panicking unnecessarily.

Then he saw through the front-room window that the television was on. Not only was no one watching it, but both the front door and the door to the kitchen were open.

By the light flooding the two rooms from the blaze of lamps and wall lights, Harry realized exactly what was wrong – while most of the curtains were pulled across to keep out the night's gloom, two of the drapes in the bay window were hanging at an angle, suspended now by only one or two hooks.

Whether he was looking at an attempt to flee or gain entry, one thing was clear, Pierre and John Kersley hadn't been in the house alone.

Giving little thought for his own safety, Harry grabbed his ASP and PAVA, got out of the car and ran towards the building.

Chapter 65

'Lili,' rasped Anna, 'you have to get out of here.'

They were both still staring at the corpse of the man who, only minutes ago, had expected them to entertain him by digging their own graves.

'Me?' she said, eyes opening wide, the pitch of her voice unnaturally high. 'Me? What about us? What about you?'

'Firstly, I don't think I could make it, not the state I'm in. Secondly, if you get out of here, you can send help. The police would be better than nothing. I'd only slow you down.'

Anna once again sank to her knees on the cold, hard ground.

'What are you doing?' Lili said. 'Don't touch him. There's blood everywhere.'

'I'm covered in blood anyway,' said Anna as she deftly went through his pockets.

As she rifled the few belongings Pock-mark had, she looked over at Lili, concern etched onto her young protégée's face.

'You look like death,' Lili said.

One hand in the dead man's jacket pocket, Anna held the other up to silence Lili while she frantically searched.

It was another movement that caused a searing pain in her side, and which she would surely pay dearly for later. Right now, her fight mode was about to switch to flight mode, the adrenalin the only thing keeping her functioning.

She fished around from pocket to pocket as she knelt beside the still-warm corpse, blood oozing from its neck and slowly seeping into the hard, cold earth.

'Ironic,' she muttered, 'that it's his blood on the ground.' Her forehead was creased in concentration until finally her fingertips touched the cold metal keys. She looked up at Lili who was busying herself keeping a look out. Quite why, Anna couldn't initially figure, as beyond their spotlight it would have been impossible to see anyone approaching.

'Got them,' she said, showing the minibus keys to Lili.

Then the reason for Lili's behaviour became clear: she didn't want to look at the dead man.

'You've gone very pale,' said Anna. 'You're probably paler than me. You okay?'

'Fine. I've never been very good with the sight of blood.'

Despite the extra pain it caused her, Anna put her head back and laughed.

When she'd finished, she slowly got to her feet, with no help from her accomplice.

'You're telling me that you're squeamish?' she asked. 'You had a broken bottle in your pocket that you were going to use on me—'

Once again, Anna put up her hand to stop Lili from speaking. She carried on.

'The sight of my blood would have been okay, I take it. His is a different matter, I suppose.'

Without another word, minibus keys clasped in her hand, Anna lumbered towards the far side of the building, where she hoped and prayed to find her means of escape, with or without Lili.

Chapter 66

It seemed like an eternity as Harry waited in the kitchen for the paramedics. He knew full well it was only several minutes before they were bound to arrive, but it didn't stop his rising concern. He left the line open while he spoke to the emergency services on the phone. His instinct was to rush to Pierre and give the best life-saving CPR he could manage, leaving John Kersley to the mercy of fate.

It was a cruel choice he was faced with: give first aid to a member of the public with possible head injuries who didn't seem to be moving or breathing, or attend to a police officer who looked as though he was taking shallow breaths, yet seemed to be groaning. That was a good sign, surely?

Harry ran through his first aid checks, safe in the knowledge that he was doing the best he could for them both.

Pierre's face was a mess, clotted with blood, skin grey, although his eyes seemed to be flickering beneath their lids. He heard an animal-like groan come from his throat, guttural and unlike anything Harry had heard before.

Kneeling on the floor, Pierre prostrate in front of him, John visible through the kitchen table legs, he felt a tug of duty to check on the witness. From where he was, Harry couldn't even tell if John had head injuries, although something was clearly causing the man to be on the ground, not speaking or moving.

John was lying on his front, one arm tucked beneath his body, legs twisted at an awkward angle. His face gave nothing away: lips clamped shut, eyes closed and no sounds at all.

One thing that Harry was absolutely certain of was that he couldn't look after them both. He had a decision to make, one he hated.

'I'm sorry, P,' he whispered to his friend, 'you'll be okay. I promise you'll be all right, or I'd not leave your side.'

He scooted across the floor in a childlike movement, the sort made by a playing toddler, anxious to get to their building bricks. Except this was no game.

With one last glance at Pierre, Harry set about the task of administering CPR to John.

He clamped his mouth over John's, hoping that the day wasn't going to end in a death. He counted out the chest compressions to thirty, paused, and began again with rescue breaths, another cycle of chest compressions, only stopping briefly to look across at Pierre who now didn't seem to be moving or groaning at all.

Harry heard the ambulance operator calling to him

over the mobile phone. Momentarily, he had forgotten the line was still open.

'I can't hear you counting,' she said. 'I need to hear you counting out loud so I know you're doing it right.'

He wanted to scream at her, *Of course I'm fucking doing it right. I'm a copper. I'm trained.*

Instead, all that came out of Harry's mouth, face tilted towards Pierre was, 'I think I'm watching my friend die.'

Chapter 67

Hazel Hamilton, detective constable of some years, very rarely acted unexpectedly. It would have been fair to have referred to her as predictable and safe, a little boring even, so when her earpiece brought news that officers were in need of urgent assistance, and made it clear exactly who those officers were, what she said to Alexa Gabor was very out of character.

The woman had been standing in front of Hazel telling lie after lie, looking down her nose and demanding that the police get out of her house or she would be forced to call her legal team.

'And another thing,' she said as she jabbed a finger at Hazel's chest, 'I've—'

'Shut up, woman!' Hazel half shouted at her, before she turned her back on the stunned, bloodied and almost bald victim of crime.

The officers nearby heard her over their Airwaves radios, some pausing in what they were doing, others carrying on with the task at hand, but not without exchanging a look. The sergeant in charge of the search said only one thing to Hazel, 'Go, we'll take care of things here.'

Simon Mannering, one of the uniformed search team, followed Hazel out of the house, keeping tabs on her as she ran to her police car.

'Can I come with you?' he said as she reached out to open the car door.

'That's a good idea,' she said as she jumped into the driver's seat.

'You've known me years, Haze,' he said, 'so trust me to drive us there.'

'I'm an advanced driver,' she replied, key already in the ignition.

'Look,' he said, 'I know you're a superb driver, one of the best, but it's not my boyfriend calling up for urgent assistance for an unconscious police officer.'

She paused, hand on the gear stick, about to pull away.

'And I know you and Pierre are good mates. Let me drive.'

Without another word, Hazel got back out of the car, stood in front of Simon and said, 'Okay, but we go now. Not in five minutes, not in two minutes. We go now, or I go alone.'

'It's a deal.'

By the time he had slid into the driver's seat, Hazel had run around the Skoda, got in the passenger seat and had her seat belt on.

'Shall I let the control room know we're coming?' she asked as he pulled away from the kerb.

He took his eyes off the road for a second to look at her.

'The sarge has probably done it, but let's make sure: I'll call up the control room to let them know.'

She knew exactly why he wanted it recorded properly: this wasn't an ordinary crime scene they were on their way to. This was an injury to one of their own, with another calling up for urgent assistance. These kinds of calls were far from everyday, and never had one given Hazel such cause to cry, scream and want to vomit, all at the same time.

Not twenty minutes earlier, she had texted Pierre to tell him that she would gladly swap places with him. It didn't bear thinking about what was happening to him at the time.

It wasn't long ago that Harry had found an old friend of his on her kitchen floor, most of her skull and brains all over the ceramic tiles. With a feeling of rising despair, Hazel had a sense that Harry was once again tending to a mortally wounded friend. Pierre was her friend too, yet she had only known him a short while. Harry had known him years, and she wasn't sure he was up to losing anyone else. He was more fragile than he made out.

Aware that Simon was saying something to her, she tried to focus, bring herself back to do what her job demanded of her, irrespective of whose life was in danger.

'Sorry,' she confessed, 'I wasn't listening to you. What did you say?'

'I'm not surprised your mind's elsewhere. I was saying that Harry'll be okay. If I was in any sort of danger, he'd be one of the first I'd want by my side. He's helped me out on more than one occasion.'

Hazel glanced out of the window at the street signs flashing by and tried to work out where they were before she looked across at Simon.

'Really,' she said. 'Recently?'

'Over the years,' said Simon as he rounded a bend, car positioned in the middle of the road. 'Once, a long time ago, I was going through a bit of a messy divorce. Him and Mrs Powell put me up for a few weeks.'

'Wow, I had no idea.'

'He's never told you?'

'Not one word.'

She sat mulling this over for a few seconds. If he hadn't told her about something so innocent as a colleague staying at his home, what else might Harry have kept from her?

She wanted Simon to stop talking, concentrate on driving them. She would have driven faster, taken risks.

'I don't think his missus was all that chuffed about it,' said Simon. 'Their kids were still quite young then so, as grateful as I was, I thought it was about time to get myself together. Even then, he helped me move my furniture, what was left of it anyway, to my new place.'

He gave a small laugh. 'Then, a year to the day after my divorce was through, he sent me on secondment from his CID team. Best thing anyone ever did for me.'

'A career highlight?' she guessed.

'No, I met my new wife. Later, he claimed that he knew we'd be perfect for each other, that's why he picked me. Personally, I think it's because he realized I would never make a detective all the time I had a hole in my arse. I still let him think it was all down to him.'

She opened her mouth to say something, then it dawned on her that she couldn't find the right words.

'I can see a number of flashing lights up ahead,' said Simon.

After a couple of seconds of silence, he needlessly added, 'We're almost there.'

The atmosphere in the police car was strained: Hazel didn't want to talk, didn't want to discuss what might have happened to one of her friends, and what mental torment her boyfriend might now be going through, and Simon had switched from telling her positives about Harry to stating the obvious.

'Paramedics are here, plus firearms, dogs and response teams.'

She just wanted him to stop the bloody car so she could get out and run inside the house.

As they drove down the unmade track to the side of the property, flanked by dense, dark woods, she wondered who on earth thought it was a good idea to put a witness who someone had tried to kill in such a desolate spot with only one unarmed detective constable for protection.

Even if it meant the end of her own career, she would

make sure that someone paid for such a stupid and thoughtless act.

This was her last thought as she flung the door open of the still-moving Skoda and ran along the rutted path towards the house of horrors, her heart in her mouth.

Chapter 68

For a time, Harry couldn't say how long, he had sat on the floor in the kitchen, Hazel beside him, one of his hands in hers, the other grabbing at his own hair. His usually straight back was rounded, his knees up in front of him, eyes down.

Harry always took charge.

Harry always knew what to do.

Right now, Harry's mind was elsewhere.

Even for a man whose pale complexion and freckled skin hated the sun, almost as much as his heart hated injustice, his pallor was deathly.

He tried to speak, was sure his lips were moving, no sound.

Hazel leaned closer, turned her head to follow his gaze to where Pierre had been lying only moments before, until the paramedics rushed him outside to the air ambulance waiting nearby.

The paraphernalia cast aside by the emergency services was strewn across the kitchen floor, blood from

Pierre, John Kersley and who knew what else pooling and congealing.

Ordinarily, Harry and Hazel would have been ushered from the crime scene to other parts of the house, a police car, the nearest police station, but tonight no one was arguing.

The uniformed inspector, Josh Walker, stood in the kitchen doorway redirecting anyone away who dared approach.

As soon as Harry's eyes met Hazel's, he knew that his secret was out: he was a broken man.

The two of them remained camped out where they were for some time, their legs losing all feeling as they huddled together: detective inspector and detective constable, boyfriend and girlfriend.

A noise at the doorway drew Harry's attention away from his friend's blood on the tiled floor.

He watched without seeing Senior Crime Scene Investigator Jo Styles tiptoe across the threshold to sombre looks from Josh. Jo was saying something in a funeral-parlour whisper.

Harry again tried to speak, felt Hazel's hair brush his face as she moved her head closer, ear towards his mouth.

'What?' she breathed. 'Please don't say that.'

For the first time since she had arrived at the isolated hell hole, Harry really looked at her.

'It's true, Haze. I sent Pierre here knowing I couldn't properly protect him. And that's not the worst of it, I almost sent you. You were my first choice to come here.'

Chapter 69

The last thing John Kersley remembered before coming to with a detective inspector pummelling his chest, was Pierre trying to drag him through the front door and then being hit from behind.

What happened after that was anyone's guess.

He had spent the first couple of seconds of consciousness attempting to work out where he was, then waiting until his eyes came back into focus to look for Pierre.

The man had tried to save his life, and from what John saw on waking, had possibly paid the ultimate price for it.

He saw the looks Harry Powell was giving him as the paramedics gathered round him, police hovering, asking him endless questions. He had tried to find out how Pierre was but no one had answered.

He didn't pursue it: some of the police looked angry, some upset, one or two even in tears. Harry himself had gone very pale and was huddling next to a blonde woman, younger than him. From the look on their faces, John assumed things were very grave for Pierre, and it was all his fault.

There was no choice but for him to tell them: they would find the phone where he'd dropped it in his bedroom and they would look at the calls.

That was it, the phone calls.

'Harry, Harry,' he said as he tried to sit up, one of the paramedics telling him to lie still.

'No,' he insisted, 'I have to speak to Harry. Please, it's important.'

From his vantage point on the trolley, flanked by paramedics and police, he watched Harry slowly get up and come over.

'This is all my fault,' he started to say as he watched the detective inspector try to look as though he was about to disagree. Everything about the officer's movements said fatigue. He moved as if he didn't know how to use his limbs any more.

I've done this, thought John.

'Pierre tried to save me, drag me out into the woods to hide, and it's my fault they knew we were here.'

Harry took a step closer, leaned across the trolley, one hand moving towards John's throat. From the corner of his eye, he saw a paramedic step a little nearer.

If Harry was about to try to throttle him he could hardly blame him.

'My phone—' began John.

'Your *what*?' said Harry, spittle landing on John's face. He made no attempt to remove it.

'I truly thought I was helping,' John said, tears

running down his cheeks as Harry, his face a mask of fury, looked down on him. 'I'd been talking to someone I thought was the cousin of the Hungarian guy, Marton, I'd been hiding, only—'

'Only, you told the people who'd already tried to kill you once exactly where you were.'

Incapable of arguing, even if he had wanted to, John lay on the trolley, anticipating a hand around his throat at any moment. Not for the first time, he wondered if the other officers would try to stop the murder of someone who had led evil straight to one of their own.

Whoever the blonde woman was, she touched Harry's shoulder, the lightest of caresses. He immediately stood back, ran a hand over the stubble on his chin.

'Okay, John,' he said. 'Thanks, we'll get straight on to that. You get off to hospital.'

Within seconds, his trolley was being pushed in the direction of the door and the waiting ambulance.

His head was pounding and most of his body hurt. How many times he had been beaten, kicked, assaulted, he would probably never know.

As the ambulance doors were slammed shut, he closed his eyes at the pain that was coursing through his skull. He tried to focus on why he was here, why he had risked his own life, and now Pierre's, to rescue pitiful strangers.

Decades of broken nights' sleep had been his punishment for his earlier cowardice.

His old schoolfriend, Dibron, the one he had abandoned when the chips were down, was never far from his mind.

And then there was Dibron's sister, Adrianne. John could still picture her beautiful smile. It lit up any room she walked into. She captivated those around her with her wide-eyed innocence and love of life.

Well, to a point, until the school bullies had come for her too and taken that innocence. All five of them.

Another occasion he would rather forget.

Another occasion he stayed down when punched, no matter what, although that time had been different: he had been fully aware of what was going on, could still hear Adrianne as she pleaded and begged until they silenced her too.

The irony wasn't lost on John that if he hadn't been trying to atone for his cowardice in his earlier years, Detective Constable Pierre Rainer wouldn't now be in the air ambulance heading for emergency neurosurgery.

Chapter 70

Walking was excruciating. Anna couldn't describe the pain or manage to block it out. She had toughened up over the last five weeks or so, but still, physical searing agony wasn't something she had endured much of before arriving in England.

And there didn't seem to be any end in sight.

She hadn't thought the plan through. In fact, until that ugly, malicious bastard had told them to dig their own graves, there hadn't actually been a plan, except to stay alive.

That she had certainly done; only thing was, she had expected it to be either her or Lili walking away, not both. Now she was dragging her feet towards the side of the building where she hoped the minibus would be.

A noise behind her made her stop, try to hold her breath, although with every intake her breathing became shallower and shallower.

She closed her eyes. A shudder ran through her at the thought of Pock-mark having an accomplice, or worse still, not actually being dead.

'Anna,' called Lili, 'please wait for me.'

The relief was immense: there was no way she could have found any more strength, fought anyone else, protected herself.

Slowly, she turned where she stood and watched the youthful, beautiful Lili bound towards her. She still looked captivating, despite the ordeal of the last few days.

'I was like that once,' Anna said.

'What?' said Lili as she came to a stop beside her. 'What did you say?'

'Nothing. It's not important. It's amazing how life can change you ... Come on. We need to get out of here.'

'I'd go and get the minibus,' said Lili, 'only I don't know how to drive.'

Anna gave her a sideways look from under her fringe.

'Don't worry, I don't think it's much further.'

They made slow progress towards the barn at the side of the disused factory, one of the many outbuildings, yet only one of a couple with unchained doors.

'If you like,' said Lili, 'how about you rest here and I'll take the keys. At least get the heating on in the bus.'

'No, no, it's okay,' said Anna. She had no intention whatsoever of entrusting her only means of escape to someone who, only minutes ago, was prepared to slash her jugular open with a broken bottle to secure her own freedom.

'Don't you trust me?' asked Lili, an almost teenage sulk to her tone.

'Let's get out of here and then we'll talk about it. How about that?'

The last thing she wanted to do was ignite the situation because right now they needed each other.

It seemed to take for ever to get to the barn. The doors were unlocked, just pushed to, which was about the first piece of good fortune either of them had encountered for some time. Anna rested against the side of the minibus while Lili pushed the doors open. She was panting now, aware that if she didn't get some sort of medical help her days on earth were most definitely limited.

With more help than she wanted to accept from her companion, Anna climbed into the driver's seat. Lili closed the door after her and ran around to the other side to get in.

Anna saw her worried glance through the windscreen. She needn't have worried as there was no chance of Anna having enough time to even get the key in the ignition, let alone drive off without Lili or run her down.

Still, Lili had watched her cut a man's throat, it was bound to make her nervous.

'Okay, then,' said Lili as she grappled with her seat belt. 'Where are we headed?'

'Once we get away from here, we'll decide,' said Anna, mind already made up that she had to get herself to a hospital before it was too late, or even a police station. It was something she didn't want to share with Lili in case it freaked her out. She knew that she couldn't trust her, so the best she could hope for was to keep driving and hope she saw a sign she could read. The pain was so bad, Anna was ready to risk it.

The problem was, Anna had only driven a couple of times before, and nothing as hard to handle as the antiquated minibus.

'You're going to have to help me,' said Anna. 'I'm not sure I can get my foot on the clutch, and I definitely can't do that and change gear. Don't look so petrified, I'll talk you through it.'

'This isn't a great idea,' said Lili.

'Nothing I've done since I decided to leave home has been a great idea. Now come on, we need to get out of here.'

The decrepit minibus lurched and chugged along, shuddering its way along the weed-strewn dirt track, past their former prison, a place where at least one of them would have been murdered, and finally made it onto the road.

It was completely unlit, no street lights or illumination from anywhere nearby. For one brief second, Anna felt a glimmer of hope. There was a chance she would get home, back to her child if she wasn't too late, back to a life that had to be better than this one.

Anna glanced across from the driver's seat and said to Lili, 'We're going home. I don't know how we'll do it, but we're going home.'

She tried to turn the steering wheel left, mainly because it was less effort than turning it to the right, and not because she had any idea where they were going. That was the point her insides felt as though they were on fire.

It was as if something had burst inside her; it seemed to send shock waves from her core to just about every part of her as she slumped forward and desperately tried to keep control of the minibus.

She was aware of Lili beside her, shouting, possibly screaming, and trying to grab her legs, get her feet off the accelerator. Except she didn't quite manage it, and careening down the dark road was likely to end only one way.

Anna was on the verge of passing out from the pain in her stomach when the minibus hit the signpost at a T-junction. Everything went black in Anna's world.

Chapter 71

Alexa Gabor wasn't cut out to sit in a police cell. She knew it, her solicitor knew it, and virtually every officer in the station knew it once she had finished telling them that there was no way she should have been arrested for kidnapping. As if.

She wouldn't even sit down, pacing the floor in custody-issued plimsolls, baggy grey jogging bottoms rustling with her every move.

After several hours, which felt much longer, not only for Alexa, but for the other prisoners and custody staff who had to listen to her tireless ranting, DC Tom Delayhoyde had the unenviable task of visiting her cell to let her know what was about to happen to her.

She merely stood and stared at him as he opened the heavy door, looked him up and down, from his ridiculous floppy hair to his poncy shiny shoes and, hand on her hip, said, 'Are you going to let me out of here?'

'Well,' he said, 'that's what I've come to tell you. After I interviewed you, a few things came back on forensics and other enquires, and . . .'

With growing impatience, Alexa watched him scratch at barely visible stubble, before he added, 'As things currently stand, we've got no further grounds to keep you here.'

That was all she needed to hear. She flounced past him, standing looking gormless in the doorway, and strode towards the custody desk and freedom.

'You haven't heard the bloody last of this,' she called.

Fifteen minutes later, Alexa found herself sitting in the police station front counter foyer, mostly bald head held high, refusing to give in to tears.

She watched the door open and the man-boy police officer step towards her.

'You could have waited around the back of custody where the bail room is,' Tom said to her.

Alexa stood up, her face inches from his. She pointed to her head.

'Why would I do that? Does it worry you that people might think the police did this to me?'

'No,' he said.

There was a pause and she felt obliged to fill it.

'I'm not hiding away. What am I supposed to do now if you're still searching my home?'

Tom paused.

'Well?' she demanded. 'I've got nowhere else to go!'

He seemed to consider her situation before he said, 'You say you've no family nearby and no friends?'

Despite receiving her most intense stare, he didn't falter. Alexa wasn't sure if it was his police officer status or that she simply couldn't intimidate people she hadn't enslaved. Whatever the reason, she stood her ground.

'Then it'll have to be a hotel,' said Tom, 'if you've nowhere else to go.'

She thought this over for a few seconds. A hotel wouldn't be the best idea ever. She would be a little too exposed there. The message she had been sent was a very clear one: she had messed up and had to make amends or life was over for her.

There was only one place she could think of where she would be afforded some safety until she was ready to tackle matters. Marko would help her. He had a soft spot for her, and besides, she was still his boss.

'A hotel, then,' she said with some disgust at the idea.

It seemed such a simple plan. All she had to do was get hold of Marko and he'd come running.

Chapter 72

It took some time before Hazel was able to coax Harry away from the crime scene. He could see officers hanging around, no doubt desperately wanting to get him as far away as possible. Few had the courage to approach him, and the hushed tones and doleful eyes of those who were brave enough gave away their own damaged hearts.

Eventually, Inspector Josh Walker approached Harry and Hazel, still crouching on the floor.

He bent down to their eye level.

'Harry,' he said, 'I can't begin to imagine ...'

It was no doubt the intensity of Harry's stare that made Josh look away and glance across at Hazel.

Harry turned his gaze to his girlfriend. Her usually composed features didn't require much interpreting. She was clearly suffering as much as Harry, doing an equally poor job of masking her torment.

'We really need to get you two somewhere where you'll be warm and looked after,' Harry heard Josh say.

Josh had been a friend of Harry's for a very long time; they knew and understood each other, and he recognized the words for what they were: more than a mere gesture as a police officer – Josh was trying to help out a mate, as well as secure the crime scene. Other than John Kersley's mobile phone records, it was the best chance they currently had to find whoever had caused such horrific injuries to one of their own, as well as an innocent witness.

With a minuscule nod, Harry tried to get to his feet, cramp, age, shock and the cold all playing their part. Hazel seemed to fare slightly better, yet still took her time.

'How you doing, Haze?' asked Josh.

'Yeah,' she shrugged. 'Can't stop thinking about Pierre.'

A single tear rolled down her cheek. Harry put a hand out to wipe it away. She moved her face into the gesture.

'I really need to get you two out of here,' said Josh. 'Apart from practical reasons, I don't think it'll be long before the press hear something's going on.'

They both gave wretched 'We understand' replies.

Harry moved his hand towards Hazel's as she made a grab for his, as if each were clinging on to a lifeline.

'What is it?' said Harry, as he saw Josh put his hand to his earpiece accompanied by a frown. 'Is it Pierre? Is there an update?'

'No, it's under control,' he said. 'We've got calls coming in: one's about a Nissan Qashqai on fire three miles away, plus there was an accident involving two foreign females in a white minibus. It looks like we might have found our hostages.'

Chapter 73

As he got nearer to the site of the accident, the blue flashing emergency lights steered Tom Delayhoyde to exactly where he needed to be. The road was blocked in both directions, partly by the emergency vehicles already in attendance, and partly by the white minibus itself.

Tom pulled his unmarked Ford Focus over on the same side as the crumpled minibus, marvelling at how the driver had managed to embed the middle of its bonnet into the black-and-white pole.

The pole, designed to point passers-by in the direction of East Rise and its surrounding villages, was itself at an angle, its concrete base no longer rooted in the ground.

He got out of the car and made his way to the uniformed PC on the cordon.

'Hi,' he said, 'I'm Tom from Major Crime. How's the driver doing?'

After examining his identification, the young officer shrugged her shoulders, moved in close and said, 'Not looking too good, although ...'

She paused, thumbed over her shoulder and added, 'I'm not convinced by her injuries. I was one of the first here and although she had loads of blood on her clothing, I don't think it was caused by the accident – I couldn't see where it was coming from.'

'What do you mean?'

'The other one, she's in the car with the second paramedic, well, she doesn't seem to have any injuries at all, and she's certainly not covered in blood like the driver.'

'Any idea of where they were coming from?'

'No,' she said, 'they don't speak English. The passenger kept looking over there, though, like she was expecting someone to be following them.'

Tom turned to look where the PC had indicated. He could see a very faint light somewhere in the distance, about two hundred metres back from the road.

At that moment, he heard the unmistakable sound of an unmarked diesel police car, engine straining under its 110,000-mile history.

Sophia pulled the car to a stop on the other side of the cordon, got out and shouted at Tom over a gap of fifty metres or so, 'Want me to come over there?'

'The foghorn's with me,' he said to the PC. 'We'll go and take a look at the building with the light on. Do me a favour? Ask the control room to send more patrols. I've got a bad feeling about this.'

He hurried over to Sophia, told her to get her personal protective equipment on, and then said, 'Rural location, old disused building, two injured women with not a word of English between them.'

'Okay,' said Sophia, 'let's go and see what we have.'

He got into Sophia's car and they crossed the short distance to the top of the rutted track. It was wide enough for a lorry, yet it was clear to both of them it hadn't seen much commercial use of late.

Driving into the unknown, armed only with PAVA spray, handcuffs and ASPs, the two officers sitting side by side were aware of the nervous tension between them. Sophia drove as cautiously as the pot-holed track would allow, following the light to the rear of the old factory.

'What's that?' said Tom, pointing straight ahead into the darkness, eyes nowhere near accustomed to the night.

'Looks too big to be a badger or a fox,' said Sophia.

'Bloody hell,' said Tom, cracking open the door to jump out. 'It looks like a person.'

'Be careful,' shouted Sophia after him. 'We've got no idea what's gone on here.'

Knowing that this could be a trap, and with what happened to Pierre at the forefront of his mind, Tom wasn't about to leave someone dying on the ground, even if it put his own safety in the balance.

He ran to the body, stopping short of stepping into the river of blood seeping from the man's neck, illuminated by the car headlights. His shoes at the edge of a dark, nasty pool of blood, Tom came to the conclusion that, although not medically qualified to declare death, he knew a corpse when he saw one.

Chapter 74

It wasn't long before more officers made their way to the disused factory. Everyone not already dealing with something in connection to Pierre and John Kersley was making themselves available for this new major incident.

Officers and staff had already been called in to work on their rest days, many had telephoned East Rise Police Station offering to work, and a number attended their local stations as soon as they heard what had happened to one of their family.

A hastily put together search team carried out a sweep of the factory and its grounds, headed up by all available dog units. No one wanted to take any chances, so a call was put in to bring out the cadaver dog, trained to sniff out corpses, body parts and blood.

If Tom hadn't been so traumatized by the events of the last few hours, he might have found it amusing that dozens of burly officers, all in stab vests, with Alsatians chomping at the bit to get away from their handlers, were all to be silenced by the arrival of the cadaver dog. It was an ordinary-looking Springer Spaniel, less than half the size of its snarling counterparts, yet with a skill set all its own.

PC Mick Hannigan and his crew member, Police Dog Benny, made their way through the throng over to where the search team had indicated Benny would be best put to use. Tom overheard the dog handler's brief instructions as Benny strained at his currently short line: find any other casualties or bodies.

The last words Tom heard as they disappeared towards the building were 'some sort of slaughterhouse'.

'Better check what they want us to do,' said Sophia as she drew level with Tom. 'Feel like a spare part just standing here. I don't think I've ever felt so helpless.'

'I know what you mean. Heaven only knows what they're going to find in there.'

PC Hannigan couldn't fault his dog's keenness. He was definitely straining to get stuck in and use his canine sense of smell, one hundred times greater than any human's.

The putrid fug hit him as soon as they descended the steps. Some of the smells assaulting the officer's nose were a mixture of human excrement and urine; it was the other ones he wasn't so familiar with.

Benny didn't seem offended. Mick would even go so far as to say that tonight was a great night for his four-legged colleague. It wasn't too often he got to feast on a variety of smells such as this.

He let Benny off the lead, allowed him to go where

his nose led him. He paused at each doorway along the dimly lit corridor, didn't stop for long at any of them. The search team had already carried out a sweep of the area, so Mick wasn't surprised that Benny hadn't yet indicated anything out of the ordinary. He knew his training. Number one was find a person, preferably a live one.

It was a completely different story when Mick opened the heavy metal door that led to the main part of the factory floor.

Benny stopped in his tracks, sat down, nose in the air. Mick watched him shudder and then howl.

The dog's behaviour made the officer stop short and caused a shiver to run down his spine.

There had only been one other occasion when he had seen Benny behave like that. That single time was in his early training.

The day Mick took him to the body farm.

Chapter 75

Wednesday 14 February

The following day, the incident room witnessed one of the oddest atmospheres possible.

DI Harry Powell was back in his office and DC Hazel Hamilton at her desk. Neither was talking to anyone, both preferring an occasional nod or smile. Both had black rings around their bloodshot eyes, an edge of uncertainty to their every gesture.

The others tiptoed around them, while trying to do what they were trained and primed for – investigate murders.

'Soph,' said Tom, guiding her by the arm, out of the main door and down the corridor to the kitchen. 'What are we going to do? Everyone's so lost.'

'God knows,' she said, biting her lip. 'Normally, we'd all look to Harry. But he's broken. Perhaps DCI Venice is on her way here for the briefing, not that anyone wants to go to it and hear the details of what happened to Pierre.'

'No one does,' said Tom, 'but we're investigators and we need facts. So we have to go and hear what's happened.'

'I think I'm going to be sick,' said Sophia. 'Will Harry and Hazel be at the briefing?'

'No,' said Tom. 'They've been told not to. It all got a bit heated apparently and they're not allowed to talk to any of us about it.'

Not appearing to like this, she bustled past him back towards the incident room.

'Soph,' he called, following her, 'where are you going?'

She didn't stop until she got to Harry's office and saw him in his chair, looking like he was about to face his own execution.

From the doorway, Tom watched her falter, then she leaped across the tiny office space and grabbed hold of him, pulled her DI into a bear hug.

'No one can believe it,' she sobbed.

'Soph, we're—'

'I know, I know,' she cried into his chest as he sat in his chair. 'This was no one's fault. We all love Pierre. You know that.'

They stayed where they were, a physically awkward embrace but both equally lost in the moment.

Neither of them were aware that Hazel had slowly made her way across the well-worn carpet of the incident room and was now standing near the window into Harry's office.

Tom moved to her side, watched her take in the scene in front of her.

'How are you holding up, Haze?'

'He wouldn't let me hug him like that,' she whispered.

'What?' said Tom.

'When we eventually got home last night, he slept in the spare room.'

It was a little uncomfortable that Hazel, who Tom didn't know very well, was letting him into her private life. He wasn't sure he wanted to know the finer points of his detective inspector's sleeping arrangements.

A noise behind Tom made him look over his shoulder. His detective sergeant Sandra Beckinsale was standing at an uncharacteristically discreet distance.

'Er, Tom,' she said, cheeks flushing, 'if you and Sophia don't mind, would you come to the conference room. It's not an actual briefing, more to give the team an update.'

She looked at Hazel, put a hand out, possibly to touch her arm, appeared to change her mind halfway through and then said, 'Hazel, would you stay here, please? I'll update you and Harry afterwards.'

The three of them stood in an awkward triangle, the unprecedented horror of what had happened finally starting to hit home.

Hazel merely nodded. Tom stepped towards the office, knocked on the open door and watched Sophia peel her face from the front of Harry's sodden, mascara-stained formerly clean shirt.

Harry and Hazel locked eyes, each of their faces a mask of despair.

Tom, Sophia and Sandra started out in the direction

of the conference room, all glancing back over their shoulders to the heart-breaking sight of Harry and Hazel not having a clue what to say to each other.

A couple of minutes later, the conference room was full to capacity.

The silence was crushing. A few blinked away tears, a few cried openly, most just looked livid.

With a nod from Sandra confirming everyone who should be there was present, Detective Chief Inspector Barbara Venice took a deep breath and began.

'Hello. You all know that, last night, a person or persons unknown attacked Detective Constable Pierre Rainer and a member of the public, John Kersley, in a police-owned property.'

She paused, looked to the ceiling and said, 'The sustained attack on Pierre has resulted in severe head injuries. I'm so, so sorry to be telling you this, but he's officially been declared brain dead. He won't be waking up.'

Chapter 76

Tom Delayhoyde drove to Queen Elizabeth the Queen Mother Hospital, parked in the same police bay where Pierre had parked only days before. He looked up at the building, wondering at the heartache and death that was taking place within.

At least Pierre wasn't here at this hospital, drawing his last ventilator-assisted breaths. Frank and Pierre's families were miles away at his bedside, waiting for his final moments. It made him want to weep, the thought that he would never see his colleague again. He hadn't really been a friend, but he was a wonderful man, always cheerful, and a constant source of advice and help.

With a resigned shake of his head, he threw his *On official police business* card in the window, got out and locked the car, walked to the hospital entrance and went inside. On the second floor, he headed to the respiratory ward and asked for directions to their witness's bed. It was more out of politeness as he could see the uniformed officer sitting on a chair outside the curtained cubicle, texting away, looking very bored.

They nodded at one another while Tom waited with as much patience as he could muster. He tried to listen to the conversation taking place on the other side of the curtain with as much discretion as he could manage. The smirk from the uniformed officer told him that he was doing a bad job of it.

The officer felt compelled to add, 'You're wasting your time, they're not speaking English.'

'Who's in there with her?' said Tom.

'Medical staff,' he replied. 'They found a Hungarian-speaking nurse.'

'And you didn't think to tell them not to talk?' said Tom, feeling as though his blood pressure was about to go through the hospital roof.

'She's being asked about her injuries.' He stood up and came towards him. 'I know what happened to Pierre. I'm still doing my job, but the staff have got to know what's wrong with her to be able to do theirs. It's just that little bit more personal for us.'

As Tom was about to respond, a cry came from behind the NHS disposable curtain and the sound of raised voices.

'Police,' said Tom. 'Can I come in? Everything all right in there?'

A slightly flustered-looking young woman in nurse's scrubs appeared in the gap in the flimsy curtain.

With a very faint accent Tom couldn't place but guessed was Hungarian, she said, 'I think it's a good idea you're here. Please come in.'

With a shrug and a glance behind him to the

PC, Tom left him waiting and stepped behind the curtain.

The stricken face of Anna, ghostly pale where she wasn't bruised and bleeding, stopped Tom in his tracks. He knew this wasn't the person who had hurt Pierre, and couldn't in any way be responsible, yet he couldn't help but feel that if it wasn't for this wretched woman, his comrade might still be alive.

'What's happened?' said Tom, unable to stop himself, before remembering procedure. 'Oh, and please let her know that I'm a police officer and I'll make a note of everything she says.'

There was some exchange of words in Hungarian before the nurse said, 'I've been translating, asking Anna about her injuries and how she got them.' She looked over at Tom and said, 'I've tried to keep it as neutral as I can, but ...' She turned her head to Anna before looking back at Tom. 'She ... well, she didn't take the news about her broken ribs bringing on pneumonia very well. I understand it's not something anyone wants to hear. But she took the news better when I told her that she'd lost the baby.'

Tom tried to take this information in his stride. He was a police officer, after all, and was used to being given updates that were a little out of the ordinary.

What came next, however, did knock him off track.

'And,' said the nurse as she stepped towards her, 'she said that the best thing she ever did was slice open the throat of the baby's father.'

Chapter 77

Evening of Wednesday 14 February

The only reason Alexa Gabor had stayed alive and, most importantly, financially secure, was because she was smart and didn't panic.

This situation was a little unusual for her, to say the least. The police had her car, her house, her passport, her history. She had had no choice but to get rid of her phone with the incriminating blackmail photos.

Even though she'd deleted them, there was no way she could risk them falling into the wrong hands.

Frustrated at being unable to contact Marko and let him know where she was, Alexa headed for the town. She would simply make her way to another of her houses. Alexa was the Controller of nine different properties in East Rise, more than any man in the county. That thought made her stand taller as she strode through the town centre. Her bald head might have attracted more stares had it not been for the sideshows of orange women, men wearing vest tops in a chill of six degrees and the feral children.

First stop, a hat. While she didn't care what others thought, her head was cold.

She then walked towards Heggarty Street, far enough out of town that it didn't attract attention, close enough that she could easily move her workhorses around without looking out of place.

It had always been one of her favourite houses, mainly because it was huge and made her a fortune, but also because it had convenient parking for her Audi. A rarity in this crappy town.

Try as she might, Alexa could not shake the feeling that her plans in the UK were going to have to be abandoned. It was such a shame as her English was coming on well, and starting again in France, Germany or Holland didn't really appeal. As she turned the corner into Heggarty Street, she gave a sigh at the injustice of it all and straightened her hat.

Too late, she saw the darkened figure step into her path a couple of metres from her. With a glance, she saw that someone else was gaining on her from the other direction. Trapped, she quickened her pace, tried to cross to the other side of the road.

That was a mistake.

The kidney punch would have floored her had the assailant not grabbed her by the elbow and dragged her back up to her feet.

Winded, Alexa tried to ask what was happening. Not that it mattered: these people weren't to be negotiated with.

Anything else she might have been about to say was knocked clean out of her head by a blow to the top of her skull, in exactly the same place as the last beating. She refused to black out, had refused to even when they kicked her repeatedly the last time. The blows they'd rained down on her had had less than twenty-four hours to heal. These ones might do her permanent harm.

With one hand around her throat, the other across her chest, Alexa found herself being dragged along the pavement to a grey Vauxhall Astra.

For once, she willed the people of East Rise to open their eyes and see what was happening on their own street, outside their homes. She was being forced into a car by two men and no one was paying any attention.

Surely, someone somewhere must care about a fellow human being.

The irony wouldn't have been lost on her, except she felt herself slipping away and blackness creeping into her peripheral vision.

A hand slapped her face and Alexa felt herself opening her eyes against her better judgement.

Everyone had a boss, someone to answer to, and Alexa had two.

As her vision returned, the world came into focus. Or at least the dank, lonely part of the world she now found herself in. A disused commercial building of some sort, probably used by the homeless and junkies if the smell and debris were anything to go by.

Tonight it was doubling up as the place she would probably die in.

The headlights of the nearby Vauxhall Astra lit up the three of them, the beam shining in Alexa's face affecting her ability to see her tormentors clearly, although she was only too aware of what they looked like.

The two Russians sat side by side in relaxed poses as if they didn't have a care in the world. Most of the worries they should have had were on Alexa's shoulders, or those of the other slave-controllers up and down the country.

With as much poise as she could muster slumped on the ground, Alexa glared at one then the other.

The one on the left gave a deep, short laugh.

'Look at her, Viktor,' he said. 'We only gave her a beating and shaved her head some hours ago, and she's trying to give us attitude.'

'What's this about?' she said. 'The fucking police have been to my house and arrested me because they thought I'd kidnapped those women. The same two women you gave me a hiding for losing. You made yourselves quite clear about the 400,000 euros. It's in hand. I haven't done anything to let you down.'

'Except you have,' said the one on the right. 'Not only have the police found the two runaway women, putting us severely out of pocket, but who knows what they're telling them.'

'I told that fucking stupid driver to take care of them,' she said, focus moving from one to the other, rapid eye movement an indicator of her so far well-hidden hysteria.

The pair of them sat like bookends, both short, robust, muscle-bound, with shaved heads and attitudes to match their chosen careers.

'That's not really our problem,' said Viktor. 'Me and Viktor here don't like losing stock, and we definitely don't like our operation being interrupted. You know, one of the many wonderful things we've come to love about the Great British culture is its wonderful language. Here we are chatting away in English and I get to use some of the interesting phrases I've learned. Such as, "Is the juice worth the squeeze?" When it comes to you, I have to say no.'

'I'd agree with that,' said the other Viktor.

Mounting panic forced the next words from her lips. 'Whatever you want me to do, I'll do it.'

'We know,' said left-hand side Viktor.

'That's why we've got something special for you,' said the other Viktor.

Alexa maintained her glare as best she could.

'We have our own ways of keeping our ear to the ground and we know that bastard ugly driver of yours is dead, although we're not clear why you thought it was a good idea to kill him. That's not—'

He stopped himself on seeing the expression on Alexa's face, sat back and said, 'Ah, you didn't know. So it wasn't you. That's a good start.'

She watched the two of them exchange a look. What the look meant wasn't important, what was important was the realization that these two had brought her to the middle of nowhere for a reason, and they weren't going to let her go until she had delivered something for them.

She tossed her head back, a gesture she should probably forgo for the foreseeable future.

'And you want what from me? You haven't tied me up so far, haven't punched or hit me since trying to strangle me, so I would say that you're either going to tell me what you want and let me go, or kill me. If it's kill me, please get on with it.'

'I didn't know Hungarians had such a great sense of humour,' said Viktor on the left. 'What we want you to do is very simple: go to the police and tell them that you're behind the recent influx of Eastern Europeans who've been working here illegally and staying in shit accommodation.'

'Then explain how you did it,' said the other Viktor. 'And, you will, of course, leave us completely out of it.'

'How would I include you?' she asked. 'I don't even know your real names. Viktor and Viktor? As if I could tell them any more than that about you.'

'That's why we've kept it nice and clean,' said the first Viktor. 'It was so you could never tell the police who we are.'

'Even if I was able to and I did,' she said, 'you would surely kill me.'

'True. Without hesitation. And in case you ever thought about trying any kind of stupid takeover, there's always the mammoth collection of revealing snapshots that could find their way to your family.'

'That would be low, even for you,' Alexa shouted at them.

'Don't be so embarrassed,' said the other Viktor. 'You made a fine whore, one of the best we've ever had, didn't she?'

'Fucking superb,' said his colleague, 'and if you didn't look such a total mess, we'd even think about giving you your old job back, but in the meantime, we've something else for you.'

He leaned back in his chair. His associate leaned forward.

Like figures on a weather clock, Alexa thought, though didn't dare to share.

'You go to the police, you tell them how you did it, arranged for them to come over, set them up in work. Look on it as a good thing that your driver was killed. He took a lot of them to banks to open fake accounts, claim for allowances for non-existent children, so blame him for any of it you can't make up the details for.'

'I'll go to prison,' she said.

'Look on the bright side: no one will mess with you looking like that. And by the time you come out, your hair will have grown back.'

'What about my home, my car?' The panic was building up for Alexa.

They both laughed at that one.

'You still don't get it, do you, you silly bitch?' said Viktor one. 'The police will take all that. You've no legitimate means of income. They don't do much well, but they can seize assets like there's no tomorrow.'

The Viktors stood up. Viktor one said, 'It's why we needed you. We needed you like you needed the slaves.'

'There's always someone worse off than you, and there's always someone to answer to.'

Chapter 78

Thursday 15 February

As scared as she was, Lili felt better than she had in weeks. Although a police officer stayed with her the entire time, the upside was she was being medically treated, fed, clothed and hadn't been threatened. All those things were a massive improvement.

She wasn't entirely sure what was happening to her, although the officer had handed her a telephone so that a Hungarian interpreter could explain exactly what a crime scene investigator was and why they wanted to take her filthy, torn, smelly clothes and rub some sort of cotton bud all over her hands and arms.

Lili co-operated, still in a daze, but she hadn't done anything wrong. Well, not really. There was a possibility she would have killed Anna if it had come down to it, but she hadn't. Anna would have done the same to her, that she was sure of, especially after seeing what she'd done to the driver's neck.

Lili shuddered at the thought of it. Still, better him

than her or Anna. She looked across from her bed to where the uniformed police officer was sitting watching her. She tried to smile at her, thought about asking after Anna. Other than not knowing enough English to form the question, let alone understand the answer, she didn't think the officer would tell her.

The officer stood up as one of the hospital staff came over. The nurse or doctor tried to explain to Lili that she could leave the hospital, but had to go with the policewoman, or at least, that's what Lili thought she was telling her. She knew that she should feel more distressed about the idea of getting into a police car than she did. From the stern look on the police officer's face, she realized that not only did she probably have no choice, she didn't have anywhere else to go.

Twenty minutes later, Lili found herself sitting in the back of a marked police vehicle, driving through rush-hour traffic, marvelling at the scenery. East Rise had never seemed real: it was a place she slept in, occasionally ate in when she was allowed, and where she was worked like a dog. Now she looked at it through new eyes, saw the laughing schoolchildren on the top deck of buses, sharing jokes and mobile phones, saw the people in smart office attire driving to work, saw the mums with pushchairs and buggies wheeling them into supermarkets and shops. It was all so normal, yet these things might as well have been taking place on another planet, not a mile from her damp shared mattress.

Without realizing she was doing it, Lili started to

cry. Her face became wet and her nose started to run. She wiped it on the sleeve of the grey sweatshirt the policewoman had given her to wear. The sleeves were so long on Lili's tiny frame anyway, she thought she would get away with rolling up the snot-covered parts. It was the cleanest thing she had worn for some days, and she had been allowed a shower.

All she wanted now was Denis, and to go home.

They pulled up at a barrier, the driver swiped a card against the sensor and waited for the barrier to rise. She glanced over her shoulder at Lili.

'You okay?' she said.

Lili was far from okay but had no way of explaining how she was feeling.

She simply nodded and waited to see what would happen to her. It surely couldn't get any worse.

Once they were parked and out of the car, Lili shivering against the cold and biting wind, she followed the policewoman across the car park to a large metal cage, not too dissimilar to the one she and Anna were going to fight to the death in. Only this one didn't smell of blood.

The officer led Lili to another door and gestured for her to go inside. She walked through the secure metal door into a large, well-lit area, wooden benches along two walls that ended in a huge metal gate.

She didn't need an interpreter to know that she was going to be questioned by the police about Pockmark's murder.

The only thing was, should she tell them the truth about Anna, or lie to help her friend?

Chapter 79

Sophia and Tom made their way back to the hospital to formally question Anna.

'I can't believe that she coughed to murder so easily,' said Sophia. 'You must have had your frightening face on.'

'You're so funny,' said Tom as Sophia fished around in her handbag before finding some mints and holding the packet across to Tom. 'I was the other side of the curtain when she told the nurse she was the one who'd killed him.'

'Still,' said Sophia, 'the checks that came back from Hungary were certainly interesting.'

'Couldn't agree more,' said Tom as he parked the car. 'No wonder she was here looking for work. After stabbing her ex-boyfriend to death, she wasn't likely to get the job of her dreams at home. Shame we can't find the bastards who murdered Pierre so easily.'

'Don't you think,' said Sophia, 'there's an air of misery in the incident room, and I don't mean only because of P's death. I mean over the investigation itself. I don't think anyone expects to get to the bottom of it.'

'I know exactly what you mean. We've got little to go on so far.'

'Let's hope something comes back on the forensics,' said Sophia. 'Come on, let's go and find the interpreter and speak to Anna.'

Tom lugged the weighty portable recording equipment with him as they made their way to the respiratory ward via the main entrance to collect the Hungarian interpreter, Zoe. Sophia and Tom gave her a brief rundown of what Anna was under arrest for and to say that it would be a normal police interview, except the suspect would be in a hospital bed.

When the three of them arrived on the ward, Tom left Sophia and Zoe and went to find the sister.

'Morning,' said Tom as he showed his identification, 'we're here to speak to Anna Bogdan. She's in the side room with that haggard-looking PC who's been here all night.'

'Oh, hi,' said the sister, 'she should be okay for you to talk to. We think we've got her pneumonia under control and her breathing is a lot better. We've drained a fair amount of fluid from between her lung and chest cavity. It was also infected, so she must have been in a ridiculous amount of pain.

'It's fortunate that she's fairly young and otherwise healthy. We've gone over her medical history with her, kept her under observation and she's had a chest X-ray, which showed her decreased lung size because of the pressure of the fluid. The pneumonia was brought on by the broken ribs she has. She claimed she was kicked, although wouldn't go into any more than that.'

'Well I'm hoping she's going to tell us everything,' said Tom, 'and that's something we'll certainly cover. Anything else I should know?'

The sister thought this over, checked through the paperwork in front of her. 'She's been given intravenous antibiotics and painkillers, but she seems lucid, all things considered. And I know she's desperate to talk to you.'

'Really?'

'Yes. Twice today she's said, "Police, please." About all the English she knows, I think.'

'That makes a change,' said Tom. 'Look, we won't wear her out. How long is she likely to be here?'

'Unless things change rapidly, I'd say about five or six more days, but that's an average.'

'Thanks,' said Tom. 'I think we'd better get cracking.'

Once everyone was ready, Sophia acting as camera and sound woman, Tom one side of Anna's bed, Zoe the other, Tom began his interview.

Introductions, legal rights and formalities out of the way, Tom asked, 'Did you murder Marko Kozma?'

The answer wasn't as satisfying as it should have been, coming, as it did, via Zoe.

'Yes, I killed him, but only to protect myself and my friend, Lili. He and the Controller woman were going to make us fight to the death for money. One of us was going to die and, for his sick amusement, he took us from the underground rooms to make us dig our own graves.'

Tom concentrated on Anna's face as the English translation of her words was spoken. Her breathing was rapid, although not as bad as the day before. She looked painfully frail and weak. It seemed incredible that a woman in her physical condition had been able to inflict the injuries Tom himself had seen on a healthy man.

Tom and Anna stared at one another. Although Tom was used to interviewing murderers and violent people, it didn't stop him feeling sorry for the young woman lying there, explaining why she took another's life.

Without waiting for the next question, Anna continued to talk.

'Both the driver, Marko, and the Controller, I don't know her name,' translated Zoe, 'had told me that Lili and me would fight for entertainment, to make them money. They said it was nothing personal, it was only business. Marko told me that I wasn't likely to make it to the end of the week. At some point, he must have given Lili a broken bottle. I suppose it was to attack me with. Perhaps he'd forgotten she had it, but when he took us outside to dig our graves, Lili put her arms around me and I took it from her pocket. It was hers, but I stabbed him straight in the neck. It had nothing to do with Lili.'

Chapter 80

The two men sat on a long wooden bench at the back of the bar. It was one of the newest to open a stone's throw from St Stephen's Basilica. Neither of them was interested in religion or views, only business.

'Part of the problem has been taken care of,' one said.

'And?' said his superior.

'Well, someone was caught up in the clean-up. The new problem we have is that that "someone" was a police officer.'

Few things fazed his boss, but this was very bad news. He beckoned his subordinate to come closer.

'Any police officer being taken out is bad enough, it brings us unwanted attention. They don't even carry guns over there. Now we've got more mess to clear up because of those fucking stupid Russian bastards. Find out where they are and pass it to your British police contact. Sort this out. Now.'

With that, he got up and went outside.

Chapter 81

Harry Powell wouldn't normally have gone out on a warrant, especially one at ten o'clock at night, but other than the insomnia that seemed to have taken hold since Pierre's death, he couldn't settle in the office. Everything reminded him of Pierre. He couldn't walk past his desk and he wouldn't allow anyone else to sit at it either.

It had raised a few eyebrows when he said he was going on the warrant, even though he couldn't see what all the fuss was about. He needed something to keep himself busy and hadn't been allowed to work on the initial shooting of John Kersley since Pierre's murder. No one would even tell him how things were progressing. He might as well go out and keep occupied.

The uniformed inspector was Josh Walker, a situation that cheered Harry up, albeit not to the point of actually looking as though he was pleased. That would have been a step too far.

He sat beside Josh as his friend drove them along behind the marked police Sprinter van.

'Don't you normally go in the bus with your team?' asked Harry.

'Yep. Thought you could do without being bounced around in the back, and besides, I've been meaning to talk to you. You know, about Pierre and what happened.'

Harry let out a sigh, looked out of the window into the night.

'How are you doing, Harry? I mean, really doing.'

'Like one of my team, my friend, got killed, and by killed, I mean beaten to death when all he was doing was his job. Not to mention, I was the one who sent him there in the first place.'

'You're not responsible for his death, you do know that?'

'Actually, I am,' said Harry, turning in his seat to look at Josh for the first time since their journey began. 'I was his governor, I should have risk-assessed it better than I did, and I shouldn't have sent the two of them to a bloody house in the fucking middle of nowhere without firearms.'

'But you did send firearms to them,' said Josh. 'Someone else called them away, not you. It's an operational balls-up, but it's not your fault.'

'It still feels like it, and let's be honest, if I hadn't sent him he'd still be alive.'

'I'll agree with you on that front, but they would have still got to Kersley some way. They went to the extent of nobbling the alarm system so it didn't go off. They weren't amateurs. Anyone could have been caught in the cross fire. You said you were there earlier that day, could have been you too, H.'

'It would have been better if it had been me,' said Harry. 'It's difficult to feel so bloody guilty when you're dead.'

'Don't say stuff like that … We're here now, but tomorrow we'll go for a pint and talk about this.'

'Okay,' said Harry as he unfastened his seat belt. 'Let's go and rescue some of these poor bastards.'

The entire team covered the modest three-bedroom house, front and back. Officers in plain clothes from East Rise's anti-slavery and human trafficking unit stood beside their uniformed colleagues. Harry tried to keep out of the way, despite itching to get inside the dilapidated property.

He ran an eye over the frontage and took in what looked like boards up at the windows and couldn't see any lights on. There were a couple of bags of rubbish in the front garden, otherwise the place looked empty.

Anna and Lili had told them a different story.

A polite knock on the front door got them nowhere, so on the count of three, a uniformed officer with a metal door-opener cracked open the flimsy wooden door with one swing. As he moved to the side, the team ran through the door. Shouts of 'Police. Stay where you are' filled the air.

Harry stood outside on the pavement waiting to be

summoned inside. It was times like this he wished he smoked. Instead he stood with his hands inside his coat pockets for warmth, glad he was out of the office, away from its sombre air, yet never far from his own sombre thoughts.

Just as he was about to lose feeling in his feet, Harry was beckoned inside by Josh.

'Things are pretty grim in here,' said Josh. 'All of these people need to come out. Now.'

As Harry went with Josh into the house the stench hit him. If he wasn't mistaken, it was the stench of human waste.

Regretting not taking more fresh air into his lungs when he had the chance, Harry followed Josh upstairs.

The first door opposite the staircase was clearly the bathroom. Or what would have been a bathroom had it had a bath, or a toilet that worked, judging by the smell. Harry caught sight of a bucket in the far corner. From the mess on the bare boards around it, it had clearly been knocked over a number of times, or its users had failed in their aim.

Wondering what else this house had to show him, Harry moved across the landing to another doorway which Josh had stopped in front of.

'Back bedroom, 'said Josh. 'This is the one that both Anna and Lili claimed they slept in.'

Harry took a step inside the room. That was about as far as he could get, what with the entire floor being covered with mattresses. There were no sheets or pillows; some mattresses had a blanket on top, most were covered with coats and jumpers. All but one of the six mattresses had a person lying on them.

The five women had two things in common: not one of them appeared to be concerned by the appearance of police officers, and each of them looked out through dead eyes.

Harry was looking at the faces of truly lost souls.

'Do any of you speak English?' he said.

More blank looks.

'Do you know Anna? Lili?'

Still no one spoke.

'Guv,' called a voice from the next room. 'This bloke seems pretty grim. We need to get a nurse to take a look at him.'

Harry and Josh both turned their attention to the front bedroom. This one had eight mattresses crammed into it, all occupied, seven pairs of eyes watching the newcomers, one person doubled over in pain. What was visible of his face as he lay on his side, arms wrapped around his stomach, showed skin blotchy and sweaty despite the cold of the room.

'He's very sick,' said the man on the mattress closest to the door.

'You speak English?' asked Harry.

'No much. He sick since arrive England. He is Dominik. My name Tamas.'

'Well, Tamas,' said Harry, 'think of today as the day your luck changed. Now, where's that bloody nurse got to? She'll take a look at your hands too. Don't tell me, chicken catcher?'

Tamas stared down at his own pus-filled, infected fingers and back up at Harry.

'You've got a young lady called Anna to thank for finding you,' said Harry. 'We wouldn't have found you without her help.'

It wasn't often Detective Inspector Powell got to see a fully grown man burst into tears.

Chapter 82

Despite his 3 a.m. finish, Harry was determined to be at the 8.30 briefing. He made it with enough minutes to spare, and was able to grab a coffee and take a seat beside Detective Chief Inspector Barbara Venice.

He knew that it was no longer his investigation, it couldn't be after Pierre's death, yet he couldn't walk away from it. It all felt too personal.

'Morning, everyone,' began Barbara. 'Thank you for coming, especially those who had hardly any sleep.' She seemed to make a point of avoiding looking at Harry as she said this.

'Anyway, updates. Let's start with Lili. I'll have to give you those as the interviewing team aren't here.'

Barbara scanned the room and said, 'Most of you already know that we've released Lili. She told us what happened on the night of Marko Kozma's murder and what happened in the days leading up to it. All of this has been substantiated by Anna Bogdan who has admitted to killing him.

'I took the decision to release Lili and she's been referred to the National Referral Mechanism so she gets the right support. For those of you who don't know, she's been offered a place in a government-funded safe house.'

Harry couldn't tear his eyes away from Barbara as she told the team about the safe house. He didn't need to be able to read minds to know that every single person in the conference room had the same opinion of them.

'Lili will have several weeks of a reflection and recovery period,' continued Barbara, 'so she can try to come to terms with everything that's happened and decide whether she wants to go home or stay here and co-operate with us regarding her trafficking ordeal.

'She's also asked to be reunited with her boyfriend, Denis Boros.'

This was something Harry wasn't aware of. He sat contemplating the mixed emotions the young man he had met a few days ago would no doubt feel on hearing that his girlfriend was looking for him. With everything that had happened to his own staff, Harry had forgotten about the car washer's scrotum.

He at least wished them both a happy ending.

He stopped listening to most of the updates Barbara gave from that moment on. It was only when she said, 'And who's got the latest from John Kersley?' he refocused his mind, as he was bound to.

'Me, ma'am,' said Sandra Beckinsale. 'I had the pleasure. He can be a little hostile.'

Despite the atmosphere in the room, most people had a small smile to themselves at this character take from the county's most miserable employee.

'He's now been moved to another part of the country,' she continued, an embarrassed look down at the blank page of her notebook. 'He'll stay there until the arrests are made and the trial over, before being moved somewhere else.'

She gave a cough, looked even more uncomfortable and said, 'I'm only one of two people in the department who knows where he is.'

The blood pumped through Harry's ears. He got the message: they weren't to be trusted, including him. Perhaps it was *especially* him. He fought the urge to get up and leave the briefing. What good was he if he couldn't be told the facts?

Unsure whether he could take much more of what he took to be personal criticism, he inspected his fingernails, linked his fingers, tried everything he could to appear nonchalant.

The first stroke of luck he'd had all day was that his mobile phone started to vibrate in his pocket. He took it out and saw a number he didn't recognize.

Normally, let alone in his current frame of mind, PPI callers or imbeciles telling him he'd been in an accident would get it both barrels. Today he decided to take the call.

Shrugging at Barbara and mouthing 'Sorry' as he left

the room fooled no one, he knew. Still, it was an escape route and he took it.

Safely the other side of the briefing-room door, he answered and said, 'Hello, Harry Powell.'

His stomach lurched as he recognized the sweet, honeyed tones of the caller.

'Harry, don't hang up. It's Martha. Martha Lipton ... Harry, are you there?'

'I'm here. Just when I thought my week couldn't get any worse—'

'Please don't,' she said. 'It's about Pierre.'

'Pierre?' he said. 'What the fuck has Pierre got to do with you?'

He didn't want to listen to anything that despicable woman had to say, yet she had said the one thing that would get him to speak to her on today of all days.

'I know you hate me,' she said, 'but please, I need to talk to you. We can help each other. I can definitely help you.'

'If you're bollocking me about I'll nick you for wasting police time, perverting the course of justice, being an unholy mother of sick fucks. Whatever, you'll get time.'

Her tone took on a sharpness and she slowed her speech.

'Pierre was decent. Don't talk to me like that when I'm trying to help you.'

He caught his breath. As much as he hated Martha Lipton and all her kind, what if she knew something? She lived in the block of flats where John Kersley had lived.

'Okay,' he said. 'What do you know?'

'Not that easy, Harry. We need to meet and I'll tell you what I know once you've listened to what I want.'

He bit his tongue. 'When and where?' he eventually said.

'Twenty minutes in the Seagull Pickings. You know it?'

'I know it,' he sighed. 'I'll see you there.'

What was it with ex-cons and the worst-named eatery in East Rise?

Chapter 83

Only the thought of doing something to help Pierre's family made Harry go back to his office, put on his overcoat and head for the front counter. He could have chosen to go out of the side gate, slip away unnoticed, avoid any annoying public, but he didn't.

He still felt bad for walking out of a briefing, let alone out of the station. Barbara would forgive him, probably never mention it. The others knew he couldn't stand to sit and listen to endless updates in a room where no one had a clue who had kicked one of their family to death.

Harry let himself into the foyer with his security pass, smiled at Ian Davis behind the counter typing away, and took in the empty space.

He was about to make a comment about Ian having a peaceful morning when he noticed a woman approaching the front of the building.

Her slow, lumbering gait would have made her stand out, even if it hadn't been for her partially shaven head, randomly spaced tendrils flying around her face in the wind.

Fascinated, Harry waited as Ian got to his feet, and she walked through the door and up to the counter.

What she said, as she tried to muster as much dignity as possible, one uncertain hand on the counter top, took both of them by surprise.

'I think you need to ... er ... arrest me.'

Both Ian and Harry stared at her.

'For what?' said Ian, finding his voice first.

'I have been trafficking people from Hungary and making them work for me for next to no pay. You need to arrest me.'

There was the briefest of pauses before Harry said, 'I think you need to take a seat. My colleague will get an officer to speak to you in a second.'

For only a moment, Harry was torn. He knew that this woman knew more than she had so far told them, and no doubt would ever tell. However, he felt the urge to get out of the station and away from everyone, find out exactly what Martha Lipton had to say to him, or else arrest her for being the scourge of the earth. Or more likely, something he could actually get past the custody sergeant as reasonable grounds for nicking her.

'Can I leave this with you, Ian? I have something important I need to take care of. Tannoy Sophia Ireland or Tom Delayhoyde, get them out of the briefing.'

'Of course.'

With that, Harry made his exit and, collar turned up, walked to the Seagull Pickings.

*

The windows were steamed up when Harry got to the grotty café. It was probably for the best that no one saw inside until they were committed and over the threshold. It was no doubt how they got most of their customers. That and, so it seemed, criminals wanting somewhere out of the way.

Harry definitely had no intention of eating.

He scanned the room, saw the beautiful, disgusting Martha Lipton in the same seat Joe Bring had occupied what seemed like a thousand years ago.

He half smiled at the waitress and said, 'Hello, De Niro, a white coffee for me, please.'

Her eyebrows shot up in annoyance, but she moved towards the coffee pot anyway and poured his drink before pushing the mug across the glass counter.

He put a couple of coins on the counter in preparation for a quick get-away and then sat down opposite Martha.

'This wants to be good,' he said.

'Hello to you too.'

Unable to meet his stare, Martha looked down at her own mug of coffee.

'When I broke the law—'

Interrupted by laughter, she broke off, then said, 'Don't scoff at me, and don't judge me.'

'Don't judge you? Really, Martha? I didn't judge you: a judge and jury did that and they found you guilty of holding down your own daughter and watching your boyfriend rape her, so don't you dare say to me "When I broke the law" like it was some sort of fucking traffic violation.'

Martha leaned across the table, pushed her face to his and spat her words at him. 'Who do you think dealt with me all those years ago? Pierre Rainer, that's who. He was decent, he was good to me, he didn't make me feel like you are now. You know the difference, Harry, between Pierre and you? He didn't make me feel like shit for what I'd done. I've been to prison. I've tried to make amends with the Volunteer Army. And will you wipe that smirk off your face?'

He sat upright, palms face down on the salt-covered, ketchup-stained table.

'Go on.'

'Whatever you think of the Volunteer Army,' she said, 'and I know it's not much, we've got contacts. There are more and more children being trafficked across Europe in the sex trade. Thirteen-, fourteen-year-old kids being sold into prostitution. I can't give you details, but we have police informants, you know that. We do what we can.'

Once more, Harry sat and listened. He knew, as much as he hated to admit it, that she was telling the truth about registered informants passing on invaluable information. No one would ever tell him, but she was probably paid for a lot of the stuff she gave the police. This one seemed to be for free.

'I've heard that Russians were behind Pierre's death,' she said. 'The people traffickers have bosses too, someone to answer to. They step out of line and they're in for a good hiding or worse. I've heard all sorts about cage fighting and heaven knows what.'

She paused, took a sip of her coffee; Harry's was left untouched in front of him.

Feeling a slight thaw from her audience now, she continued. 'I'll never come forward and tell anyone I gave you this, but the two men you're looking for go by the name Viktor. That's both of them. I know they burned out the Qashqai they were in when they killed Pierre. Now they're on their way to Manchester in a Vauxhall Astra.'

'That's it?' he asked after a brief pause that Martha didn't fill.

'That's it,' she said and drained her coffee mug. 'You're the detective, you work it out. I don't know much more, and besides, if I tell you, they'll know the source and I'm dead. They already tried to shoot my neighbour, so they know where I live, and if you couldn't protect him and Pierre, you definitely won't save me. I'm only here because of Pierre.'

She stood up. 'Bye, Harry.'

She pushed out her chair, did up her coat and picked up her handbag from the floor.

'Bye, Martha.'

She made a move past their table.

Harry failed to hide the shudder as he said, 'And thank you.'

Chapter 84

Evening of Friday 16 February

With the thought of the previous evening's prostitutes in Manchester put to the back of their minds, Viktor and Viktor made their way to their next port of call: Newcastle. The motorway traffic was flowing well considering the Friday evening rush hour, and they were making good time.

Ready to put behind them the misfortunes of the last week, the two were in better spirits than they had been for a while.

'Manchester was a good place,' said Viktor, cigarette hanging from his mouth, lighter in hand. 'Market is a little overcrowded, but we can maybe make it work.'

'Well, we need to move away from the south-east,' said Viktor. 'We've lost a fortune this week and if we don't make the money back, we'll get more than a few punches to the face and a shaved head from our superiors.'

'Neither of us have any hair.'

This made them both roar with laughter.

'So why Newcastle?' said Viktor, as he looked across at his business partner leaning against the passenger side door.

'I've never been. Looks interesting, that's all, and in a few miles we'll find out.'

He blew cigarette smoke towards the car roof.

'Don't do that,' said the other Viktor from the driver's seat. 'I want to keep this car, so let's not drive anywhere we'll end up killing police officers and having to burn it. We've got to be more careful.'

'Like they'll have any chance of catching us. We left no fingerprints, no DNA, we've burned out the car we used. How would they ever know it was us?'

'There are blue lights behind us,' said the driver, eyes fixed on their reflection in the rear-view mirror.

'Are you speeding?'

'No, I'm under the limit. They're right behind us and there are several cars, some vans.'

Twisting round in the passenger seat to see for himself, Viktor said, 'What the fuck are they stopping us for? Just say nothing. This has to be a coincidence.'

Both men were more concerned than they let on to each other: both knew they had cocaine and alcohol in their system, both knew they had left two of the prostitutes in a very bad way.

They were still prepared to do anything to get away.

'What are you doing?' said Viktor, as the passenger crawled onto the back seat.

'I packed the weapons,' he said as he frantically tried to release the rear seats and get to the luggage.

'What the fuck did you do that for?' he yelled.

'In case we got stopped by police.'

'We *are* getting stopped by police. This isn't going to end well. There are far too many of them for this to be random. Someone's grassed us up.'

With Viktor back in the front passenger seat, the other Viktor put his hand out to grab one of the handguns from him, put his foot to the floor, and tried to gain some distance. None of that really mattered when it dawned on them both that, not only was there a sea of blue lights ahead, but the unmistakable sound of a helicopter above them.

Chapter 85

Evening of Monday 26 March

Harry had never been good at showing his emotions, sharing what was going on beneath the surface. It protected those around him, but most of all it protected him.

Anger was positive: it meant he hadn't given in, let life beat him down, despite its perpetual effort to do just that.

Lately, the spark seemed to have left him. Things were going wrong and he wasn't entirely sure he knew how to put them back on track.

As he moved around his kitchen, stirring the contents of saucepans, checking the oven from time to time, it didn't escape his notice how much homelier his house had become since Hazel moved in.

He even tolerated the scented candles he wasn't allowed to light and the bowl of fake fruit. Quite why anyone would have such unnecessary crap on display, attracting dust, he couldn't fathom.

Yet Hazel loved it, so he loved it. He loved her. Simple.

That thought made him pause as he opened the fridge to get the champagne out.

He did love her, loved being with her, loved having her at work, apart from lately. The strained atmosphere in the office had seen two members of his staff transfer to other departments, one resign, and one go off with long-term stress. The rest carried on with cracked hearts and burdened minds.

Still, they would get through this.

He checked the clock on the wall.

Hazel had said she would be home at 8 p.m., so at two minutes to, she would walk through the door. He could rely on her for that.

He took the bottle from the fridge and placed it in the ice bucket, another surprise gift from Hazel some time ago, when it still felt as though they had something to celebrate. He went to the freezer, took out the ice and, to his surprise, found he was humming.

Of late, he tended to mutter under his breath, sometimes even growl.

Whenever Harry thought of Pierre, he could easily cry, but life had to go on. Not as before, that would never happen. It would be different, and as good as he could make it.

At 7.58 p.m., Harry heard the door open.

'Hiya. You in the kitchen?' she called.

'Sure am, sweetheart.'

He stood next to the kitchen table, the same table that he and Hazel had sat at while she talked him through finding his murdered friend's body.

He went to sit down, changed his mind and felt conspicuous in his own kitchen, as if his arms were too long for his body.

Tight smile on her face, Hazel walked through the door.

'I've missed you,' she said.

'Bloody meetings all day at HQ,' he said.

'No,' Hazel said. 'I didn't mean today. I meant over the last few weeks. Where have you been?'

'Right here, darling.'

He opened his arms. They stepped towards each other. Caught one another.

'I can't stand that we're not talking,' she said. 'We have to talk about what happened to Pierre, and you can't keep blaming yourself.'

She held him at arm's length, studied his handsome, world-worn face.

'We're going to destroy each other if we continue like this,' she said, 'and I can't—'

For the first time, Hazel looked past Harry at the table.

'Our table,' she said. 'Where it all began.'

'Don't tell the IOPC, for fuck's sake,' said Harry. 'If you remember rightly, you were still on duty and I kept trying to get you to drink brandy with me. They'd have my bollocks for that.'

'You're kind of taking the edge off the romantic gesture,' she said as she let go of him and reached out a hand to caress the top of the champagne bottle. 'And you've got my favourite.'

She grinned at him and picked up the cardboard certificate.

'Well, most men would buy their wonderful girlfriends flowers, but I know you hate the waste.'

She read from the certificate: '*Gladys is one of our long-term residents at Gilly's Goat Sanctuary. For your year's sponsorship, we'll send you photos and updates and invite you to open days.* I love it,' said Hazel. 'Can we go and see her?'

'Any time you want,' he said. 'There's just one more thing . . .'

He cleared his throat, took a small blue box from his pocket and said, 'Hazel, will you marry me?'

Epilogue

Without fully knowing why he was there, Harry Powell, police officer for longer than he had been a civilian, made his way to the viewing point overlooking the Channel. The day couldn't have been any more glorious: the sun was working so hard, it even managed to make East Rise look like a bustling, thriving seaport full of tourists and trade. For one moment, Harry managed to forget that it was a haven for drug dealers, people traffickers, those with no future prospect or hope of a living. He so desperately wanted to see the good in people and the wonderful things the human race was capable of when it tried.

The warmth of the day touched his face, stubble and all, as he strained to look towards the foot passengers snaking towards the ferry.

It didn't take much of an effort to spot them. The two of them huddled together, not for warmth today, solely for the physical comfort it no doubt gave them. A couple of things gave them away: for one, the tentative steps Denis Boros took as he navigated his way across the expanse in front of him, all that was separating him from getting on a boat to start his journey home. The other, the Salvation Army red jackets and woolly hats both he and Lili wore.

For one glorious moment, Harry turned his face skywards, enjoying not only the physical feeling of the sun's rays, but the soar of having been in the presence of so many people prepared to carry out selfless tasks for total strangers with little or no thanks.

He felt his fingers close around his mobile phone as it started to ring. No one would ever think to ask him if he had watched Denis and Lili walk out of the country right under his nose. But then no one would think to ask Denis exactly why most of his testicles had been washed away down a drain at a roadside car wash.

Life really was unfair.

Harry, arms crossed, standing at the edge of his vantage point for spotting day trippers, holidaymakers and fleeing slaves, watched as the two young Hungarians disappeared from his view towards the security checks.

Denis and Lili had been completely oblivious to his observation, and Harry too was unaware that someone had been watching him.

Even though she was about a hundred metres away, his every gesture, face tilt and movement had been monitored. Most of it photographed too.

Detective Constable Gabrielle Royston was, by most people's admission, a fairly strange young lady. Even by her own standards, following her detective inspector along the cliff tops to peer down on ferry foot passengers was a very odd thing to do.

Snapping photo after photo of him with the most powerful lens she owned was even weirder.

Still, she'd been after a photo of Harry for ages.

This one was just perfect.

ACKNOWLEDGEMENTS

As ever, there are so many people to thank, most importantly the readers. Without anyone picking up the book, taking the time to read and share your positive comments, there is no point. Thank you.

I'm so grateful to all the team at Simon & Schuster for your help, work and enthusiasm in helping the book along. Without the brilliant assistance of editors extraordinaire, Jo Dickinson and Rebecca Farrell, and the copy-editing skills of Mary Tomlinson, I'm not sure where I'd have ended up. So much work by so many people, from cover design to the production team, is the only way books ever find their way to readers.

The wonderful S&S team would have had slim pickings to work with had it not been for the guidance and knowledge of Lys Ford from the Gangmasters and Labour Abuse Authority. Lys, I'm indebted to you for wading through an early draft of the book and steering me in the right direction – not for the first time.

Huge thanks too to Detective Inspector Gary Scarfe, from the Serious and Organised Crime Unit for your assistance and words of advice regarding the tireless and superb work carried out by yourself and your dedicated team.

Ian Davis, thank you for agreeing to be a character in the book. Working at a police station front counter is a dim and distant memory for me in my uniformed days, but it never ceases to amaze me at the knowledge required of Public Enquiry Staff. No one should know that much! I haven't done your role service – you could have your own novel.

Last but no means least, another massive thank you to Caroline Leighton, wonderful lady with a wealth of medical knowledge. Any medical inaccuracies are due to me and I'm grateful for your assistance once more for broken rib advice.

I wrote *Lost Lives* after finding out that trafficked slaves were housed all over beautiful, green, leafy Kent. While it didn't come as a total surprise to me that I was a stone's throw from modern-day slaves, the sheer scale of the situation, horrific conditions human beings were being held in, along with the complete dominance they faced, made me question why society was so blind to what was going on.

If you're reading this book in a café, hotel, shopping centre, you're probably extremely close to a trafficked worker. I can't shop for chicken or vegetables without thinking of what went on behind the scenes. And I never use a car wash.

DON'T MISS THE BRAND NEW CRIME
THRILLER BY LISA CUTTS

GRAVE RISK

COMING SOON

Read on for a gripping exclusive extract ...

**SIMON &
SCHUSTER**

Autumn 1993

I knew that I was taking a big chance – a massive one – not to mention one with an outcome that could end it all. Potentially my life, *definitely* my freedom. Still that was why I did it: the rush was like nothing on earth, well nothing legal, anyway.

I had taken my time, watched the premises, scoped the route, timed the comings and goings of anyone likely – or stupid – enough to try to stop me.

I had upped the game, there was no doubt about it, but the trouble with this particular game was that not only were the stakes high – so was the win.

Still, it wasn't the first time and it certainly wouldn't be the last.

I sat in the car, trying hard to steady my breathing, and I took the key from the ignition. To those scuttling past on the pavement, crossing the road in this shitty little town, right at this moment I was nothing more than a man parking his battered Ford Cortina. No one ever paid me any attention, and right now that was what I wanted.

I leant across to feel beneath the passenger seat. My fingers grasped the edge of the woollen balaclava before reaching the sawn-off shotgun a couple of inches further away. My nicotine-stained fingertips grazed the surface of the crumb-riddled, black, plastic floor mats, the gun knocking the empty cigarette boxes and discarded takeaway wrappers out of the way.

With the blood pumping in my ears and my heart rate racing, I tucked the shotgun inside my deliberately too large jacket and rested the balaclava in my lap.

This was the part where I had to take my time, take control and focus.

I did all that and more as I ran what was now a well-practiced eye over the glass front of the building society.

Bradford and Bingley was my financial establishment of choice, most likely because of their adverts on television. They always seemed to appeal to the right people, the sort who had money.

Once more I took a few deep breaths, made sure I had a tight grip on the balaclava in one hand. Over the last few months I had perfected the art of leaving the right one free for the shotgun when the time became right.

One last glance along the almost empty Tuesday lunchtime pavement before I got out of the car.

For one stupid moment it crossed my mind to lock the car, but as there was no one I trusted enough to be my getaway driver, locking it would cost me precious seconds when I'd need them most.

Without giving anything else much thought, adrenalin now off the scale, I cleared my mind of everything that didn't involve executing the perfect armed robbery.

I walked the two hundred and fifty feet towards the building society, one hand on the balaclava, the other on a loaded shotgun.

I strolled along the pavement, face down, collar up, palms sweating. Even before I opened the door and stepped inside, I knew there were only two customers and one middle-aged woman working behind the counter.

Ideal.

One elderly man stood to my left, busy trying to fill in some piece of paper with a pen chained to the desk he leant against. A young woman of about twenty stood in front of me at the counter, foot tapping at presumably annoyance at how long her transaction was taking.

That was all about to change.

I almost felt sorry for these people: they had no idea at what was about to happen; the impact the next few minutes would have on the rest of their lives, wondering if today might have been their last.

Still, I had a job to do.

I stepped forward to the bored customer, unnaturally close to her. She was wearing a cheap perfume, something sweet that reminded me of old ladies, all flowery and sickly.

She turned her head, annoyance on her face, about to tell me to step back, and then her features changed dramatically as she realised what was happening.

Her mouth formed a perfect, tiny round, her eyes the size of saucers, her skin a deathly white as she took in my balaclava. Until this point, she hadn't even noticed the shotgun I had pulled from inside my jacket.

Now that I was pointing it at her head, she most definitely had.

'Hands on the counter,' I said to the woman behind the till. She looked terrified too, but that was the point.

'Money, now,' I shouted to the woman. She was mid-forties, attractive in a Mumsie way, shaking like a shitting dog.

She fumbled, unsure of what to do, even though her staff training would no doubt have instructed her about how to behave, what to do if someone were to come into your provincial branch and point a gun at a customer's head. Supposedly this stupid bitch thought it would never happen to her. Except now it was and she should get on with it. I hardly had all day.

'Fucking do it,' I shouted at her as I grabbed the petrified younger woman's arm.

I glanced behind me at the old man, saw the pen in his gnarled, liver-spotted hand, face a mask of horror, then I turned my attention back to the counter.

'Notes only,' I shouted at her again. 'Fives, tens and twenties.'

Fifties were too difficult to get rid of. Keep it simple, always.

I let go of the young woman's arm to pull a Sainsbury's carrier bag from my pocket, then threw it across to the cashier and watched as she stuffed the cash inside.

I lunged across towards the bag, grabbed it by the handle and turned and ran towards the door.

My whole body was coursing with adrenalin, pumping around my system, making me feel more alive than I ever felt possible.

I ran towards the car, shotgun back inside my jacket, balaclava pulled off my head as soon as my feet hit the pavement.

Then I was back to a brisk walk, not looking behind, not trying to draw attention to myself. Just a man with his collar up to keep the cold out on a chilly afternoon in the south east of England, shopping bag at his side, car keys ready to shove in the ignition.

I almost laughed as I opened the car door, threw the bag down next to me and pushed the shotgun back under the passenger seat.

I indicated and pulled out of the parking space, driving away, the sound of police sirens growing louder.

Discover more gripping investigations from
Lisa Cutts . . .

MERCY
KILLING

The violent death of a local sex offender puts intense
pressure on the police officers at East Rise incident
room. Under constant scrutiny, they must treat
this case like any other murder. But how can they
feel sympathy knowing the terrible things Albie
Woodville did?

However, as the investigation progresses, it becomes
clear that this isn't just a one-off killing – someone is
out for revenge . . .

AVAILABLE NOW IN PAPERBACK AND EBOOK

**SIMON &
SCHUSTER**